Praise for *Heading Out to Wonderful*

"Deliciously dark and dangerous." —*O: The Oprah Magazine*

"I love Robert Goolrick's *Heading Out to Wonderful*. The novel's seductive power and the beauty of his writing create a delicious feast for the reader." —Kathryn Stockett, author of *The Help*

"A suspenseful tale of obsessive love." —*People*

"Beautifully written, striking in its imagery, *Heading Out to Wonderful* is a passionate and tragic story of a love affair that is entirely consuming yet completely forbidden. Robert Goolrick has crafted another rich, evocative, and sometimes unsettling story."
—Garth Stein, author of *The Art of Racing in the Rain*

"[A] soulful and heart-wrenching tale of love that knows no bounds."
—*Family Circle*

"With understated delicacy, Goolrick . . . creates a mesmerizing gothic tale of a good man gone wrong . . . Goolrick effortlessly creates a timeless, erotically charged tale of illicit passion and peoples it with a unique cast of characters . . . Finely crafted fiction from a captivating writer." —*Booklist*, starred review

"*Heading Out to Wonderful* reads like an Appalachian ballad . . . Goolrick is an atmospheric writer, and he builds the tension well."
—*The Christian Science Monitor*

"Haunting . . . Goolrick's novel has the economy and mournful grace of an old mountain ballad, and its repercussions echo far outside the little valley."   —*The Columbus Dispatch*

"A lyrical meditation on the magnified elements of small-town life: friendship, trust, land, lust, and sin . . . Goolrick creates a timeless town where memory of an affair and crime can haunt forever. A lyrical yet suspenseful novel."   —*Library Journal*

"A multilayered novel that manages to be a tragic love story, a coming-of-age tale, and a bit of social commentary on a bygone era all at once . . . Beautifully written."   —*The Louisville Courier-Journal*

"In *Heading Out to Wonderful*, novelist Robert Goolrick vividly evokes two lovers doomed by their place and their past."
                                   —*Richmond Times-Dispatch*

"Goolrick's tale of doomed love resonates like a folk ballad, with the language of the Blue Ridge Mountains and its people giving this novel its soul . . . Like any good ballad, the narrative builds slowly to its violent climax, packs an emotional punch, and then haunts readers with its quintessentially American refrain."   —*Publishers Weekly*

"Always lurking, as in Goolrick's previous novel, *A Reliable Wife*, is the dark undercurrent of suspense, as we hurtle toward finding out what happens. And we hurtle—the book is hard to put down . . . It's a beautifully told story of human failings and yearnings, and redemption sought but never quite attained."   —*The Wichita Eagle*

"Simply superb . . . *Heading Out to Wonderful* is so humane, so filled with generous people who want to do the right thing, so accurate in its sense of place, it is sure to be on all 'best of' lists for 2012 . . . The story's explosive conclusion builds for pages, and even when you know something has to happen, it's a jolt for the reader. But the generosity and decency of the townsfolk gives this story a poignancy that will break your heart."   —*St. Paul Pioneer Press*

"Landscapes are painted in lusciously vivid detail, and scenes unfold at a dreamy pace . . . Conflict builds in the background like an un-watched, covered pot rattling on a hot stove, threatening to explode. We know something terrible will happen, but the gasp-inducing re-sult is one we never see coming and is something we'll never be able to forget."   —*Virginia Living*

"*Heading Out to Wonderful* is a literary novel with complicated characters that invite discussion, making it an ideal choice for book clubs—one certain to lead to late night talks about Goolrick's characters, and their motives."   —*The Washington Missourian*

"The Southern novel comes in two main varieties: The first is the Gothic, best typified by William Faulkner's enervated lyricism. Then there's the sharp and sorrowful style of which Robert Goolrick is shaping up to be a master."   —*Minneapolis Star Tribune*

"Robert Goolrick is a master of emotive, suspense-driven drama."   —*Flavorpill*

"*Heading Out to Wonderful* is exactly that. Wonderful. That is, it's filled with wonder. Robert Goolrick, author of *A Reliable Wife*, has once again dug beneath the surface of lives, unearthing mystery and motive that, when combined, drive this impressive, hypnotic tale relentlessly forward . . . Gorgeous."
—*January Magazine*

"Powerful . . . There is much pleasure-giving psychological truth along the way . . . Arresting."
—*Kirkus Reviews*

"Told in [Goolrick's] lyrical prose, *Heading Out to Wonderful* is a pleasure to read—heartbreaking but inspiring and unforgettable."
—*BookPage*

"Goolrick set a frigid Wisconsin winter afire with passion in his first novel, *A Reliable Wife,* and he brings the same talent to bear in *Heading Out to Wonderful* . . . Through his memoir and novels, Goolrick returns again and again to the undercurrent of private passion that can roil beneath the smooth surface of our public lives."
—*The Salisbury Post*

"Goolrick's prose is rich, wise and beautiful . . . Such fine writing carries the doomed story up to its very end."
—*Historical Novels Review*

"[A] poetic tale that simmers with foreboding atmosphere."
—*Chicago Tribune Printers Row*

HEADING OUT TO WONDERFUL

ALSO BY ROBERT GOOLRICK

A Reliable Wife
The End of the World as We Know It

ROBERT GOOLRICK

Heading Out to Wonderful

A NOVEL

ALGONQUIN BOOKS OF CHAPEL HILL   2013

Published by
Algonquin Books of Chapel Hill
Post Office Box 2225
Chapel Hill, North Carolina 27515-2225

a division of
Workman Publishing
225 Varick Street
New York, New York 10014

First paperback edition, Algonquin Books of Chapel Hill, January 2013.
Originally published by Algonquin Books of Chapel Hill in 2012.
Printed in the United States of America.

There is an actual town of Brownsburg, Virginia, and it is a beautiful town,
one of my favorite places on earth. But it bears no resemblance at all to the
Brownsburg in my book. The parameters, population, and other specifics of my
town are completely fictitious, as are the lives of the citizens. There is also,
by the way, a town called Ordinary, Virginia, and I would have set the
book there, but nobody would have believed it.

LIBRARY OF CONGRESS CATALOGING-IN-PUBLICATION DATA
Goolrick, Robert, [date]
Heading out to wonderful : a novel / by Robert Goolrick.—1st ed.
p. cm.
ISBN 978-1-56512-923-8 (alk. paper) (HC)
1. City and town life—Virginia—Fiction. 2. Butchers—Fiction.
3. Virginia—History—20th century—Fiction. I. Title.
PS3607.O5925H43 2012
813'.6—dc23   2012002948

ISBN 978-1-61620-279-8 (PB)

10 9 8 7 6 5 4 3 2 1
First Paperback Edition

This is for my remarkable and beloved cousins
John Esten, Alexandra, and Sally Page Byers
And for Stephen Carrière
Who is my true father

It wasn't the cold river bottom I felt rushing over me
It wasn't the bitterness of a dream that didn't come true
It wasn't the wind in the gray fields I felt rushing through my arms
No no baby, baby it was you

—BRUCE SPRINGSTEEN, "Valentine's Day"

HEADING OUT TO WONDERFUL

PART ONE

The Man Who Sins

CHAPTER ONE

THE THING IS, all memory is fiction. You have to remember that. Of course, there are things that actually, certifiably happened, things where you can pinpoint the day, the hour, and the minute. When you think about it, though, those things mostly seem to happen to other people.

This story actually happened, and it happened pretty much the way I'm going to tell it to you. It's a true story, as much as six decades of remembering and telling can allow it to be true. Time changes things, and you don't always get everything right. You remember a little thing clear as a bell, the weather, say, or the splash of light on the river's ripples as the sun was going down into the black pines, things not even connected to anything in particular, while other things, big things even, come completely disconnected and no longer have any shape or sound. The little things seem more real than some of the big things.

People still ask me about it to this day, about what happened and why I think it happened, as if I knew even now after all this time, when everything's been over for decades except the talk and the myth, I don't know what else you'd call it. I'm not young any more, so sometimes I can't tell what things are the things I remember and what things are just things that other people told me. They tell me things I did, and a lot of them I don't remember, but most people around here aren't liars, so I just go on and believe them, until it seems that I actually do remember the things they say.

But I still ask myself sometimes late at night about what happened, how it all turned out, about the life I've led, you know, everything. I ask myself the same questions they ask me, these people who've only heard about it, who weren't even around when it all took place. What happened and why did it have to happen in the way it did?

Was I damaged by it, they want to know, wounded in some way? And I always say no. I don't think I was hurt by it. But I was changed, changed deeply and forever in ways I realize more and more every day. Anyway, it's too late now to go back, to take that rock out of the river, the one that changed the course of the water's flow.

The story began this way. And it began here, more than sixty years ago.

This was a town where no crime had ever been committed. Disasters had happened, of course, natural disasters had occurred in the course of things, barn fires, floods, house fires, terrible illnesses. So many fine young men from the town who didn't come back from the war, or came back from France and Germany bruised and wounded and shy and scared of sharp bright electric sounds in the dark. And sin. Envy and greed and covetousness and pride, there was terrible pride. But no crime. Not in this town.

Brownsburg, Virginia, 1948, the kind of town that existed in the years right after the war, where the terrible American wanting hadn't touched yet, where most people lived a simple life without yearning for things they couldn't have, where the general store had tin Merita bread signs as door handles, and, inside, slabs of bacon and loaves of thin-sliced bread and canned vegetables and flour and flannel shirts and yard goods and movie magazines for the dreamers and penny candies in glass jars on the counter for the children. Cokes and brightly colored Nehi pop nestled in a metal box that was filled with iced water, and you got your drink by sliding it out of the metal slots through the icy water, dope, my mother called it, sometimes saying to my father, "Let's go down to the store and get a dope." She was a teacher, Latin to unruly and unwilling boys and girls, but she longed for another time. She liked the way it had been before the war a whole lot better. She saw everything that way, as though change were not happening faster than her heart could beat.

The general store stood in the middle of a thin short row of others like it, a butcher, a barber, a bank, a hardware store with bins of nails and screws and simple tools and wiring, and lumber in the back, but everything else you had to drive to Lexington to get, twelve miles of two-lane twist away. It was a town where people expected to live calmly and die and go to heaven in due time.

On a hill behind the town there was a school that went all the way from first grade to graduation, the ones who made it that far, with a small, thinly stocked library built alongside it. That's where my mother taught the stories of the wars and the gods. *Arma virumque cano / Troiae qui primus ab oris.* The school was heated by wood stoves, and sometimes it was so cold in the winter that the children got the day off, even if it wasn't snowing, and school let out in early May so the children could help with the planting.

There weren't any stoplights. The streets, the few of them that there were, were straight and smooth and didn't go very far. Nobody drove fast, except the occasional stranger who drove through town, lost on his way from someplace to someplace else that wasn't Brownsburg.

There were two advertising billboards, one at each end of the town. Crudely painted, they said, identically, CHARLIE CARTER CLEANS CHIMNEYS, and underneath, *Recaps, Liners, Repairs.* That's all. No phone number, no address, so unless you knew who Charlie was and where he lived, there was no way in hell you were going to get your chimney relined, if you needed that. But Charlie Carter lived right behind one of the signs, anyway, so the few people who had need of his services didn't have much trouble.

The people here then, they believed in God and The Book. They believed that the Word was made flesh and dwelt among us, that the Word was truth—no, that it was fact, as it was given to the prophets and the saints. The faith of their fathers passed through them mother to son, son to daughter and son, until it peopled the towns they made.

They hoped for their own salvation, and they feared for their neighbor's perdition.

They didn't divorce. There was not one divorce in the whole town, never had been. The church preached against it, and custom didn't allow it.

THE HOUSES IN BROWNSBURG sat with straight and honest faces toward the street, brick mostly or clapboard, built within a twenty-five-year span of one another about a hundred years before. They had shallow yards running along the street, and bigger yards to the back. These yards became a kind of unspoken, amicable battleground between neighbors, in every house gardeners, and every gardener seeing who could make the best show, flowers on the street side, vegetables behind, the women and girls to the front, the men and boys out back, victories measured out in continuous, radiant bloom, and in the number of jars of vegetables put up on hot summer days, to be eaten in the dead of winter.

In the evenings, the mothers and fathers would sit on the porches, drinking iced tea and talking in soft voices about the day's events, while the girls sat on the lawns making chains out of dandelions, and the boys made lonesome bleating whistles with blades of grass squeezed between their thumbs. They listened to the radio, in the evenings, but since there was only one station anybody could get, the town became, for that hour or two, like a stereophonic symphony.

There were five hundred and thirty-eight people here, then, and it rarely changed, the number of births pretty much keeping pace with the number of deaths.

No doors were ever locked. No dogs were walked on leashes. On a snowy day, children sledded in the street. Most of the men smoked, and some of the women, who had picked it up when their husbands went off to war.

The black people, about fifty adults and twenty children, lived in clean neat wooden houses clustered together, not quite outside the town, but not quite inside it either. They worked hard, and they pretty much kept the town running, the houses clean, the laundry fresh and crisp, and the fields flourishing, with not one word of thanks and very little in the way of money, and they spent the money they made from the white men at white men's stores. They had their own church, a storefront down at the end of Main Street, and a preacher who came every other week to lead them in services of prayer and song that went on from ten in the morning until six at night with a break for lunch. The children learned to read and write and do their sums at home. Their knowledge of the world stopped pretty much at the edge of the town limits.

Nobody went on vacations. The idea just didn't occur to them. Trips were limited to funerals, the occasional wedding, and family reunions.

Children remember summer best; they feel its pleasures on their skin. The older you get, it's the winters that stay with you, down deep in your bones. Things happen in the winter. People die in February.

Children remember staying up late. Grownups think about getting up early.

A particular town, then, Brownsburg, in a particular time and place. The notion of being happy didn't occur to most people, it just wasn't something they thought about, and life treated them pretty well, and even though at least two or three men got drunk every week night and slapped their wives and children around and children were punished hard when they were rude or misbehaved, the notion of being unhappy didn't occur much either.

They just accepted their lot, these five hundred or so men, women, and children, black and white, the blacks knowing their place, as they said then, which meant that the whites knew their place, too, and were pretty pleased with their lot in the evolutionary parade. The people moved about their daily business and did the things that life laid out for them to do, always aware of the mountains that ringed them in, blue in the summer twilights, the light turning from white to gold to rose as they sat on their porches. In the black winter, they sat in front of their wood stoves and listened to the sad and joyous songs of mountain women and plains cowboys on the radio before they went to their early beds.

They belonged to the land, to this particular place, the way their cars or their tablespoons belonged to them.

The people were religious people, and their faith got them through whatever fell on them, that and the land and the mountains that cradled and gave a salvation to anybody who had the grace to live nestled in their ancient soft hollows.

DAPPLED, THEN, AND GREEN in the summer, when Charlie Beale arrived, the days hot and the rain regular. Everybody complained about the weather most of the time, except for rain, which stopped everything useful but always made people think that it was needed, even if it had just rained three days before.

Charlie Beale drove into town out of nowhere in an old beat-up pickup truck. On the seat beside him there were two suitcases. One was thin cardboard and had seen a lot of wear and in it were all of Charlie Beale's clothes and a set of butcher knives, sharp as razors.

The other one was made of tin and it had a lock because it was filled with money. A lot of money. Charlie wore the key to the lock on a chain around his throat.

He paid Russell Hostetter a dollar a night to let him park his truck out in a field by the river, three miles outside of town, and he slept in the flatbed, sleeping on one old quilt, covered by another, and he bathed in the river in the dark with soap and a towel he bought at the general store. The summer moonlight filtered through the willow branches and made shadows on his pale, glistening back. The black, cool water sparkled as he shook out his wet hair, turned from brown to the black of the water and the starlit night. One thing about Charlie Beale, he was always clean. He dried his wet skin with the rough towel, rubbing until it was red, as though he had been slapped.

Every night, before he slept, before he turned down the kerosene lamp he kept with him and lay back to marvel at the vastness of the sky, he drank a glass of whiskey and smoked a Lucky Strike, and then he wrote in his diary. Mostly it was just the state of things, the temperature, the amount of rainfall, little things. Hot today, he would write. Snow, twelve inches. Or, Saw an eagle. He wasn't a poetic man. Thirty-nine years on the planet had beaten the poetry out of him.

As he wrote, he would start to remember what it had been like, growing up where he grew, the people who were his people, and other people he met along the way, and he would note down things, finding as he wrote a kind of simple eloquence, always referring to his friends only by their initials, just so, when he got old, he would have some way of looking back on the days that were passing, the places he'd been. He'd done it since he was a boy, when his fascination with the world was greater than it was when he came to town, and even though the passage of his life didn't interest him nearly as much now that it was happening as it had when it was all just waiting to begin, he still kept at it, out of habit. Sometimes, in reading back, he would come across a set of initials he'd written down, and not be able to place the person, the face, or the reference.

Keeping the diaries was his way of judging how far he stood from what he considered to be goodness, as he understood the term, and most nights he would add a little plus or minus next to whatever he'd written, just to gauge the distance, his recorded moral compass. There were eleven of these diaries in a box in the truck, numbered by year. He was working on his twelfth.

Then he knelt by the truck with the singing of the crickets loud in the dark and the murmur of the night moths like a fluttering in the heart, and he said his prayers, even though he knew deep down he had lost his faith somewhere along the way. He prayed for his family, he prayed the bright hopes of his childhood would return to him. He prayed that things would finally turn out better, and that this would be the place he could feel at home.

◆　◆　◆

He bought a loaf of white bread at the store, and some sliced baloney and peanut butter and jelly and a carton of Cokes, and he ate sandwiches out by the river, keeping the drinks cool in the dark flowing water.

Every day of the first week he walked the streets of the town, seemingly without purpose or direction. He nodded hello to everybody he passed, politely, but he didn't talk to a soul. He just looked with a quiet, even stare at the shops: from the dry goods store down to the barber shop with its striped pole twirling endlessly. He looked closely at every house, at the neat picket fences and gardens. He looked at the faces of the people of the town, as they in turn looked at him, and he pictured these faces as he lay in the dark out by the river, just thinking about whether or not these were people he would like to know.

Some days, he got in his truck and drove aimlessly around the back roads of the county, his suitcases on the seat beside him. He would stop and look out at the mountains, across the farm fields now gray-gold with the end of summer heat and drought, the second-cutting hay all done, the golden stubble sticking straight out of brown dirt. He just watched the land. He looked at the county from every angle.

Everything he did was noticed. What was he looking for, they wondered all over town. What was he looking *at*?

They were waiting. They were waiting for him to do something, and until he made the first move, nobody would hold out a hand to shake, or give anything back to his gentle stare.

He was the scarecrow in the garden.

After one week, Charlie Beale started doing things. He got up with the first light, a sliver of moon still in the sky, and shaved in the rearview mirror of his truck. He put on a clean white shirt, and he went and sat with Russell Hostetter at the breakfast table and arranged to buy the fifty acres of river land out where his truck was parked.

He paid him one thousand dollars in cash.

"Planning to build?" Russell asked.

"I don't think so," said Charlie. "It's just peaceful. I just want a quiet place."

"Well, it's pretty peaceful out there," said Russell. "I got to tell you," he said, eyeing the stack of one-hundred-dollar bills, "that land ain't good for much except peace and quiet."

"That's all I want."

"Flood plain."

"I'm not building out there."

They shook hands and Charlie said he'd arrange to have the survey done and the deed recorded. Then Russell went back to his breakfast and Charlie got into his truck, the leather seats already warm from the morning sun, and just drove and sat by the river, his land and river now, until it was late morning. He took off his shirt to let the sun warm his skin.

He felt complete peace, watching the water flowing by, knowing that wherever he put his foot, the land under his shoe belonged to him. When the water rose, *if* the water rose, and sooner or later it would, it would flood his land.

At the beginning of his second week in town, he got out his

knives and sharpened them again, then drove into town and parked outside Will Haislett's butcher shop. Stores were already shutting for lunch, shopkeepers going home to their dinner.

He got out, locking the truck, and walked over to the entrance and pulled open the door handle that said GWALTNEY'S HAM, and stepped inside. The bell over the door jangled. There was a small boy standing in the middle of the store, shorts, T-shirt, bare feet on the sawdust floor. Charlie Beale didn't see anybody else, just the child, his blond hair cut close to the skull, almost glowing in a shaft of light from the street, the glare from a passing car's windshield, motes floating in the brilliant air around his still and golden head.

They stood silently, a grown man and a small boy. Everything stopped for a second except the buzzing of the flies, the tiny bits of dust floating in the air, the man suddenly awkward, drawing lines with his foot in the sawdust on the floor, the child freezing him with an intent stare, as though he were seeing through Charlie and into some other landscape, as though Charlie weren't there. A tiny slice of time in a small town a long time ago.

"I'm Charlie Beale."

"Beebo" was all the child answered, shaking his head, looking past Charlie, into that other landscape, dead serious.

"I know who you are," said a voice from the back of the shop, as the heavy door to the meat locker swung open. "Everybody knows who you are. Nobody knows what you want, but ain't a soul in this whole town don't know your name is Charlie Beale. Not since the day you bought Russell's land. We know your name, we know what you paid for it. Question is, what do you intend to do with it? Why are you here? That's the question, Mister Beale."

"I'm a butcher, Mr. Haislett. A good one. I'm looking to work. That's all I want. Just a job."

"You see a big crowd here? You see a lot of people just standing around waiting to be served with nobody to wait on them? Cause if that's what you see, you got a world better eyes than I do."

"A good butcher. I have experience all over the place. There isn't anything I don't know."

The boy never took his eyes off Charlie, just shuffled over to the white-haired man and held on to his pants leg.

"Hell's bells, son. *I'm* a good butcher and I run a nice clean shop, and people come and they go and nobody complains and I've been doing it for more than thirty years, ever since I was just out of the army, learned everything from my father who learned it from his father."

The little boy laughed. "Beebo," he said, delighted. "Beebo. Beebo." His father looked down, rubbed his head.

"This here, Mr. Beale, this here is Sam Haislett. He is my son and he is five years old and he is the light of my life. Shake hands with Mr. Beale, boy."

"Beebo!" The boy laughed again, then stepped forward and held out his hand, watched as it disappeared in Charlie's broad palm. "Pleased to meet you, Sam. It's a real pleasure. Call me Charlie."

"I'm going to call you Beebo, sir. Okay?"

"Whatever suits you, son. Whatever you think best."

Sam returned to stand by his father's leg. Will picked up a butcher knife, wiped it down with a clean cloth.

"I'll work for free."

"Free work is worth exactly what you pay for it."

"I'll work for free for one month. Then you'll decide what you want to do. If you still want me around. I'm worth it, you'll see."

"Why would you do a fool thing like that?"

"I mean to settle down here, Mr. Haislett. I've seen enough of the world. I just want my own little corner of it. A place to feel at home again."

"And where's home?"

"Nowhere, now. Came from up north. Born out in Ohio."

"Why'd you leave?"

"You know the story. Came back from the war. Daddy dead. Mama moved in with relations. Family scattered. So I went traveling. Saw the country, looking for I don't know what. Yes, I do. Something wonderful, I guess. Someplace special. I saw Brownsburg. I've been here thinking hard on it for a week."

"Let me tell you something, son. When you're young, and you head out to wonderful, everything is fresh and bright as a brand-new penny, but before you get to wonderful you're going to have to pass through all right. And when you get to all right, stop and take a good, long look, because that may be as far as you're ever going to go. Brownsburg ain't heaven, by any means. But it's perfectly fine. It's all right."

"I mean to stay. I've got nobody and nowhere I want to be. I need something to do with my days."

"And money don't mean nothin'?"

"Like I said, sir, I have nobody. I have what's in my suitcases. I mean to find a house, make a place to lay my head and all that takes money and it takes work, and butchering is what I know."

"Slaughtering?"

"Everything. I can slaughter a cow so fast she looks as peaceful as if she died in her sleep. They say it makes the meat sweeter, more tender when the animal goes quickly and peacefully."

"Hell. I don't know. Tell you what. It's almost dinner time. Go in there and get some of that beef and cut us off some steaks and come home to eat with us. My wife Alma's smarter than me. She's a schoolteacher. She'll know what to do. I'll call her now."

Charlie stepped into the cool of the meat locker, listening to Will speak in hushed tones on the wall telephone. He picked a side of beef and swung it out and onto the butcher block without even getting his shirt dirty. He opened up the leather pouch holding his knives and laid them out one by one on the counter.

"I've got my own knives."

"That I can see."

"From Germany."

He picked out a knife, tested the blade against the side of his thumb.

"T-bones? Sirloin? Tenderloin?

"T-bone. Pan steaks. You know."

"Bone in?"

"Yes. But thin."

"How many?"

"Four."

Using a knife and then a hacksaw for the chine, Charlie cut four steaks, pulled on the roll of white paper over his head, tore off a square and wrapped up the steaks as neatly as a Christmas package.

"That'll do?"

"That'll do fine. Let's go eat. We'll ask my wife what to do about you. She'll know. She knows everything."

They stepped into the day, now hot, and Will carefully locked the door behind him.

All around them, in the hot stillness of Brownsburg at noon, people were sitting down to their dinner. They walked along Main Street. It was the kind of town that had only one of everything it had, and a lot of things it didn't have at all. They didn't talk.

They stopped in front of a tall Victorian house, neat as a pin, with zinnias growing around the steps that led up to a high porch, gingerbread trim fretted and heavy with wisteria vines, the blooms long gone. The buzz of summer noonday flies; the smell of hot black tar about to bubble. The house was a sturdy building where a family lived out its life, its loves, its sorrows, its small everyday inconsistencies and mundanities. All of it Charlie Beale breathed in as though it were the sweet heavy musk of a night blooming flower.

Will Haislett opened the door, and Charlie Beale stepped into the dark warm hall. With his first breath, he could tell that everything in the house was clean, clean all the time, the tables dusted, the glasses in the cupboards clear and spotless, the sheets on the beds taut and smelling of bleach and fresh air. It was like nothing he remembered, had nothing to do with his own reckless childhood, but it was somehow as familiar as his own skin, like something he had known was there his whole life but had never tasted or smelled.

A home, something Charlie didn't have, shelter and kindness to every living soul who slept there, bonded by blood, and every friend and stranger who passed through its doors. It was in a constant state of readiness, a readiness to welcome.

In those days, there were no antiques. There were just new things and old things, things brought from the home place, things cared for through the years, through the rough-and-tumble of life, things bought when the marriage was new, things bought for a lifetime.

The furniture in the sitting room where Will Haislett led Charlie was mostly old, covered now by summer slipcovers of chintz and linen, made by Lula Hall, who knew every piece so well by now she didn't even have to measure when called on to make covers for the sofa or the big, comfortable chairs.

Will didn't offer Charlie a seat, and they stood awkwardly, five-year-old Sam holding on to his father's leg, the face the same in man and boy, the same blue eyes. Charlie could smell things cooking, good rich fresh things, could sense a bustle going on somewhere in the house, even though everything where they stood was perfectly still.

"Alma?" Will called softly. "Alma, I've brought him home for dinner."

And with just the slightest movement of the warm summer air, just a sigh, there she was, as she was every day at fifteen minutes past twelve, and all she said, looking at Will, was "Darling," and there is no earthly way to tell you the sweetness of it, the soft accent, schooled, not country, the voice breathless with the anticipation of his company.

She was forty years old, just a year older than Charlie Beale was then, and fourteen years younger than her husband. Her red hair was just beginning to go soft, pale like fall leaves in November, and her pale gray eyes seemed expectant, surprised, as though something wonderful were just about to happen.

She raised herself on her toes to kiss her husband, then knelt on the floor to kiss her son, who wrapped his arms around her neck, hiding his face in her shoulder.

She looked up. "Of course," she said. "Charlie Beale," as though she had known him all her life, "you're here." As though he already held a place in her heart as one of the many good men and women who filled her days. Then she stood up and held out her hand to shake his, and said, "You're more than welcome in our house."

"This is my wife, Alma," Will said. "She came along and saved my sorry ass from ruin and destruction."

She laughed. "Oh, Will, don't be so dire, darling." Again that word, darling—Charlie felt it and it filled him completely, as tangible and soft as a kiss good night.

" 'Ruin and destruction.' Forgive us, Mr. Beale, but around here we spend so much time in church we talk like preachers quoting scripture."

She let go of his hand. "Welcome to our house. Those must be our steaks."

He handed them shyly to her. "Thanks for inviting me in. I

was getting awfully tired of sandwiches out there by the river." He hadn't talked to a woman in months. He had forgotten how, he realized, forgotten the simple graces. He especially didn't know how to talk to married women.

He had turned away from his past, his reckless ways, but he hadn't turned toward anything new except the restless unceasing driving that had taken him all through 1948, ever since the end of the war, really, until it landed him here, in Brownsburg, Virginia, in the sitting room of people he didn't know, with nothing to say to them at all, no way to say what was in his heart, to say that he had forgotten, forgotten the pleasure of company, the beauty of children, the smell and sense of clean warm hearts in clean bright houses.

He wasn't used to being welcomed. He wasn't used to being looked at with anything other than weariness or fear or distrust. Suddenly shy, he felt the blood rush to his face.

She stood close to him, uncomfortably close. She looked into his eyes, her gaze too long, but unexpectedly, too kind. He glanced away.

"Mr. Beale," she brought him back. He looked into her gray eyes.

"Charlie," he said. "Please."

She continued to look at him. "Mr. Beale, are you a Christian?"

"Not really, ma'am. I used to . . . but that's been a while."

"But are you a good man?"

"I try. I guess you never know until it's over."

She reached up, touched his skin the way a blind mother might explore the face of her only child. Her eyes never left his. He reddened further and his skin felt hot. She must have felt it with her cool hand, like a fever.

"He wants a job," Will said.

Without breaking her gaze, she said, over her shoulder, "Of course, Will. Of course he'll do. You could use some help. I don't know why you needed to ask me."

She turned away, knelt down to hug the little boy. "Now let's have our dinner."

And it was done. Whatever it was, whatever Will had wanted her opinion about, it was over and done with.

And that's how the story began.

CHAPTER TWO

CHARLIE STILL STAYED out by the river, except when it rained, and then he would stay after supper and sleep in the Haisletts' spare room, next door to the boy, who kept a wary distance. Sometimes, on the nights out by the river, an unexpected storm would roll in in the night, and then he would crawl under the truck, and he would think of Alma's clean sheets, crisply laid, smelling of laundry soap and sunshine.

He liked it better out by the river. He was used to being alone, and the weight of all those bodies around him gave his sleep an uneasiness that left him tired the next day. Most nights and noons he ate what Alma made for him and was grateful that he wasn't living on sandwiches and Cokes any more.

Driving back to the river, in the dark, he would smoke and watch for animals. He liked to fling the burning end of his cigarette out the window and watch as it hit the road behind him, sending up a meteor shower of sparks receding in the distance, a sudden orange flare in all that racing blackness, the flint striking steel, momentary but staying in his eyes long after the speeding truck had left the sparks behind. Such magic in the rearview mirror, his eyes, the speeding road, the sparks of a Lucky in the dark.

One time he was letting go of his cigarette just as his headlights lit up the still body of a deer, a big doe, hit by a car, dead on the roadside, its eyes frozen in a fixed shock of terror. After that, every time he saw the shower of sparks, he thought of that dead deer, and of the permanence of fear, of how, once it got into you, it never let go. He hoped it never got into him.

He thought of his brother Ned, who always had that look of a deer frozen in the headlights, stunned. He hadn't seen Ned since right after the war, but now his face came back so clear and true he might have reached out and touched it. Now every night when he threw the cigarette out the window and watched the display vanishing behind him, he said his brother's name to himself, and the shower of sparks became inextricably linked to his brother's face and name. One day, he would think, I'll see what he looks like now, grown. But then the sparks would be gone, and Ned would be gone, too, until the next night, the next Lucky on the blacktop.

By the river, on his own land, he woke up every morning before the sunrise, warm in his quilt and the rising heat and his usually pleasant dreams. The days seemed like good ones, mostly, and he rinsed his face and shaved in the river with a light heart.

He was at the butcher shop when it was just light. The thing he liked about being alone was that you could have things exactly the way you wanted them, with nobody looking over your shoulder.

He used the hour before Will appeared to clean the shop, sweeping the wood floor and laying down fresh sawdust, every morning. He sprinkled salt on the butcher block, and scrubbed it down with a steel brush, scrubbing away yesterday's steaks and chops and roasts, yesterday's blood. He washed the marble counter with bleach and warm water. He checked in the cold locker to see what was there, what was needed, what was selling and what wasn't.

It was too early for the radio. The distant, staticky station didn't come on until nine, so Charlie hummed to himself as he got everything ready, old songs he remembered his grandmother singing to him, and songs he had heard just yesterday on the radio, new songs out of Nashville.

All this country music was new to him, and he liked it. It felt like home, the thin, high mountain voices singing about heaven and hell and betrayal and loss. There were songs about love and murder. Something about these songs made Charlie remember what it was like to be in love, made him want to feel that way again.

He laid out the thick strips of country bacon in neat rows, bacon Will had smoked himself, so rich, so salty, and put sprigs of parsley around the cuts left over from yesterday. He made clean butcher's bows to put on yesterday's chops, flipped the steaks and roasts so they looked fresh, as though they'd just been cut. Will tried not to have a lot left over at the end of the day, but whatever was left, Charlie made it look brand new.

Just as the other shops were beginning to open, Charlie uncurled

the hose from the side of the building and washed down the sidewalk outside the store, the bricks turning from dusty rose to deep
bloodred and drying in the sun to an ancient pink, the same color
as most of the houses that lined the streets of the town.

When Will appeared, always with the boy, he brought Charlie
a fried egg sandwich and a few strips of bacon, wrapped in wax
paper, and Charlie sat in the one chair and ate his breakfast while
Will went over the figures, called the slaughterhouse, counted the
money in the cash register, sometimes taking a huge roll of cash out
of his pocket and either adding some to it from the cash register,
or peeling off some of his own to add to the drawer. Then he filled
out his bank deposit slip and went across the street, leaving Charlie
to eat in peace, while the boy sat on the floor, still in his summer
shorts and T-shirt, drawing faces in the sawdust.

Will always brought two sparkling white butcher's aprons—he
said Alma could get blood out of anything—and Charlie would
be just slipping his on when Will came back from the bank, and
the first customers opened the screen door, tinkling the bell.

The black women came first, ages nineteen to eighty, in their
thin dresses smelling of hand soap and galvanized washing boards,
as though they wanted to get their business out of the way before
the white women stirred from their houses. Sometimes they had
extra shopping to do for the white women they worked for. They
rarely came alone, usually with a friend or a cousin or an aunt,
and some mornings, they were all there at once, at the door before
the sidewalk dried, and gone just as quickly, their neatly wrapped
bundles in their hands. Sometimes they came with children, children who stared at Sam and didn't speak or say hello.

They ordered as much, if not more, than any of the white women, and Charlie treated them all with the same respect, although he never learned any of their names, and they didn't ask his.

He looked at their hands, looking for wedding rings, and he called them Miss, or Ma'am, depending on how he figured it. They never smiled, and he never smiled back, just looked at them with his honest eyes, and treated the exchange as seriously as they did, watching as they counted out the money for Will, sometimes in bills, sometimes in coins.

Usually they were gone by the time the first white women came, and if they weren't, they stepped aside and looked away as the white women entered, then left quickly, silently.

Fanning themselves with paper fans from the funeral parlor or the Methodist church, the women of the town came. It wasn't that there were more customers since Charlie had started working at the butcher shop, since the customers were basically every woman who lived in the town, along with the few single men, but their visits seemed more social, and they started to buy just for the day, or just for their midday meal, so they could come back tomorrow or even later in the afternoon. Most of the women had electric refrigerators now, so they could have shopped for a whole week, but they chose not to. There were some, a few, not many and mostly Negro, who had iceboxes. And there was still an ice man who made his dwindling round of the town every two days, hefting a massive block of ice with pincers, the sweat showing between the shoulders of his shirt even as he stepped out of the frigid air of the back of the truck, his huge forearms glistening as he carried the blocks into the houses, to put them into the bottoms of the oak boxes lined with tin.

One man came in every day, a fat man Will called Boaty, although anybody else who was in the shop at the time called him Harrison or even Mr. Glass. He was about the same age as Will, although it's hard to tell with fat people, and they treated each other the way men do who have grown up together all their lives, watching as their lives, once so identical, changed paths and led one this way, that one another.

"Charlie Beale. This is Boaty Glass. Sorry. Harrison. Harrison Boatwright Glass."

"Morning, Mr. Glass. Good to meet you."

"Harrison and I were babies in the cradle together."

"We were that," said the fat man. "We did a lot of adventuring, back in the day."

"Boaty doesn't trust his own wife to pick out his supper for him."

"My wife can cook anything, but she's not exactly what you'd call an early riser. And then it takes her about two hours to get ready to come into town, and by then all the good stuff might be gone."

"You always thought ahead, Boaty. Admirable quality. Always give Mr. Glass the best there is, Charlie. He worked hard for it. And he deserves it." Will couldn't help himself. "And, obviously, he deserves a lot of it."

"Bastard," said Harrison Glass. "You always had a mean streak, Will."

"Not a mean bone in my body, Boaty. You've got the appetite a man your size ought to have. That's just a fact. Not an unkind thought in my head."

Boaty Glass did get the best, and he didn't pay, just watched as Will wrote down his purchases in a book, and, because he bought a lot, Will always gave him a little off, although Boaty Glass didn't look like he needed any kind of discount on the things he paid for.

Boaty Glass was the kind of man who told jokes, like a nervous tic. Often vulgar, but, in mixed company, usually just dumb old country jokes he'd heard on the Opry or read in the *Grit* paper.

"So old Torkle McCorkle walks into Manley Brown's black-smith shop the other day, and Manley's just finished pulling a red hot horseshoe out of the fire and laid it on the anvil. This fella walks over to the anvil, picks up the horseshoe in his bare hand, then puts it right back down again. "'Burned you, didn't it?' says Manley. 'Nope,' says Torkle, 'just don't take me very long to look at a horseshoe.'"

He'd laugh so hard at his own joke you could see the back of his throat and his thick, coated tongue hanging out of his mouth. A man's man, some might have said. A buffoon, others might have called it more accurately. A fat clown.

He usually came on his way to Staunton to take care of his business. Everybody treated him with a kind of deference, as though he, like Charlie, were a stranger to them, even though they'd known him their whole lives.

"Nobody likes him," said Will one day, after he'd gone. "Sad. Not even me. Not any more. He's no more like the boy I knew than Eleanor Roosevelt. And it ain't just because he's rich. He was a nice boy, big, but not like he is now. Now he's just plain gross. Got a hillbilly wife he wears like a ring on his little finger. Nobody else would marry him, and god knows he tried. Imagine, rich as he is, still nobody would have him. Maybe that's what turned him so mean. He's sharp in his dealings, don't treat people with respect. Skinned every man who had a hide in two counties. Thinks he's better than he is, and everybody knows exactly what he is, just a fat, rich man who's forgotten everything he learned from his mother, who was a good Christian woman, rest her soul.

"One day we were friends. The next, he decided I wasn't good enough for him. We'll get together next week, he'd say, but next week never came, and finally he stopped asking, and I stopped caring.

"It's a sad thing to watch your best friend turn into somebody you don't know any more. Or even want to know. Still, you've got to pretend. Make the best of it. The thing about small towns is, you *live* with these people, see them every day. No point in fighting. Everybody is always just there, every day, so you've got to make your peace. And he spends good money. Still. Sad.

"Just goes to show you that having a good name and coming from good people don't actually make you good people yourself. I don't know him from Adam, any more.

"And that wife of his. Just you wait. She's a piece of work."

They all called him Mr. Beale, the white women, and he gently told them not to, every time, until eventually they all called him Charlie, although he continued calling them by their married names, even though they asked him to stop.

Charlie was a better butcher than Will, and the women were impressed, although they didn't say anything, so as not to hurt

Will's feelings. Charlie's steaks looked better, trimmed with just a fine thin layer of fat at the edges, and he would tie up their roasts for them with twine, so they looked tight and neat, covering the pork roasts with neatly laid strips of bacon.

So Charlie cut the meat and charmed the ladies, one by one, but, more than charm, he treated every one, black and white, from the richest to the shoeless poorest, from dollars to dimes, with the same deference and shy kindness, and he won their hearts while Will took the money and read to Sam from the *Richmond Times-Dispatch,* read it to him cover to cover every day, even the captions on the pictures, everything from politics to sports, and how to keep your stockings from running by keeping them in the freezer.

Sam was crazy about sports, even sports he'd never seen, like tennis, and of course he liked the comics, which he could just about read for himself by now, even though he didn't start school for another year.

He talked about Joe DiMaggio and Steve Canyon and Popeye and Harry Truman in exactly the same way, as though they were people he actually knew, as though they might all be coming to Brownsburg any day now. His special hero was Jackie Robinson, and he talked endlessly about how Jackie could hit and run and play the field, a triple threat was the phrase he used, although where he had picked it up, nobody could say for sure. There are some things boys just know.

At the end of Charlie's first work week, on a Friday in late August, 1948, a woman walked into the shop, and that's when the story becomes more than just another story, becomes instead a tale that's passed down from father to son as a warning, from mother to daughter in that year when the daughter first begins to dream of romance, the kind of romance seen in the flickering light of the movie screen: The lights go down, the movie starts, the silent flicker as the frames go through the sprockets, and even the most ordinary gesture becomes extraordinary. Everything stops, and something you can't explain begins.

The bell over the door jangled, everybody turned to see who was coming in, the way they always did. She walked silently into the butcher shop, and everybody stared at her and they didn't turn away and start talking again, the way they usually did, and nobody, not one woman, said a word of greeting to her.

Charlie had never seen her, not once, and he thought he'd seen everybody. It was obvious she was different from the other women. She had a country face, young, probably not much more than twenty, if that. She wore a wedding band and an engagement ring, so that much was clear, but she looked as though she had stepped into the shop from another part of the world, from one of the cities Charlie had visited during his days and nights of travel.

She wore a white linen dress, it was still before Labor Day, and such things still mattered then, a white dress with an olive green belt at the trim waist, the neckline cut low with a certain sophistication and style that said she had not bought it anywhere near Brownsburg. Her lips were a crimson slash, her hair pulled up in gleaming blonde waves on top of her head, held with tortoise-shell combs studded with rhinestones. She wore dark sunglasses, a thing no other woman in the town even thought to own, and espadrilles, tied with grosgrain ribbons around her ankles, on her small feet.

Her only other jewelry was a small gold cross she wore around her neck on a delicate chain, and she carried a small green leather bag under her arm.

She walked quickly into the center of the store, and nobody said a word to her. Charlie stopped slicing the pork chops he was cutting for Helen Anderson, and wiped the blade of his knife with a clean cloth. It glinted in the light as he laid it quietly on the counter.

Will, sitting in his chair with the boy on his lap, finally broke the silence and the stillness. He greeted her softly as he stood up and put the boy down on the floor, "Morning, Sylvan. How're you doing? How's Boaty?"

"We're fine," she said. "It's lovely. Everything's just the same as always."

She had a sweet, girlish voice. She couldn't have been much more than a teenager. She didn't sound like she was from around Brownsburg. She spoke in some faraway accent, like a princess, or an actress.

She took off her dark glasses, very slowly, bowing her head to do it, gentle, graceful. She looked up at Will briefly, nodding hello. Then she just stood, and she turned her head slowly to stare at Charlie Beale. Five seconds. Ten, maybe, no more, but it seemed forever.

His hands were on the counter. He felt the urge to do something, to wipe the butcher block, to jingle the change in his pocket, but nobody moved, and he didn't either.

"May I help you, ma'am? Is there . . . ?"

"No. No thank you. I'm not hungry for anything." She spoke with the sort of fake English accent Charlie had only heard in the movies, those glowing women on the screen with the sparkling hair and the black lips.

Five seconds.

"At the moment. Not hungry at the moment."

Then she turned and headed for the door. The bell tinkled as she left, and she shielded her eyes for a brief moment in the sudden brightness of the street. She put her dark glasses back on and let herself into a black Cadillac, started the engine and drove away.

He wanted to look. You could tell he wanted to follow this woman with his eyes, a quick light came into them, but then it was out, just like that, and he went on with the next customer. He came awake like a man who'd been in a deep sleep, and was late getting where he was going. His blade sliced into a chop, the ladies began their chatter again, watching him not watch her leave.

"That woman," Will said, "walks like a farmer."

"How's that?" asked Charlie.

"She walks," said Will, waiting, "like she's got a bale of hay on one hip and a bale of alfalfa on the other, and when she walks," he paused for effect, "she's rotating the crops," and all the women laughed, even though they had heard the same old joke since they were girls, and Charlie laughed, too, although he found the joke vulgar when he thought of the way it didn't even begin to describe the majesty and poetry of that girl's way of walking.

As if the movie were over, everything went back into motion, the ladies chattering as though she had never been there, Charlie finishing the chops and wrapping them neatly in clean white paper he ripped from a roll over his head, his hands shaking, his whole body electric beneath his clothes, the boy and Will sitting again and playing at Cat's Cradle, the chair creaking as the father and the son intertwined the string in more and more complex ways.

"Poor Sylvan," said Eleanor Cooke.

"Poor Boaty Glass, you mean," said Mary Page. "He sure got what he paid for."

"If you lie down with the dogs, you get up with the fleas," Eleanor said, ending it, and all the ladies nodded in agreement.

But Charlie Beale had heard her name. Sylvan Glass. She went off in his head and his heart like a firecracker on the Fourth of July. Something dazzling. Something stupendous.

Something, finally, that was wholly and mysteriously wonderful.

CHAPTER THREE

A SHIMMERING AND A *stillness, all at once. Charlie moves across the land, humming a song, but compared to the landscape itself, he is still and mute as a rock. Compared to the animals that, unseen, surround him, moving, feeding, breeding, he is a statue.*

The thousand thousand grasses, dry now in the late-summer heat, bristle like the brittle pages of a thousand ancient books being turned by invisible scholars. Every blade and leaf and rock speaking of loss and endurance, the birds settling down for another night or two before their long, familiar hegira. The landscape he walks is an endless cascade of loss and dying and coming to life again, and he feels the immense silence of the dead and the eternal pulse of the living in the soles of his feet.

He is in the valley of the Blue Ridge Mountains of Virginia, on flatland by the Maury River. He is cradled in the valley as a mother holds an egg in the palm of her hand.

His quilts are spread out on the ground, sandwich eaten, the speckled tin plate washed in the river, the last light now the thinnest veil between him and the mossy blackness of the night. He hums the song he heard two days before, the old guys singing it sitting on the porch at the general store, brothers, overalls, dung-smeared boots, the brothers white-haired and bearded, a five-string and a mandolin, the same face no more than two years apart, playing and singing a song they had been singing together for years and years, singing separate lines of music that flowed together like the water around him into a single river of sound. The words come back to him, the sound of their wavering voices, infused with a belief in what they knew to be true.

> Life is like a mountain railway
> With an engineer so brave
> You must make this run successful
> From the cradle
> To the grave
> Watch the curves that fill the tunnels
> Never falter, never fail
> Keep your hands upon the throttle
> And your eyes upon the rail.

It was music. It was gospel. It was their hearts' true belief, those old men, and Charlie, listening, believed, not so much in the gospel, but in the foreverness of the thing, the music, the brothers, the valley itself, and that was more forever than any man could take into his mind.

What does he believe, he wonders now, humming and thinking the words of the song he made them sing three times until he got most of it down. He believes, at this minute, in this valley, this land he is walking on, in this water that flows nearby and through his life, the passing of afternoon into evening into night, this blackness of safety and solitude. He believes in the peace of it, the eternity.

Blessed Savior, that will guide us
'Til we reach that blissful shore

But this here, the valley of sweet Virginia, this is the blissful shore. There is no more to reach for. But, humming, he knows. He knows what he believes. He believes in the strength of muscle, the pleasures of the body, the goodness of the heart. He believes in goodness, and this is a new thing, a gift to him from the river and the land and the blue light now almost black, the ink of the sky pocked with stars. This is what the valley and its waters whisper into his ear, in this evening into night. He believes at this moment, and he will always believe it, that people are good, and that he is good among them.

Where the angels wait to join us
In God's grace forevermore.

Now he knows the angels have joined us, have joined him, are in him. Such a surprise, after all. So many living things, snake and bird and fish and man, each working to create the whole, this brilliance of sound and silence, these voices of man and animal that flow into one voice, and that voice is the whole southern world, is this loss and this living. For what else has the land done but persist, and in the face of that, what else was there for him, for any of them, but to persist along with the soil that gave them bread and fed, as well, their hearts?

Lying down on his quilt, he remembers it all, it enters into his body and he knows that he has become the thing he will be from now on to the end, unless something terrible, something unimaginable, happens, but believing that it will not. There is such deep silence. There is such a roar of noise inside that silence. There is just so much.

He thinks, as he does every night before he sleeps, he wonders, what is the point, what is the reason for all his wandering, for his solitude in a peopled world, if he's not, one day, to have children, a child of his own, a son, whom he might teach and train and raise up to be a scientist, or a butcher, or a baseball star? He misses, as he does every night before he sleeps, the soft and peaceful breathing of his imagined son sleeping clean beside him.

He closes his eyes and he sees the dream that waits for him ahead, and he hears the brothers, finished with their laughing over his foolishness, realizing that they are in the act of converting a sinner into a believer, so they sing with conviction and grace and then wave him on, no more, they wave, no more, you're on your own. That's enough, they wave. If you don't get it now, then we have failed and you cannot be saved.

> As you roll across the trestle
> Spanning Jordan's swelling tide
> You'll behold a Union depot
> Into which your train will glide
> There you'll meet the Superintendant
> God the Father, God the Son

He sleeps now, cradled in peace, his right hand cupping his ear, in sleep hearing but not hearing any more the final words the old men gave to him so graciously:

> With that hearty, joyous plaudit:
> "Weary Pilgrim
> Welcome home."

CHAPTER FOUR

THE ANNUAL OYSTER Supper at the Ebenezer Baptist Church, just outside of town on a low rise by the highway, was pretty much as good as it got. Every white person in town went, and some from as far away as Lexington. It started at three, with games and gossip until suppertime, and it went on until dark, with old Rooster Ruley playing the fiddle, and the ladies of the church cooking all day long.

The oysters came from down on the Chesapeake Bay, shipped in a few days before in big wooden barrels filled with shaved ice, and they were kept in the cool dark of the church basement, where the ladies fed them with cornmeal every day, thinking it would make them fatter, and maybe it did.

They made oyster stew, scalloped oysters with cream and butter and nutmeg—so rich it threatened to stop up every artery almost immediately—oyster fritters, and fried oysters. There was a raw oyster bar, where men shucked oysters and other men slurped them down directly out of their shells, smothered in a sauce so hot it burned your tongue.

Oysters in a land-locked valley weren't so much a food as they were a rarity, an exotic way to while away a late summer afternoon.

There were hot biscuits with country butter, soft and rich gold in color, and corn on the cob, picked that morning, and tomatoes from the vine, and cole slaw and sweet iced tea and lemonade.

And there was ice cream, two kinds, mixed from Louisa Stephens's grandmother's recipe, butter pecan and peach, made with heavy farmer's cream and sugar and barnyard eggs. It was made the night before by the teenagers of the church, cranked by hand in old wooden barrels packed with shaved ice from the ice man, and rock salt to make the cold set, the boys and girls cranking in turn until their arms hurt and then passing the job on to the next one. Then it was packed in more ice, and wrapped in muslin, and stored in the chill of the basement, and brought out, vat after vat, all day long.

There was softball in a freshly mowed field in back of the church, and the boys played all afternoon, and in the evening the men played and even some of the women, the ones who had just begun to wear pants and smoke during the war.

Even the twins came, Elinor and Ansolette Gadsden, old maids so identical that they could hardly tell themselves apart. The line that divided them as people had long since disappeared. They looked alike, of course, the creases in their sixty-year-old faces matched line for line. They also dressed alike and walked hand in hand and finished each other's sentences.

When they were young, they were beauties, the old ones said, the people who remembered them as girls, and Elinor and Ansolette still had a certain quality about them, a refinement, that set them apart. Their people, of whom they were the last, the end of the line, because of their stubborn refusal to marry and thus be separated, had lived in the town since the town began. They were highly sought after because they were aristocrats, and because they had buckets of money, and they were the only Gadsdens left.

It was said that the reason they never married was because they used to tease the boys, changing places now and then, so that, when a hapless young man asked for Elinor's pledge of marriage, he was met with a peal of laughter, only to find he was reaching out for Ansolette's hand. They were both called Miss Allie, by everybody in town, and even Boaty Glass treated them with extreme respect and even affection.

The old ladies played softball. They didn't field, they just took a turn at bat, once a year, going in turn and striking out at the soft, easy pitches the men threw to them. They swung identically at any pitch that was thrown to them, in their identical dresses, and, in six swings, their athletic endeavors were over for another year.

But that day, that day in 1948, it was Charlie Beale on the ball field who won every heart. He played tirelessly, with the boys, with the grownups, and it was a thing of beauty. He took off his white shirt, and played in his strap undershirt, so you could see the size and shape of his body, not big, but strong and slender and young, his neck and shoulders rosy from exertion. He had the power and grace of a natural athlete, and the gleam that came into his eyes whenever the ball was near him, or the bat was in his hands, was something to behold.

He could stop any ball that was hit his way, catching a ball on the first hop, jumping and swiveling in the air to rocket it to any base before the runner got there. He would dive and roll in the grass for a hard-hit grounder, and he would be up in a shot and his aim never missed its mark.

Sam Haislett was entranced. He couldn't be coaxed or begged away from the edge of the field. He just had to watch every move.

At the plate, the bat seemed a natural extension of Charlie's long arms. He took a stance like a pro, legs wide, angled far back from the plate, and when the ball was pitched to him, even by the fastest of the fastball pitchers, he would lean slightly back, and smack that thing into kingdom come, every time, any pitch.

Sam watched his every move, and he fell in love. His Beebo was all the baseball pictures in all the newspapers come to life. He was Jackie and Joe together. To watch him swing, or swivel and throw, his eye unnerved, his aim true, gave Sam his first sight of the power and possibilities that lay dormant in his tiny body. He had never seen anything so beautiful.

Nobody had. The edges of the diamond filled up with onlookers, and they all picked up on the nickname Sam shouted out, until every time Charlie swung the bat, every breath was caught, every voice yelled out, "BEEEEEBO!!" at the crack of the hard

wood bat on the scuffed leather of the ball. They were seeing something they'd never seen before, man or woman, not in real life, and
nobody there ever forgot it, and the nickname was fixed in their
minds from that day on, like Babe, or Joey D.

"Must have played some ball, that boy," said one of the men.
"Maybe even pro."

"Probably not. Maybe Triple A. But he's played."

When he finally came off the field, Charlie Beale's neck and his
shoulders were rosy and running with sweat, and the crowd drifted
away with him, losing interest once he'd left the field. Without
him, the game was over.

Somebody grabbed a towel from the trunk of a car, and he thanked
her, and wiped himself down, and put his shirt back on, and every
woman watched him until the last button was buttoned. The men
stood around, clapping him on the back. Way to go, Beebo. Way to
go. It was their way of saying Beebo was fine with them, wherever he
came from, however strangely he talked, he was okay.

With the crowd drifting off, Charlie noticed Sam, and he walked
him on to the field, and knelt behind him in the batter's box, and
gave the boy his first lesson in how to hold a bat, how to keep his
eye fixed on the ball and never waver, and swing from the hips. Sam
never again swung a bat in his life that he didn't feel Charlie behind
him, Charlie's hands on his, Charlie's arms leading him back and
forward again and into the ball, sending it into the far reaches of
the field where the eye couldn't even follow it. For the rest of his
life, every time he waited for a pitch he heard Charlie's voice in his
ear, telling him that the power came not from the arms but from
the hips.

Later, cooling off, Charlie sat with Will and Alma, while Sam still hung out at the edge of the ball field, waiting for the minute Charlie might pick up the bat again, not wanting to ask but not wanting to miss it, and Alma told him everybody's story.

"They seem like nice people," Charlie said, looking out at all the folks, everybody in clean shirts and dresses, greeting each other as though they hadn't seen one another for a long, long time.

"I'll tell you a story," Alma said. "A story my mother told me, from back in the Depression. The town drunk is sitting on the courthouse steps. A tramp walks into the town, like this, like any town, and he stops and says, 'What kind of town is this?' he asks, and the drunk lifts his eyebrows, looks him over, and says, 'Oh, it's a terrible town. It's full of liars and cheaters and people who live for nothing but being mean.'

"And the tramp thanks him and moves on to the next town, hoping for better. A little later, another tramp stops by. 'What kind of town is this?' he asks. And the old drunk tells him, 'It's a wonderful town. The people are kind and good, and take well to strangers, and bring their children up right.'

"So the tramp decides to stay a while, and he finds a handout or two, and then he finds some work, and then some more work, and pretty soon, as times get better, he's got a wife and a little house and some children of his own. And he, like the rest of the town, brings them up right."

They watched the crowd for a minute, then Charlie looked at her. "Is that story about the town, or the drunk, or the tramp?"

"I think it's about finding the thing you expect to find. What do you expect to find, Mr. Beale?"

"Are you ever going to call me Charlie?"

"Lord, Alma, the man sleeps under our roof."

"Will, things will be this way between me and Mr. Beale. At least for a while. These are good people, Mr. Beale. I teach their children. You can tell a lot." She turned and smiled at Charlie. "I'm just shy, Mr. Beale. Will doesn't like it, but that's the way I am. It's the way you are when you don't meet many new people."

"However suits you, ma'am."

She laughed, and touched his hand. "Just because I'm shy doesn't mean I'm your mother, either. Call me Alma."

"Seems a little unbalanced."

"It won't be long. One day, just by accident, I'll call you by your name."

"I'm patient."

Will turned to him. "Alma's right. Good people. Happy, by and large."

"And we have good manners. That makes up for what happiness doesn't provide."

Will laughed. "Sam Mohler said to me once, when I was real young, 'You know,' he said, 'I think people pretty much decide early on how happy they're going to be. And then they just go on and be it.' Course, that was just a month before he got run over in his own front yard by Jackson Taylor's son, who was driving drunk at the age of sixteen. Jackson Taylor sold cars. Jack Junior had borrowed one from the dealership seven minutes before he ran Sam over. It's not all peaches and cream, whatever Alma says." He stood up. "Speaking of which, let's get some ice cream. Get out amongst 'em."

The women, Charlie knew from the store. The men, Will introduced him to, and so Charlie gradually put the town together, husbands with wives with children, and they all greeted him with the same friendly distance, and nobody asked him how he had ended up working in a butcher shop in Brownsburg, Virginia.

Will got three bowls of ice cream, and joined Alma and Charlie, where they had moved to a picnic table in the shade, the ice cream already starting to melt. A long black car pulled up and parked, and Boaty Glass got out of it, and went around to the other side, and opened the door—men still did that—and then she got out, and there she was. Brand new all over again.

She was wearing a full-skirted dress, royal blue, silky, sleeveless, a cocktail party dress, not the kind of thing you'd wear to a social in the backyard of a Baptist church. She had a perfect figure, rounded, soft and fleshy for a young girl, although she seemed willowy next to her bulky husband. Her legs were long and beautiful, and her blonde hair was tied back with a ribbon in a way that reminded Charlie of someone else, some other girl, perhaps in a magazine.

She was tall, taller than her husband. If she'd been standing next to Charlie, she would have been just slightly taller than he was, especially in those shoes.

She looked like the kind of pinup girl men had carried pictures of off to the war, and looked at in the lonely nights, after they had written to their sweethearts. A pinup girl in sunglasses, her eyes hidden from the world. Together, Boaty and Sylvan looked important, like people you'd see in *Life* magazine.

"Him you know," said Will. "You'll want to know about her. Tell him, Alma."

"I only know what everybody in town knows." She paused, as if she were trying to recall some tale, a myth she had heard as a child. "There's a place about fifteen miles from here called Arnold's Valley. It's hard to get to, but it's very wild and beautiful, lovely. It's untouched by time, like Eden. I've only been there once, a long time ago. The same fifteen or sixteen families have lived there for generations, since before this town even started, and they don't like strangers, and they don't much like modern life.

"Nobody goes there, except occasionally people from the state, who go and try to get them to send their children to school, and, for a couple of years, men from the army who tried to get the boys to sign up for the draft. The boys hid in the woods, until finally they were left alone. But, still, their children don't go to school, and their boys never went to war. If anything goes wrong, they decide it themselves. When they marry, *if* they church marry at all out there, or if they die, they take care of everything themselves. Nothing leaves the valley.

"Once in a while, you'll see them in town, buying shoes, or sugar, things they can't grow themselves. But not often.

"Harrison Glass was a bachelor until he was forty-eight years old. He took care of his mother, I have to say that, a difficult woman who had spells and seizures and was not only sick but a hypochondriac. Thin and romantic, like she'd been planted in weak soil. And three weeks after she died and he watched her go into the ground, he drove out to Arnold's Valley for the first time. Everybody thought he was going to buy some land there. He didn't talk to anybody, and nobody talked to him, just watched that big car of his wander the dirt roads. But it wasn't land he was after.

"He went out twelve times, they say. On the third visit, he saw a girl walking in a yard, and then he went more often, and looked for her, in the yard, in the fields, sitting on the porch.

"On the last visit, he stopped his car and got out in front of her house. He walked into the yard, knocked on the door, and spoke to her father. Then he bought her for cash, along with the farm neither one of them ever went back to I don't believe, bought her for one or two thousand dollars, although it could have been more, could have been less. She was seventeen."

"He bought her like a head of cattle," Will added.

"That was three years ago. He brought her to town, and he married her. We went to the wedding, such as it was, Will and I. Except to say 'I do,' she never spoke one word during the whole day. Then he took her to the one place she wanted to go, Hollywood, so she could get on a bus and take a tour of the stars' homes — five days out, a week there, and five days back.

"And, since that time, she's hasn't spoken much more. He bought her her own car, and she drives into Lexington every other day to go to the movies. She's crazy about the movies.

"Her name is Sylvan. Isn't that a lovely name? It might be her real name, some old mountain name, or she might have heard it on the radio or made it up out of some movie. Sylvan Glass.

"She goes to the movies and sees some getup, or she cuts out a picture from a movie magazine, and then she gets a woman in town to make a five-and-dime version of what they wear in Hollywood. That's how she learned to speak in that fancy way, first by listening to soap operas on the radio from the time she could walk, and then by watching movie stars, once Boaty got her that car.

"And, yes, that is her real hair color. Everybody in Arnold's Valley is blonde, pretty much. She'll never go back there."

"Alma drove out there once, it's that big house on the way to the slaughterhouse, and asked her to come into town and have an iced tea and a visit." Will looked at his wife.

"She said she'd be happy to," Alma said, smiling. "Sweet as she could be. But she never came. I never asked her again."

Charlie never looked at Sylvan the whole time Alma was talking. He just took it all in. From his first sight of her, that day in the butcher shop, she had burned herself into his mind, vivid and beautiful, the effect she had on most men, and women, too.

"It's a paradise out there in Arnold's Valley," Alma said. "Tended. Cared for. They have nothing, no money, no education—no regular morals, a lot of people say although I don't believe it—nothing except for their land. They don't know anything about what's going on in the world. They only care about their place, farm after farm. They never leave it. Maybe it's religion. Maybe they're just private people. The only things Sylvan knows, she's gotten from the radio, and, in the last three years, at the movies."

"She's beautiful," Charlie said as he stole a glance over to where Harrison was laughing loudly while Sylvan stood silently by his side.

"Don't say that too loud," said Will. "Boaty Glass'll cut your ear off quick as that. He was a good boy, my best friend, but he's a mean man now with a lot of money and a quick temper and a nasty disposition."

Charlie stood up. "Sam, let's go say hello to Mr. and Mrs. Glass."

He took the boy by the hand, and they walked over to where the couple stood and Charlie shyly shook Boaty's hand. Then Sam shook Boaty's hand, too.

Sylvan turned to him, took off her sunglasses so her green eyes flashed in the sun, and she, too, shook both of their hands, first the boy's, then Charlie's, without a word. But you could tell the way Charlie let his hand hang just for the moment in the air where her hand had been that something, some word of recognition, had passed between them. It was as though whatever was going to happen between them had already happened, was already over and done with.

If it had been winter, there might have been a static spark, something visible, but it was too warm. Something had been said, but she was the only one who knew what it was.

Charlie let his hand drift in the air for a moment, a long moment, watching the last of her gaze as her sunglasses went back on, and then he put his hand in his pocket, holding on to the warmth of her brief touch. Then he nodded, first at her, then at her husband, and he and the boy returned to their places.

"She smells nice, Mama," said the boy. "Like she cost a lot of money."

It was late afternoon, the second time he saw her. But twice was enough. Something had been said. The movie had started.

They didn't stay long. Harrison Glass and his wife stayed no more than an hour, Boaty eating a helping of everything, telling dirty jokes to red-faced Baptist men, laughing while the food dribbled down his chin, sweating like a pig, Sylvan nodding charmingly to everyone, but hardly speaking, staring off somewhere, one, two, glances in Charlie's direction, no more. Her vague green eyes sparking into sudden sharp focus at the sight of his face, seemingly random glances, once, twice, a third time as her husband shut the car door for her. No more than that, but that was enough.

After they left there was some more eating, and a little dancing—although ordinarily the church didn't much approve of it—until the shadows were long on the makeshift ball field and all the children were tired and the smell of cooking oil was thick in everybody's clothes and all the oysters were gone.

THE TWILIGHT BEGAN to fall and then to fade, and Christmas lights out of somebody's attic were turned on, but the children were arguing, and Ray Turner drove the Gadsden twins home to their big house, the biggest in town, because they didn't drive and he was a good, careful boy. People began to leave after that, and the Baptist men and women began to clean up whatever the animals could get at, leaving the rest for tomorrow.

Charlie waved to the Haisletts and got into his truck and drove out to his land by the river, the night clear, the stars as close as the top of the willows by the river, and he lit a Lucky Strike and wrote one word in his diary, one Christian name. Then he drank his glass of whiskey and said his faithless prayers and lay out on the ground and slept with only one thing on his mind, burning bright in his eyes and torching his heart like music.

CHAPTER FIVE

Fɪʀsᴛ ᴏғ ᴀʟʟ, this should be clear: She wasn't a bad girl. She was a dreamer, and she wanted things, something, anything of her own. What girl doesn't? What girl her age, coming out of what she came out of, wouldn't go a long way to get closer to where she wanted to be in this world? She dreamed of movie stars years and years before she even saw a movie, and only when she finally saw her first one, hypnotized in the dark in the State Theater, could she even put a name to what it was she had always wanted.

Where did she get such ideas? From the time she was six, she listened to *The Romance of Helen Trent* on the radio. Helen Trent was always in love with and never saying yes to Gil Whitney, who wanted her with all his heart, even though she was thirty-five. On the show, Helen was always and forever thirty-five, and Sylvan hung on her every word, her every refusal of Gil's love, forming the words the actors spoke, mimicking their ways, and maybe she learned it from there. For her, Helen Trent was a real person, frozen in time, speaking perfect English, and designing costumes for movie stars. Sylvan wanted to be like her, to have the life she had. Maybe the dreaming started there, maybe that's why that thing, that way of being, caught her imagination and fired it up. Hollywood. The people and the clothes. The hopelessly elusive quality of true love. The kind of love that only little girls think is possible.

Where would a girl get such notions? Where do you get porcelain skin, or blonde hair or green eyes? They're born in you, those ideas, and the patient ones wait, and the lucky ones find, and the smart ones get. She got.

You have to understand where she came from, what she came out of. If you heard the name she was born with, the one she had before she married Boaty Glass, you would laugh. Most people did. They laughed at her all the time in the first days. She was only seventeen and she knew they were laughing and she went about her life quietly, pretending to the world that it wasn't happening the way it had happened every time she set foot in town.

This is America. She had a right. She had a right to be whoever she wanted to be, and she was becoming that person every minute of every day, long before she even knew who the person was. She, like the rest of the country, was always becoming, never just being, never at rest, and because now she's part of a story, a story that gets told again and again, she just goes on becoming, even after anybody who actually knew or saw her is dead and gone. Most of us will be ended then, when we die, we will have become, but not her. So, in her way, she did get to be a movie star.

I knew her. I saw her. She was, I can promise you, a woman of quality.

She was remarkable, particularly considering where she came from, who her people were. Nowhere and nothing, that's what. She was like a buried treasure until Boaty Glass got the idea in his head that he should take a wife, and that that wife, like everything else Boaty got, should be acquired cheaply and should be of the best quality. He got to be so rich because, from the time he was a boy, he could drive a bargain like a New York lawyer, and he got to be so fat because he couldn't seem to find a limit, could never know how much was enough.

Ever notice how a fat man's shirts never wrinkle? A skinny man, he'll be a mess by noon, but a fat man's flesh holds the cloth so tight, his shirt still looks pressed when he takes it off for bed.

Now think about Boaty, lying in his bed night after night, in that big house he had lived in all his life and couldn't get rid of. After the war, people didn't want that kind of thing any more, because families that had been together on the same land for two hundred years went their own ways and left nobody except the old ones to look after what the young ones called the "home place."

Think of Boaty, forty-eight years old, five eight and 280 pounds, lying in his cold bed at night and dreaming of a young blonde girl who would be his wife and bear his children. It wasn't that he didn't understand he was a gross and greedy man, crafty enough to satisfy his greed. He just didn't care. He just wasn't built that way. Boaty was like a big round of dough that had never been baked into bread, worthless as nutrition, unfeeling and fat as risen flour paste.

Boaty had never been with a woman. Even before he got so huge, he was already gross in other ways, arrogant about his lineage, and unkempt and unruly in public and private. His knowledge of women was formed by the pages of girly magazines he bought in Staunton and kept in a box under his bed. He wore flesh-colored neckties that had pinup girls showing their breasts painted on the inside, and he thought it was cute to show these off to religious men at Rotary Club meetings.

But even Boaty Glass had feelings, although you'd never know it. Whatever else might be said about him, he'd worked hard all his life, and, rich as he was, he still lived alone. He'd seen the sad and mournful look on his mother's face as she died, looking at her son, heavy, sad, childless, and rich. He felt he owed it to her, to himself, to have a wife and children, the best wife, stunning, acquired as cheaply and craftily as everything else, and children whose futures grew more grandiose with every passing night, the royalty of his own widening realm. Tall, handsome, muscular boys and lean, well-mannered girls. Popular children, children who would be sought after and asked everywhere, and who'd grow up to be successful and respected in a way Boaty knew he never would be.

So he lay in bed and dreamed until he couldn't stand it any more, the rejections by the right girls from the right families, then he went out shopping. Picture it: touring the back roads of the county, in his black Cadillac, driving past farms, back up into hollows where they'd never even had electricity or indoor plumbing until about ten years before, where some children had never seen anybody who wasn't related to them. Picture Boaty driving and just looking, looking at every female face he saw. Girls of twelve and thirteen, fifteen at the oldest, barefoot girls wearing their mother's or sister's dresses, hanging slack from the shoulders, billowing in the breeze around where their breasts had not yet grown. He liked the blonde-haired girls the best.

He found one girl. She was fourteen. She was standing on a porch back up in a hollow, holding a baby in her arms, staring off at the sky. Boaty stopped his car, got out, and went up on the porch to knock on the door. He talked first to her mother, while the girl wandered down to look at his car, shyly putting the baby's hand on its hot, shiny surface. Then he took out a roll of money and talked to the father, he guessed it was the father, a man who looked too old and tired to be her father but said he was, who stood stooped over in the door, big arms and a puny chest, and the man listened carefully to what Boaty had to say, the offer he had to make, and then he went and got his gun and just stood without saying anything, in the doorway, while Boaty raised his hands, his money still visible, and slowly backed down the stairs and to his car. He carefully got in and started the engine and purred away without saying another word.

Two miles down the road, he stopped the car and threw up in a ditch. He shook all the way back to town, shook until he was inside the safety of his own house.

Finally, he found her, way out in Arnold's Valley. She was picking beans from a garden, dressed in a man's white shirt and pants that must have belonged to a brother. She was taller than he'd hoped for, probably a little taller than he was, and older; she must have been at least fifteen.

She was girlish but already full and wide-hipped, her breasts making a real difference inside the man's shirt. Her beautiful blonde hair hung to her waist, covering her face as she bent over to root among the vines, showing her angelic features as she stood up to put the beans in the basket slung on a leather strap over her shoulder. She wasn't exactly the thing he'd set out to find, but the minute he saw her he knew she was the one.

This time the negotiations went better. He'd learned some diplomacy that didn't cause a father's hand to reach for the shotgun right off the bat. The mother answered the door, took one look at him in his black suit, the stomach straining the buttons of his white shirt, the mother barefoot on the wooden floor and holding, of course, another baby in her arms. She took one look and said, "I'll get my husband," and backed away into the shadow of the kitchen.

He appeared, a strong blond man who must have been ten years younger than his wife, or so it looked, although with those people it was always hard to tell. The men stayed young from hard work, the women got old from having babies year after year.

"Yes sir?" the man said. He looked suspicious but not lethal, a yard dog trained to be wary of strangers.

"I'll say it straight out. I have a business proposition for you. One that'll suit us both, I guarantee."

"What kind of business?"

"Business that'll change your life. Business that'll put money in your pocket and a smile on your face."

"I don't need no life insurance, and I don't want no encyclopedia." The man started to close the door.

"This has to do, sir, with making you money, not you spending the money you worked so hard to make."

There was a long pause while the man thought it over. "Well, you better come in." So Boaty went inside, and, when his eyes adjusted to the dark, he saw it for what it was, a poor place that never got clean, the woman having no time for cleaning what with all those babies, who seemed to be everywhere, all ages, all blond.

In a clean house, the knobs of things — doors, cabinets — are the first things to get dirty, because they're always being touched by unclean hands. In a dirty house, those are the only things that are free from grime, because the hands that open and close the doors rub the filth and oil from them.

The house smelled like bacon fat and laundry detergent. The people smelled like bacon fat and pig shit and sweat.

"You want something? Whiskey? Coffee? Water?" and Boaty knew he should take something but he didn't know what because the thought of the water scared him, so he accepted a small glass of clear whiskey that would probably kill him anyway, but he had to take something. The man had a glass of the liquor sitting on the kitchen table, the open jar next to it, and the stuff hadn't killed him yet, so Boaty figured he could give it a try.

It tasted like copper and kerosene, but he drank it down quickly, because he knew that was what he was supposed to do. Then they set to talking.

"Let me be straight, friend. I want to buy your farm."

The man drank down his moonshine and just stayed put for a while. He laughed.

"This farm? My farm?"

"How big is it?

"It's a hundred and forty-two acres, all but twelve of which is shit, plain shit. Rock and limestone and dirt that's been planted and fucked over for so long it's near about dead. Man can't hardly feed his family."

"I'll pay you two thousand dollars. Cash money. But that's not the best part."

"We wouldn't have no place to go."

"That's the best part I was telling you about. You'd stay here. Nothing would change, except you wouldn't have to pay the land taxes any more."

"What's the real deal here?"

Boaty waited while the man poured himself another shot and drank it down, his lips pursing to the edge of the glass like a baby at the nipple. When he had set the glass down, pushed his hair back from his eyes and looked up again, Boaty finally spoke. He spoke very quietly, and lowered his eyes, dipped his chin so that the roll of flesh rose around his buttoned white shirt. "I want the girl."

"You what?"

"I want the girl. I want to marry her. Give her a better life."

"How old are you?"

"Forty-three." He thought of exaggerating even more, how would this man know, but he didn't want to push his luck.

"I can't do that."

"Course you can. One less mouth to feed. A better life than you could give her. Three thousand dollars, let's say; that's a lot of money. And a tractor. I'll buy you a new tractor."

The man looked wistful, helpless. Having never been offered a choice in anything he ever did, even choosing a wife, the one he had being four months pregnant when they married, after having had a single encounter after a church supper when he was sixteen and didn't even know how to do the thing with any respect or affection or thought. Again, now, he didn't know what to do and knew there was nowhere to go for advice.

"Which girl?"

"She's out there right now, picking beans in the garden."

"Sylvan. My first girl. She's got my heart, that girl."

"And what's that heart worth to her now, you reckon? How old is she?"

The man paused, ruffled his fingers. "Sixteen. I think. No, seventeen."

"What use is a girl on a farm? What good is she to you now? You want her grabbed up by some trash? Maybe she has been already. She's seventeen. I don't pay top dollar for used goods. Maybe I should reconsider."

"Sylvan is a good girl. She's special. Not just to me. Ain't nobody been near her, that's for sure. I've been careful. Real careful."

"Can she read?"

"Course she can read."

"Mathematics?"

"Some. Not division. But she's bright. Listens to all them shows on the radio."

"Good. A good girl. A little older than I hoped, but she'll do."

"You're the one that's asking, mister. If you don't want her, and I ain't saying this is a done deal, you don't want her, just walk away."

"I'm offering you, say, three thousand dollars, a new tractor, and a better life for both you and your family and the girl Sylvan."

"And I hear you and I'll think about it. Now, with all due respect, I want you to leave my house."

"There's one condition," Boaty said as he stood.

"Figured," said the father.

"If she runs off on me, you lose the farm. I take it back, and you have nowhere to go. Understand?"

There was a long pause. "What if she dies or something else?"

Boaty hadn't thought that far. "There is no something else," he said. "No divorce. No running off. But I guess if she dies, you stay put. As long as she dies my wife. So it's kind of 'for richer or poorer' for you, too. You got that?

"When she's gone, she's gone. She won't be coming back, and you won't be seeing her. Not at Christmas, not at Easter. You'll never see your grandchildren, at least not by her."

"That's pretty hard."

"Life is hard, isn't it?"

The man looked out the window at his oldest daughter, straining in the hot sun to find every last bean on the vine. The white shirt was soaked with sweat, and her hair clung in tendrils to her neck. Boaty thought she was the most beautiful thing he'd ever seen.

"I got to consider her. Whether she'd like it. Don't even know I could convince her. She's got ideas, like I said."

"When can I come back?"

There was a long pause. Two men in a kitchen, the woodstove, always hot, the flypaper hanging down, encrusted, the whiskey clear and still in the jar, the girl in the garden, the boys bawling for lunch and the baby for the teat. For three whole minutes he sat and waited.

"Sunday week."

"We understand each other? You get what I'm saying?"

"I ain't stupid, sir. I heard every word. I'll think on it."

"Sunday week?"

"That's what I said."

"I'll bring cash money."

"I asked you to leave. I'd like you to do that now."

They shook hands, like two men at a funeral. Boaty was careful not to wipe his hands on his pants until after he had gotten in the car and driven away, the girl standing in the garden, basket full, staring after his Cadillac until the dust had settled back on the road and the drone of the cicadas could be heard again, the wind rushing through the corn, replacing the swish of the car's wheels, the dust from the dirt road blowing into the girl's eyes.

When he went back in two weeks' time, the girl was standing on the porch, wearing an old dress that was clean and smelled of sun and fresh night air. Beside her was a suitcase that Boaty gently explained to her she wouldn't be needing. Her whole family was gathered around her, except the father, silent, dressed as though for Sunday church.

Inside, the big blond man sat at the kitchen table. He looked drunk, the Mason jar empty in front of him on the greasy flowered linoleum. He looked like he'd been crying, but it was hard to tell.

Boaty put a document in front of him, a piece of paper that gave Harrison Boatwright Glass the right to marry the girl, and ownership of the farm. The man didn't even ask what the paper was. He just signed his name carefully and in full.

Boaty got out the cash and then hesitated. "You made it clear to the girl that this is forever? No running off?"

"She understands that."

"It says so in the contract you just signed. So you better be sure."

"I'm sure. She knows the deal. She's yours, mister."

Then, after Boaty had put the cash money on the table, without counting it the father handed over her birth certificate, yellowed and stained, and all he said was, "When do I get my tractor?"

CHAPTER SIX

WHEN THEY GOT to the cattle guard at the end of the rutted dirt drive that led to the gravel road that led to the blacktop back to town, Sylvan touched Boaty's arm and said two of the only four words she was to say that day: "Please stop." She said it in a gentle voice with an accent that was strangely refined.

She turned her head and looked back through the cloud of dust at her family gathered on the porch. The father had joined his wife, his hand in her hand, both shy and sad. Around them, the brothers and sisters, one boy with a baby of his own on his arm, stood and stared. Sylvan looked for two full minutes, still, not moving, like she was taking a photograph in her mind, the hot breeze from the road spinning blonde cobwebs of her hair around her head. Then the family all scattered, running off to do chores or play in the fields.

The father stood alone on the porch, and the light caught the tears in his eyes as he forlornly waved at his leaving child, and she waved back, although he could never have seen her. She seemed to want to call out, to cry some last thing to him, but she made no sound at all. After a time she turned back and looked straight ahead. There were tears on her cheeks. She did not brush them away, or try in any way to hide them.

"Now?" Boaty asked.

She nodded, and they rode the twenty miles back to town in silence. At Boaty's house, a justice of the peace waited, along with Will Haislett and Alma, who had been called to be witnesses because Will was practically the only man around who would stand up for him. With them stood the foremen of two of Boaty's farms, hired hands standing awkwardly in dirty shoes and clean white shirts, buttoned at the collar, their big red hands fumbling with handkerchiefs in the heat.

Sylvan signed some papers without even bothering to read them. What did it matter what the paper said? Then they stood in front of the justice, and he said all the words, and then she said her only other words of the day, "I do." And that was that.

Louise, the colored woman, had put out some sliced ham and some potato salad and a coconut cake. Nobody ate much. Will and Boaty had nothing to say to each other any more, except to talk about the old days, and that didn't seem right on his wedding day, so they kept quiet. Alma tried to get Sylvan to talk, but she just looked pretty and nodded her head, as though she had been hypnotized. The justice regretted his own hot dinner waiting at home, and the foremen were embarrassed, for their employer and for the girl, so they ate quickly what little they ate, and then they left. Will and Alma stayed a while longer in the awkward silence, with Sylvan, now Mrs. Glass, sitting still and pretty as a porcelain doll, but they were gone pretty quickly, too, and the colored woman cleaned up while Boaty and his new bride sat in the parlor, and then they were alone and Sylvan took off her shoes.

Boaty thought he should maybe talk to her, but he'd almost never been alone with a woman except for his mother, and he had no idea what to say.

"You need a bathroom?" was all he could think of, so he showed her the way, and stood outside listening while she was in there, noticing that she didn't wash her hands after the toilet flushed. It kind of made him nervous.

When she came out, he looked at her, and, without a word, walked in and began filling the tub. He handed her some fancy French soap he'd bought, his only wedding present, and took her gently by the elbow and led her into the bathroom, then left her alone. There was silence for a long time, as though she didn't know what to do, then Boaty heard her clothes dropping to the floor, and heard her slowly settling herself into the water.

He listened to it all. She was naked in the hot water. It excited him.

After half an hour, she came out, dressed, her hair clinging to her damp neck. They went back to sit in the parlor, but he could still smell it on her, or thought he could, the pig shit, the outhouse, the moonshine that had run in her family's veins for generations. He got up, filled the bath again, and she seemed to know what to do, and he stood outside the door again, listening.

She never said a word to him all day. She didn't smile, she didn't look troubled, either. She was just blank.

He made her bathe three times that afternoon, until all the towels were damp on their hooks, and he finally could sit in his own living room with his own wife and not smell the stink of country on her. By the time she was done, clean to his satisfaction, her skin had the color of the sun setting outside, and it was time to eat again, so they sat down to two plates left out by Louise, covered in wax paper, and they ate a little, and then they went upstairs to bed.

She was so shy, and so inept, that he knew her father had been telling the truth. He hadn't expected her to rush at him, but he also realized he didn't exactly know what to do, either.

So he just took off his clothes, except for his boxer shorts, big, voluminous, patterned things, tented now, he noticed with some embarrassment. He laid his suit and tie and shirt neatly on a chair. Then he lay down on the bed, grunting with the effort to lower himself, a big, hairy melon on a chenille bedspread. After a while, she began to take off her clothes, but not before she drew down the shades, even though it was only half dark and even though it would serve to make the room even more stifling. She turned away from him, and, naked now, backed her way toward the bed. Just the way her mother had told her. She was just barely seventeen years old. She felt older than her own mother.

It caught her by surprise when the back of her knees hit the edge of the mattress, and she tumbled back against his belly, and he saw her for the first time, the first time he had seen any woman naked, in fact and, even though he knew what to expect, he was still startled,

startled by the vastness of her, her expanse of skin, her breasts, her deep pink nipples, the shimmer of her skin, pale and powdery everywhere except her arms and her face. All the women from all the magazines under his bed were now lying on him, touching his skin with skin that was sweet but strangely frightening, unlike the girls in the pictures, whose skin was glossy and inviting.

He pulled her on top of him, and kissed her. She didn't kiss him back. He rolled her over and lay on top of her as she closed her eyes, and he did what he was supposed to do, what he'd waited forty-eight years to do in his own bed. She didn't respond, but she didn't seem to mind, either.

It didn't take long. When it was over, he lay beside her in the room that was now dark, neither of them even close to sleep. She got up and went to the bathroom and, when she came back, the blood was gone from her legs, and Boaty looked down and discovered to his horror that there was also blood on his shorts, so he pulled a clean pair from the drawer and went into the bathroom and put them on. He didn't know what to do with the soiled ones. He didn't want Louise to find them in the laundry basket, so when he came out, his new blue shorts replaced with his favorite green ones, the color of spring leaves, he rolled the blue ones up and put them at the back of his closet, underneath some shoes, to be tossed out later with the trash.

When he lay back down on the bed, grunting again, she didn't even turn to look at him. He took her hand as they lay in the dark, waiting for sleep, his sweaty palm engulfing her dry one until she pulled it away and rubbed it on the bedspread.

In the dark, afterward, listening to the night, he decided he didn't think much of it. He didn't see what all the fuss was about. Maybe he'd done it wrong, but he didn't think so. It wasn't the kind of thing Boaty would think about himself, anyway, and, besides, how many ways could there be to do it?

No, he didn't think it was all that great, this thing he'd waited for and dreamed about for forty-eight lonely years, and he didn't suppose that he would make it a regular thing. Maybe once a week. Maybe.

CHAPTER SEVEN

B UT ALL IN all, Boaty Glass was pretty pleased with himself. The next day, he drove his new wife into Lexington to get some clothes, the kind of clothes that might make the other women in the town turn their heads. They went to Grossman's. Almost every Southern town has one clothing store run by Jewish people, and in Lexington it was the Grossmans who kept the ladies looking up to date. Boaty watched as Sylvan tried on the clothes, and he got more and more pleased with himself every time she came out of the dressing room. She had a nice figure on her, full and round, and the Grossmans looked her up and down and pulled out things that looked like they had been made just for her. It gave him a funny feeling in his heart, watching her, a rush to wrap it all up, the dresses and the suits and the hats and gloves she had to be taught to wear, and take her back home, dress her up, and just walk her up and down the main street in Brownsburg all day long.

In Arthur and Ginger Grossman's hands, Sylvan became the thing he had driven all those miles on all those country roads to find, had sat in all those parlors in Staunton and Charlottesville, drinking cups of condescending tea under stony unforgiving glances so he could bring her home. She might be the fake version of that thing, but, like they say, when she stood on top of Boaty's money, she stood pretty tall.

She had a natural grace to her, in the way she walked, in the way her hands moved up to rearrange her hair or smooth an eyebrow. And she seemed to take Boaty as he came, his hulking body with that faint smell of sweat, his age, whatever it was, and she didn't know and didn't seem to care—as long as he was older than eighteen, he might as well have been a hundred. He kind of loved her, but then, he loved his car the way he loved his money, and he had loved his sainted mother, but this girl was not his delicate mother. This was a flesh-and-blood woman. He'd seen her naked. He never got up the courage to ask himself whether she loved him, too.

Some things he had to teach her, like how to hold a fork and knife in the right way, how to put a napkin in her lap, but most things he only had to tell her once. She was that quick.

The first time he took her to town, to church on Sunday, she caused a stir. She turned some heads. She was by far the prettiest girl in town, and she made the other teenaged girls look unfinished, somehow. She was voluptuous where they were meager, and, of course, she was married to Boaty, and everybody knew the desperate and disastrous course of Boaty's various courtships. Nobody knew who she was, exactly, except Alma, who remembered from her days of going out to Arnold's Valley and trying to teach those children some few simple facts about the world, and Alma knew the girl wouldn't remember her, or, if she did, she wouldn't acknowledge their acquaintance, so Alma didn't say anything, except to Will, later, at lunch, and Will laughed his head off. "Arnold's Valley?" He laughed at the whole idea.

Then Will told just one or two people, and that was enough, so by the end of the week, everybody in town knew exactly who she was and where and what she had come out of. But still. But still.

She didn't talk like a hillbilly, that was the remarkable thing. She didn't talk like anybody in Brownsburg, anybody in the county. She talked like somebody you'd hear on the radio, which, of course, was where she'd learned to talk like that in the first place. She talked like Helen Trent.

Boaty liked showing her off, and so, once he felt Brownsburg had been suitably impressed, he took her back into Lexington, where they had supper at the Dutch Inn. Then they went to the movies. The movies cost a quarter apiece, but they also cost him—and Boaty didn't know this at the time, how could he?—they also cost him much much more. The movies cost him his wife, because after the lights went down in the State Theater, and the first image flickered on the screen, and she saw those enormous, beautiful faces and heard them talking in that way that didn't sound like any country except the country of the movies, Sylvan never belonged to him again. From that night on, she belonged, body and soul, to the movies.

The movie they saw was *The Big Sleep*. The plot didn't even begin to make sense to Sylvan, but then there was Lauren Bacall, a girl almost her own age who had made herself up out of her own imagination, or so it seemed, falling in love with Bogart, a man who was totally and completely authentically what he was. She felt in her heart he wasn't even acting; he was just that man who talked like that and smoked cigarettes and who was obviously old enough to be Bacall's father. She knew right away that she was Bacall, and suddenly her black silk dress from Grossman's felt drab and itchy on her skin, as though it didn't fit her right, didn't belong to her. And it was clear as a bell that Boaty wasn't Bogart.

Sylvan took in every line of every dress Bacall wore, the drape of a suit, the flow of a gown, the sparkle of a brooch, the actual words the characters spoke flowing past her as though in a language she'd never heard before, all money and music. She imagined her own hair falling like that, in soft, gleaming waves around her face. She didn't watch the movie so much as she watched the way Lauren Bacall moved her beautiful mouth, and heard the way she breathed sex and glamour into her every word. She imagined Lauren Bacall's body moving beneath those clothes, and she could see in Bogart's eyes that he was thinking the same thing.

The next day, Boaty gone, she stood in front of the mirror and lowered her chin and raised her eyes and looked at her reflection the way Bacall had looked at Bogart, trying to make with her mouth the sounds and syllables she had heard coming from Bacall. She practiced for hours, until she finally realized that she wasn't Bacall, she didn't have her body, and her neck got tired from keeping her chin on her chest all the time the way she did. She was somebody, but she wasn't Bacall.

That night at supper, Sylvan said to Boaty, "Harrison? Will we go on a honeymoon?"

The question took him aback. He figured he'd already spent enough on her.

"It hadn't occurred to me, baby."

She got up from the table, sat on his lap and wrapped her arms around his neck, "Well, Harrison, honey, I'd like to. People do. Even my daddy and mama, they did. And I want to."

He didn't say anything. She kissed him on the neck, and he smelled the perfume he'd bought her at Grossman's, Eau de Nile, by Elizabeth Arden. "I think it'd be nice." She kissed him again, and he felt her tongue dart onto his neck, leaving a small wet spot he tried not to wipe with his hand, but he did, anyway.

"And where would you want to go? I'm not saying . . . where? Niagra Falls? I hear that's popular."

"I want to go to Hollywood, California."

He laughed. "You say what? All that way? What in hell for?"

"I want to see where they live. Those movie stars. I want to eat in the restaurants they eat in. The Brown Derby. I want to go to Warner Brothers studio, if they'll let us, and see where they make those movies. Is it far?"

"It's all the way across the damned country. The whole country. Takes five days on a train."

"I've never been on a train. I want to go on a train to Hollywood and see a movie star, face to face. Please, Daddy."

He seemed confused.

"Will we sleep on the train?" she asked.

"Yes, if . . . yes, we would get a compartment and sleep on the train. And eat on the train and brush our teeth on the damned train."

"All by ourselves?"

"Well, of course, by ourselves."

"I'd be so nice to you, sweetie. I'd be just as sweet as pie."

Boaty wasn't quite sure what she meant by that, but his mind started working, and there were some things, some things he'd heard about, some things he'd heard girls could do, and while he wasn't sure he wanted to do them, he knew he was supposed to want to do them, and if Hollywood was what it was going to take to find out, then he figured he might as well give it a shot. It began to seem like it wasn't such a bad idea.

So, of course they went, five days there and five days back, in a Pullman car, and a week in a fancy hotel on Hollywood Boulevard, the Roosevelt, cost a fortune. He never talked about it, but whatever he found out about what women could do didn't seem to make him any less cranky or mean.

That was pretty much it, for Boaty. He'd seen the world, he thought, although the limits of the world for him outside of Brownsburg were forever confined to Fort Bragg, North Carolina, and Hollywood, California, and that was just fine with him. When Boaty came home from that last place, a place so vile and filled with bad food and rude people and high prices for even the smallest things and too much skin on everybody and too many teeth in every mouth, he'd pretty much had it.

But Sylvan, that's a different story. Sylvan Glass was just getting started. That's why she needed Claudie Wiley.

CHAPTER EIGHT

CLAUDETTA WILEY WAS a genius. She was born that way. She lived in a falling-down old clapboard house way out on the edge of town with the other black folks, with an idiot daughter nobody had seen since she was a baby so maybe she was there and maybe she wasn't, and maybe she was an idiot and maybe not. Claudie lived in the last house before the fields started, and her house was so crestfallen that even the other black people wouldn't have gone there if they didn't need to, and some people said it was green and some people said it was gray, but there wasn't anybody who didn't know that Claudie had a gift that was astonishing. Claudie Wiley could sew.

She was a short but majestic woman, pale-skinned and wild-haired and big featured "high yellow," we called it in those days. She had a slender frame from the waist up, but from her hips down, she was big-limbed and thick. She had eyes that looked right into you, without hesitation or the shyness that most black people affected around white people. She never deferred, because she knew the genius that was in her long slender fingers, needle-threading fingers, and she was sure of herself in a way that didn't need to say what it was she was sure of. There wasn't anybody like her, and, like Sylvan Glass, the solid being of her character and her way was fashioned out of a fantasy that had come to her as a young girl, but with a gift that could only have come from God.

Inside that house, with its bare wooden floors and its cracked windows and torn lace curtains, only one room of which anybody ever saw, the room she met customers in, Claudie Wiley dressed most of the town's women, black and white. At least she made the things they wore when they wanted to look their best. She did all the alterations for Grossman's, and she dressed every bride and bridesmaid and bride's mother in this town from the time she was fifteen years old.

Her grandmother, who raised her after her mother ran off to California in search of something other than scrubbing floors, said she was born with the gift. At four, she could thread a needle and sew dolls for herself. She made them out of any scraps she could find, dishtowels, burlap bags, old dresses, and they were always smiling, which she almost never did. By the time she was six, she was making her own clothes, dressing herself like a white girl, and it caused some talk. Little motherless colored girl, people said, putting on airs, but still, nobody could fail to be impressed.

Every Easter she put on a real show, and if this town had an Easter Parade, she would have been the star, every year. When she was ten, she started making clothes for other little girls, white girls, and they were fine, even if Claudie always saved her greatest skill for dressing herself. Sometimes she would use a pattern, but a lot of the time, she'd just make something up.

She went to the little school they had at the church, but she didn't pay attention much, since she was always doing something with a needle and thread while she was supposed to be studying history or numbers, and after a while, her teachers just gave up on her. So, in one way, she was completely ignorant of the world. But in another way, she knew everything she needed to know. Her grandmother worked as a cleaning woman, moving from house to house on different days, and the women in those houses would give her magazines that showed pictures of women of the day in dresses and evening gowns and suits, and the grandmother would give those to Claudie, who would study them as though reading scripture, sometimes practicing with empty hands on invisible material, making invisible clothes just like the ones she saw in the magazines the white women whose floors her mother mopped gave her.

The white women would always say, when Claudie brought them their new dress, "What do I owe you?"

"Whatever you think is right, ma'am," Claudie would answer, having no idea what clothes cost. And most of the women, admiring the handiwork of this brilliant child, would give her more than they had planned to. So Claudie was clever that way. By the time she was fourteen, she was one of the few black people in town to have a checking and saving account at the bank. So that set her apart as well, along with the color of her skin, pale when almost all of her neighbors were dark, and that way she had of appearing to belong to nobody, to follow no rules except the ones she found useful to her, like her unfailing politeness to customers. She never flattered them, never went out of her way to tell the women or the girls that they looked better than ever. She just left them with a sense that they looked better than they would have if they hadn't come to Claudie Wiley, and that was enough to open the purses and keep the money coming in.

Her grandmother died when she was fifteen, leaving her mostly unschooled, unable to cook, or even to clean her house. She never blinked an eye. She went on living there, taking up as little space as possible, letting the rest of the house go to ruin, receiving her customers in the one room downstairs that she kept immaculate even as the house fell apart around her.

People were concerned. Black people and white people alike talked in their houses about how something should be done, but nobody could figure out what that thing might be, and their concern rolled off her, left her unmoved. "I'm fine," she would say to those brave enough to ask. "Don't you worry about me none."

And she was fine, as far as anybody could tell. She'd grown up. She wasn't the scrawny little girl she'd been; she'd grown into a tall woman with a big behind and big bosoms. She wasn't beautiful, but she was handsome, and her skill gave her a kind of luminosity that made beauty seem irrelevant. You might have thought her ugly, until you saw her expressions when the subject turned to women's clothes, and then you would have changed your mind. And she had those fingers, those long, thin fingers like the tines of a fork, fingers that did what she wanted before she even told them to.

Women started to come to her from all over, bringing fancier and fancier ideas and more exotic pictures from magazines Claudie had never heard of. She took them all in, treated them with the same distant politeness, judging their figures and their often absurd visions of themselves with the precise eye of a surgeon, gently leading each one away from their fantasies and into what was at least possible for them, and the women were grateful for that. They paid her even more.

One of them, a woman who drove over the mountain every month all the way from Charlottesville, had an idea that Claudie should go away to a fancy fashion school. Claudie had been secretly doing fashion drawings since she was a child, and one day she shyly showed them to this woman, page after page of tall, thin white women in ball gowns and wedding dresses and luncheon suits, and tea dresses for parties that Claudie would never go to. The woman was convinced that Claudie had a great future; she saw a way for her out of this town and this filthy house and this lonely life. She offered Claudie her help and her checkbook.

She did everything for Claudie. She picked the school, way up in Boston. She edited the drawings down to two dozen of the finest and fanciest, she filled out the pages of the school application, even opened and read to Claudie the letter of acceptance that came in the spring. Claudie dreamed that night of furs and hats and jewels, of department stores, things she'd never seen even in pictures, while the Charlottesville woman sat at her own table, served by black servants, and told her husband how important this was, as a moment, to create a new life for Claudie, a life no black woman anywhere had ever had.

All that summer, her seventeenth year, Claudie sewed the clothes she would need for school in a big city up north. The woman bought her cardigans and little sweaters that went underneath, and gave her a second-rate string of pearls, picked up at the Episcopal Church Bazaar White Elephant table the year before. She gave her knee socks, all of this totally unsuitable to Claudie, who spent most of her days in shapeless dresses and bare feet, with a closet-ful of clothes she wore alone, in private, clothes that could match any clothes anywhere in the world. But she was excited at the same time, and she worked hard at turning herself into somebody she'd never been, into a fantasy of the woman she might be.

Two days before she was supposed to leave for Boston, the woman drove over from Charlottesville and picked her up. Claudie locked her house and left the town without saying good-bye to a single soul. She spent the night in the woman's guest room in Charlottesville, not even in the maid's room, and she slept in the best bed under the best sheets she'd ever felt.

In the middle of the night, she sat for a long time and looked at all her bright new school clothes in her suitcase, so neatly folded, still smelling of the stores they came from. Then she unpacked everything, and hung each piece on hangers in the closet, and then she picked up her empty suitcase and got ready to leave that house and that life and those sheets forever behind her.

She left anything the woman had given her on the dressing table, her train ticket to the future, even the pearls, and walked down through the alien streets of the biggest town she'd ever seen, past the shop windows filled with tweed jackets for the college boys and polite dresses for the faculty wives, marveling at the richness of everything. In the bus station, just another unschooled black country girl, she waited quietly for the first bus to take her back to Brownsburg. The woman and her husband didn't lift a finger to interfere. Nobody ever messed with Claudie.

So she came home, and she sewed, and nobody ever asked a thing about why she'd come back to that old house. She got older. Somewhere along the way, she had a baby of her own, a little girl she called Evelyn Hope, who was the one who might or might not be some kind of idiot, and nobody ever knew or asked who the father was.

She had to get a telephone, so her customers could call, the first black person in town to have one. She never made a call herself. She *got* calls. She was making as much money as most white people, but working twice as hard, late into the night, and traveling all over to make these dresses for rich women who no longer had to come to her. She bought herself a car. It was a Packard Super Clipper, two-toned, fancy beyond belief, even if it had been owned before her by Boaty Glass. The boys of the neighborhood washed it every Saturday, and waxed it once a month until its red and silver body sparkled in the sun. She didn't need anybody or anything, and nobody bothered her, ever. Nobody much talked to her either, except about yardage and pleats and darts, and that was just fine with her. Men were put off by her independence and her obvious lack of need for them, and women were just flat out afraid of her, of any black woman who could make her way in the world, all alone, stitch by stitch.

She drove that car wherever the calls told her to go, pulling up to big houses and going around to the back door, sometimes staying overnight in a maid's room, making dresses for well-bred women and wide-eyed debutantes all over the state. She was treated no worse than other black people of her generation, and maybe better, because it was clear, even though she didn't say much, that Claudie was something special, that Claudie had almost witchlike powers when it came to conjuring a dress out of a bolt of cloth.

The brides would walk down the aisle beaming, preceded by bridesmaids who looked themselves like princesses out of a fairy tale. The Garden Club ladies would sit down to lunch in their specially-made outfits, and accept the compliments that came their way, pretending it was nothing special, but passing Claudie's name and number along to their friends, and their friends would rush home and call. Debutantes would sweep to the floor in dresses made by Claudie Wiley, until their foreheads touched the hardwood, a Texas curtsey at the Jefferson Hotel in Richmond, while silver- and blue-haired men and women plotted the girls' matrimonial futures and fortunes.

Claudie never thought about Boston, or well-meaning white women, or what she might have done with her life. She was doing what she could, and to think a black woman in those days could do anything else seemed just as foolish to everybody else as it had been frightening to her.

She knew she was capable of great things, and her money was slowly piling up in the bank, more than any other black person in the town, more than a lot of white people, too, although she never thought about how much was there. She just waited for some part of her girlhood's dream to come true, her imagination firing up only occasionally, her hand reaching for drawing paper on the kitchen table to make a few deft lines, a suggestion of a splendor she had no reason to execute.

Then one day Sylvan Glass walked through her door, seventeen years old, a stack of magazines she'd picked up in Hollywood in her hands, and Claudie knew in a glance who she was and what she was and where she'd come from and what she wanted.

It was like an itching in her fingers.

CHAPTER NINE

I'm Sylvan Glass. I've come to see about getting some clothes made."

Claudie took it in, this tall girl standing there on her porch with a clutch of magazines in her hands. She felt some kind of something, some shiver run through her, as though she were looking at the figure she'd drawn on all those pieces of paper all her life. The lines. The curves. The carriage. Now here she was, standing in front of her on the porch next to the rotting old sofa her grandmother had died on. She took it all in, and she saw the clay she'd been waiting for all her life, the clay from which she would build her perfect model of the white women who had both mystified and fascinated her.

"Well, you better come in, ma'am."

Sylvan laughed. "Please don't call me ma'am. I'm only seventeen. It makes me feel like an old lady. Call me Sylvan. Everybody tells me you can do anything. I've been mad to meet you. Simply *mad*. Here, hold these," and she thrust the magazines into Claudie's hands, then ran to the sleek white convertible Boaty had bought her and came back with a dozen bolts of cloth in her arms.

They stepped through the torn screen door and into the dim hallway that led to the workroom. Sylvan took notice of the broken chairs, the dusty box record player tilted on its side, the remnants of other people's fabrics, the cat smell. She just hoped there weren't snakes in the house. She'd seen worse, back home. It didn't bother her at all.

In the workroom there was a big wooden table, and two chairs, and Claudie moved around the room, turning on the lights one by one until the gloom dissolved and Sylvan could see how clean everything was. There was a dress form, an old wooden box filled with every kind of scissor, a sewing box, and an immaculate new Singer sewing machine. There was no sign of life, of living, just the implements of Claudie's work. Sylvan had heard she had a daughter, but she didn't see or hear anybody, didn't sense that anybody did anything in this room except what they were doing now.

"I've seen you. You're married to Mr. Glass."

"Call me Sylvan."

"I can't."

"Why not?"

"I don't know. It's not my way. I just can't. People around here . . . What are you after?"

"Dresses. A suit. Some skirts and blouses. I don't know if you can make them."

"I can make anything."

"I heard that. From a picture?"

"From a picture. From a pattern. From some idea in your head, if you can say it clear."

"I've got pictures," she pointed to the magazines, dog-eared pages flipped over at the corners. "I just went to Hollywood, California, and I saw so many things. I think I even maybe saw Miss Joan Crawford. Looked like her, anyway. And I got these magazines all about movie stars. Miss Lauren Bacall. She's married to an old man just like me. Miss Lana Turner. Lots of movie stars. There's pictures of what they wear to lunch at the Brown Derby, what they wear at home when they have other movie stars over for tea parties or cards, everything."

"Where do you come from? Not from around here."

"I actually do. Right near here, out in the county." She made it sound like she came from some grand plantation, with servants and foxhounds. But Claudie could tell.

"And how was that for you?"

"Well, I'm here in town, aren't I?"

"You talk like somebody on the radio."

"I hope so. I been studying that thing a long time. You don't smile a lot."

"Haven't seen anything funny so far."

"Most of the colored women around here smile at me all the time."

"They're not me."

"No. I guess not."

"I make clothes. I'm real good at it. Ask anybody. Rest of the time, I just mind my own business. I don't know who that Crawford woman or any of those other women are. I've never been to the movies. Why would I?"

"You've never seen such beautiful people. Every one of them. That's why they call them stars, I guess. They just shine."

Claudie smiled finally, a broad, sweet smile that made her look fourteen. "How old you say you were?"

"I'm seventeen. But I'm married already. See, you smiled."

"You wouldn't believe some of the things I hear, the way some women fool themselves. They think they're thin when they're fat, or the other way around. They act like they're rich when they can't even pay their old cleaning woman. You. You think I can turn you into somebody you're not, just somebody you saw who looked like somebody else who makes movies. Well, I like a dreamer. I'm a dreamer. I can't tell you I can do that, turn you into Miss Cranford or whatever her name is, but I sure can make you some pretty clothes to wear. Let's see what you're after. Let's see those magazines."

So they sat down and went through *Photoplay, Motion Picture, Screenland,* and the rest, Sylvan turning the pages as if they were the pages of an ancient family Bible, her face lit up with longing and hope. She pointed out daytime dresses that were so fanciful they looked like something out of a fairytale. Suits that made Claudie want to reach for the scissors and start cutting. Elegant, lush clothes, alive with desire, worn on rich, full bodies. Claudie felt her heart beat fast in her chest.

Here was a girl who wanted to wear the kind of clothes Claudie wanted to make, who had the kind of full, womanly body she wanted to make them for. She didn't ask why, or where on earth in this town Sylvan thought she was going to wear them, she just knew this girl had an idea in mind of who she was going to be, and that excited her.

They went through every magazine. As they looked at the pictures, Sylvan told Claudie about this fantastic place she'd been, Hollywood, staying in a hotel called the Roosevelt, with maids who changed the sheets every single day, taking buses and taxis, eating a lobster, going to a movie studio, and actually seeing some of the houses where these impossibly beautiful people lived, at least glimpsing them in the distance through the thickly ivied front gates.

She'd gone to a department store, dragging her husband along. She'd bought so much material for the clothes she wanted they had to buy an extra steamer trunk, yards and yards of stuff even Claudie had never seen before. Silks, and wools so fine you could have pulled a yard through a wedding ring, and linens as sheer as a handkerchief.

They picked six things, and matched the materials to the dresses they chose. Sylvan undressed down to her slip, and Claudie took all her measurements.

"You have a good behind for clothes," Claudie said at one point.

Sylvan laughed. "Big," she said. "At least it's good for something besides sitting."

"All us colored women all have big butts," Claudie said.

"Why is that?"

"Clothes fit better. And the men like it."

"Do you have a man?"

"Men don't like me. These men around here, they don't want a strong woman with her own money and her own car. I might run off on 'em." She laughed. "Probably would, too, if I had anywhere to go."

It took all afternoon. By sunset, there were plans for twelve dresses, and Claudie already knew she'd never be paid enough for all the work she was going to put into them. But she didn't care.

That was the great thing about Claudie. She just didn't give a damn.

CHAPTER TEN

CHARLIE BEALE NEEDED a house to live in. The nights wouldn't stay warm forever, and Alma wanted him to have a roof over his head before the days got short. He wanted to live in the country, but she wanted him in town, near the shop, said he'd get too lonely out by himself, even though Charlie said he was never lonely and liked the quiet. She wanted him to be able to stroll down to work, to water his lawn after dinner the way the other men and women did, to be a part of it all.

To Alma, there was no end to the wonder, the delight of being in town. She had grown up far out in the country, a family of twelve and even though she liked it when they drove out there to visit her sisters and brothers, nothing beat town. She liked hearing her neighbors' voices on their porches at night, hated hearing the occasional arguments, late at night, from upstairs, the voices so close you could hear what the argument was about.

It wasn't very hard to find a house for Charlie. There were only three for sale in the town, and one was too big and one was too small, so that left one. Alma picked it, even though Charlie said the smaller one would be enough, she insisted, saying that he'd find a girl and then have a family and outgrow the smaller one and have to move to one of the other ones, anyway.

He paid cash for it, the way he paid for everything. Eighteen hundred dollars for three bedrooms and two bathrooms and a big wide porch that wrapped around the front and the sides. The trees in the yard were big and old, eight feet around, and Alma said they would keep the house cool with shade and breeze, even if Charlie might miss the beauty of the sunrise out by the river.

He and Will painted some of the rooms, at night, after work, and Alma got a girl in to sweep and scrub the floors. Soon, Charlie Beale had the first real home he'd had in a long, long time.

In the weeks before school started, they'd drive around the county to auctions; there were always one or two every Saturday. They took two vehicles, Charlie and Will in the pickup, to bring home whatever things Alma picked out, and Alma and Sam in the old Buick. They parked side by side in dirt fields, and by the time she got out of the car, Alma was already running with excitement.

Charlie wasn't used to the country auctioneers. He could never understand what they were saying in their rapid-fire singsong — it was like the country songs without the melody — but Alma would raise her hand when she saw something he needed, and keep it up until the auctioneer slammed the gavel down.

Ray Miller was always the auctioneer, and whatever didn't sell,

Ray would buy for pennies on the dollar. He kept it all in two big barns somewhere out near Glasgow, and he knew somehow that all this country stuff that people didn't want today, milk-glass darning eggs and butter churns and whatnot, they'd come to want a few years down the road. They'd start to miss their grandmothers and grandfathers, the old ways, the home place, and they would fill the corners and knickknack shelves of their new houses with things that were familiar to them from their childhoods, even if the stuff had belonged to other people, other childhoods than their own.

Usually, they served lunch at these auctions, and they'd sit at long tables and eat Brunswick stew or hot dogs, while prim, sad-faced families watched from the porches of the houses they were soon to leave. They were festive and sad, those auctions, eager and mournful at the same time.

There wasn't anything you couldn't buy, if you thought you needed it. Beds and chairs and tables and rugs, of course, but also plates and glasses and sets of silverware, even good old sheets and mixing bowls and egg beaters and wooden spoons. A great find was an old pine blanket chest that turned out to have eight good quilts inside it.

People, some people, were already tired of the country, tired of living with the same stuff that had been in the house for generations. After the war, they wanted a clean sweep. There was a longing for the new, the modern, and a disregard, just beginning, for lives that had been lived in faithful seclusion, fathers and sons working the same land, climbing up and down the steep stairs their great-grandfathers had climbed, had sometimes even built by hand.

A whole hotel, Alum Springs, went out of business because people just didn't believe any more in the curative powers of the waters, and Alma got for Charlie a whole set of heavy hotel silver, knives and forks and spoons for twelve, even if Charlie didn't know twelve people in the whole town. She bought him a porch rocker for a dollar, and heavy maroon velvet curtains, everything he could need for setting up a kitchen, and rugs that ladies had walked on when their skirts still swept the floor.

There was even a grand piano, and Alma raised her hand to bid, but Charlie and Will begged her to stop—nobody played, no matter how beautiful it might be or even how cheap, so she stopped at thirty-four dollars. It went for forty-eight, and Alma settled instead for twelve huge bath towels with ALUM SPRINGS written on them, two dollars for the lot.

She had a vision for Charlie's house that mystified the amused men. She wanted it not simply to house, but to attract, although who or what wasn't quite clear. It was as though she already had a vision of who Charlie would become, and was outfitting his rooms so that a woman would feel at home when she arrived.

He moved in on the last Friday in September. Most of the furniture was already there, but Will and Charlie worked all day, putting the pieces where Alma told them to. They opened all the tall windows, and the warm Indian summer air blew through the house, the men with dark sweat rings under their arms as they lugged sofas and armoires from one room to another.

Charlie picked out a bedroom, not the biggest one, but facing east, so he might still wake at the first light of dawn and smell the first breeze of the day. Alma laid out the linen sheets on the bed, tucking the corners tightly so the sheets wouldn't get all tangled up in the night. She put on the bed one of the strongest and brightest of the quilts, a pattern called Crown of Thomas, even though Charlie wouldn't need it for weeks and weeks, just to add some color to the room.

As he worked, Will smiled and sang the verses of one of the mournful old songs over and over:

> Oh, I wish I had someone to love me
> Someone to call me their own
> Oh, I wish I had someone to live with
> 'Cause I'm tired of living alone.

Finally Charlie told him to quit it, and Will did. But Alma still hummed it, forgetting, maybe, that however cheerful the melody, it was about going off to jail and dying, that song.

> Now I have a grand ship on the ocean
> All mounted in silver and gold
> And before my poor darling would suffer,
> Oh, that ship would be anchored and sold.

Mac Wiseman sang that song on the radio. It was a beautiful thing to hear.

Neighbors dropped by, bringing things, saying how glad they were that the house wasn't empty any more. They brought lunch, egg salad sandwiches on rich, fluffy rolls, and potato chips, and Mason jars full of sweet tea with mint and lemon.

Betty Fowler from next door brought a potted chrysanthemum, russet gold, a massive plant that spoke of fall and last bright fadings. She even picked out where to put it on the porch so it would catch the most light, telling Charlie to be sure to pinch the dead flowers every day, so more flowers would come in abundance. In the late afternoon light, they hung the swing on the porch, while Alma cooked dinner in the pots and pans from the old hotel.

When they were done, they were worn out from lifting in the heat, but it felt good, as though a complicated thing had been done almost by accident. They sat down at the dark table in the dining room and ate Alma's cooking, the first meal in Charlie's new house.

After supper, Charlie sat on his own porch with his own best friends, the lights on all up and down the street, watching his neighbors as they watched him, his voice joining with theirs as the people of the town sat and discussed and scolded one another for minor infractions of this or that nature, and the children played catch in the empty street.

"I've got a question," said Will.

"Shoot." Charlie sipped his tea and rocked while the others swung gently to and fro in the porch swing.

"How'd you get to be a butcher?"

"Accident, I guess. I worked in a grocery store after school when I was . . ."

"Where was that?"

"Will," Alma laid her hand on his. "Let the man talk."

"Back home. I was sixteen. You know, bagging groceries and such. Then the manager moved me into the meat department, the last thing I wanted. I liked meat. I just didn't want to put my hands on it. But I did, because that's the kind of boy I was then. I pretty much did as I was told.

"And I got to like it. I figured, if you're going to eat it, you might as well know where it comes from, so I studied up, learned where all the cuts were, learned how to cut clean and fair. I learned how to slaughter the animals, learned to walk up to them so they trusted me and they weren't afraid, so they didn't release any chemicals that make the meat tough.

"By the time I was twenty, I was the head butcher in another store. A big store. That's when I got my knives. Cost a lot, came all the way from Germany.

"But, to tell you the truth, I haven't done it in a while."

"Since then?"

"Things happened. Other things I hadn't counted on. But it's like riding a bicycle. If you learn something early, and you learn it well, you don't forget."

"That's enough, Will," Alma shushed him. "Don't push so hard." Then they just sat for a while in silence, rocking, the white smoke from Charlie's Lucky Strike floating like a ghost in the air, the boy quiet and tired on his mother's lap. Such a simple country quiet in the air, in the softness of the dark street, the porch lights on, the last moths of summer flittering into and out of the bright ring that hung above them, where the people of the town rocked and smoked and slept and talked in quiet voices.

When it was dark, the fireflies rose off Charlie's own front yard, and bats wheeled and circled the eaves of his house and in the dark, heavy branches of his trees. Charlie felt a mixture of freedom and imprisonment he hadn't felt in a long, long time.

Then they did the dishes, Alma washing, the men drying, while Sam sleepily wandered around the new house, touching every single thing, asking when Beebo was going to get a radio, where the Christmas tree was going to go, asking what had happened to the people who had lived there before. When the dishes were done, Alma showed Charlie where everything was stored, put away neat as a pin, scrubbed clean and ready to use.

Sam was tired, and Will picked him up, wheezing, "I'm getting too old for this," and they said their good nights, nodding, not touching, and left Charlie alone for his first night in his new house. Charlie closed the door behind him when they left, and took satisfaction in the fact that, when he walked through his rooms, the house didn't sound hollow, and it didn't sound new. It sounded already lived in.

That first night in his new house, he sat on the porch after supper, his porch light off, smoking a Lucky Strike and watching as the lights of the other porches went off as well, until there was only one left, across the street and down one, Old Mrs. Entsminger, sitting on her porch in a rocker, a shawl around her shoulders, her grandson at her feet on a stool with a fiddle to his chin.

The boy played eight notes, and the old lady began to sing in the high mountain voice they all used. There was such sadness in her quavering voice, such hope in the words she sang. She had been singing the same song since she was a girl younger than her grandson.

> The water is wide
> I can't cross o'er
> And neither have
> I wings to fly
> Build me a boat
> That can carry two
> And both shall row
> My love and I.

Such a sad sweetness, a sweet sadness that was born in the mountain and crept down into the valley like a gentle fog. She drifted off, it seemed, to sleep or memory, but the boy played on, and when he had played another verse through, she opened her eyes and patted his head. "Finish it, Henry," she said, "Take us home."

He was a boy; he was eleven, or twelve, his voice not yet changed. Still he had the music in him, and he sang the words that were far older than he would ever be, and what he sang filled and changed Charlie's heart.

> Oh love is handsome
> And love is fine
> The sweetest flower
> When first it's new
> But love grows old
> And waxes cold
> And fades away
> Like summer dew.

How could he know, the boy, and, knowing, how could he sing? But he knew. His child's voice didn't mean he did not know, and Charlie knew, too, knew a thing that he had not remembered for a long time.

The boy's voice trailed off. He helped his grandmother to her feet and into the house, their porch light went off, the last one of the night. Then Charlie went indoors and closed the door behind him, locking it, he knew for no reason. He climbed the stairs, a glass of whiskey in his hand, and undressed and lay in his bed and sipped the whiskey. Alma had told him never to smoke in bed, but he did anyway. The linen sheets were old and heavy without being hot, and they felt good on his body. He was small in the big four-poster Alma had chosen for him.

Whiskey done, he said his prayers, remembering, as he always did, the name and face of every person he had ever loved. Before turning out the light, he picked up his diary, spit on the end of a pencil, and turned to September 30, 1948, and wrote: Home. 126 Main Street, Brownsburg, Virginia, USA.

He closed the book and arranged the pillows so that nothing touched his body while he slept. But smooth and arrange as he might, hearing the soft whir of his new fan from Sears, he couldn't sleep. He tried for three hours, and then he gave up. So Charlie Beale got out of bed, remaking it as neatly as a nurse, and got dressed and went out and started his truck, the only sound on the street.

He drove out to his land by the river, and spread out his quilt on the ground. He was asleep in five minutes, while the silver river fish swam through his dreams.

He woke up with the first light of a new day in his eyes.

CHAPTER ELEVEN

T HERE WERE TWO things Charlie Beale wanted, and neither one was a woman.

The first thing he wanted was a dog. He said it wasn't so much that he himself wanted a dog, although deep down in his heart he felt that if you had a house you ought to have a dog, but that Sam wanted a dog and couldn't have one. That boy talked about it every single day, bringing it up time after time as though it had never been discussed before. He knew every dog on the street by name, and there was a kind of mournful, tender wonder in his eyes every time he put his hand on a dog's head to pat it.

The second thing was land. Charlie wanted to amass acreage the way boys collect baseball cards or young men collect broken-down cars, hoping to take the parts and put them all together one day into a sleek, fast, girl-attracting ride.

Maybe it was because Charlie wasn't a big man and wanted the armor that land would provide him. Or maybe because it was that, for so long, he had lacked a sense of place, of belonging. It *was* beautiful, this land in the Valley of Virginia, and Charlie hungered for beauty.

Obviously, one thing was a small thing and the other one was a big thing. But both dogs and land were everywhere around him, and at least he knew exactly which dog he wanted, the dog he thought Sam might like, because he'd seen Andy Myers's place on one of his many drives around the county when he first got there.

Andy Myers had more dogs than children, and he had a gang of children. He bred both for use and pleasure, the dogs to hunt and sit by his feet in the evening, and the children for chores. The beagles were brindled and content, the children freckled and happy with their lot.

Charlie drove out there and looked over the new dogs, a twelve-week-old litter.

"You hunt?" Andy asked him.

"Don't," Charlie said. "Not against it. I just never got the idea of killing for pleasure."

"I kill to eat."

"Well, see, that's sort of my business," Charlie said, looking at the squirming mass of puppies around his feet. He loved their spots, and the colors splashed on their skins, honey and black and white, the way their tongues hung from their mouths. He felt like he was five years old again, just picking out his first dog. "I'm a butcher by trade, and I never go hungry."

"I don't sell house dogs, or yard dogs. I sell hunting dogs."

"He can go hunting with Will Haislett."

"Oh, you a friend of Will's? His mother was my mother's second cousin. I don't know what that makes him and me, but his people and my people are buried in the same graveyard, so I guess that makes us family. Sure, you can have a dog. Male or female? There's both."

"I want that one, the strong one, the male."

"He'll make a good hunting dog. I was thinking of keeping that one for myself." But Charlie figured that's what Andy always said, just to get another dollar or two.

"How much?"

"For that one? Any other one, I'd take fifteen, but that one, I got to get more."

"Eighteen."

"Least twenty."

"I'm not going to argue about two dollars. He's the one, and twenty happens to be exactly what I'd planned on spending." When Andy saw the roll of bills Charlie took out of his pocket, he looked at it like he wished he'd started at twenty and gone up from there. Now he couldn't go back, so Charlie put the dog in the cab of his truck, squirming beside him in the quilt he'd brought, and drove on home.

Sam was beside himself that night. At first, he just stared at the dog, but then he laughed. "Can I pet him?" He looked at his mother.

"Of course, Sam."

The puppy took to him right away. Soon, they were on the floor of the porch together, rolling and tumbling. "Be gentle, Sam," Charlie said softly. "He's just a baby."

They all played with the puppy until it was time for Sam to go to bed. The next morning, the boy was back before breakfast, practically before it was light, and Charlie sat on the porch with his coffee, and he and Sam named the dog. Charlie'd been thinking about it all night.

"Sam, I've got two choices for you. We could name him Popeye. You know, from the funny papers. That's kind of nice. Or we could name him Jackie Robinson." Sam had been astonished when, a few weeks before, Jackie Robinson had hit a home run, a triple, a double, and a single, all in the same game.

Sam looked the dog in the eye. "Jackie Robinson!" he cried, and the dog cocked his head at the sound. "See? See, Beebo? He knows his name already!"

So Charlie laughed, and that was that. Charlie took the dog to work with him every day. It wasn't quite legal, a dog in a butcher's shop, if anybody looked into it, but nobody minded, and even Boaty Glass thought it was a fine-looking dog.

"Crazy name," he said. "Calling a dog after a nigger. Make a good hunting dog, though."

"Not going to hunt him, sir. Not this dog." Charlie looked up from cutting.

"Better not let him near a chicken coop, then. Those beagles get a taste of blood, they never stop. Got to hunt 'em or shoot 'em."

After he left, as he was writing Boaty's purchases in his book, Will said, "Boaty don't much care for pets. He's already got a pet."

"What's that?" Charlie asked.

"That wife of his."

So the little thing was done, and Charlie started on the big thing. The county was six hundred square miles, and criss-crossed with two-lane blacktop that went mostly from nowhere to nowhere, often deadending in desolation and wilderness.

Every Sunday afternoon, he got into his truck with his suitcase and his dog, and he drove. The roads were narrow and winding, not always paved, and he looked at everything in the whole county, even though he didn't know what he was looking for. He just knew he'd know it when he saw it.

He drove out to Goshen Pass, along the Maury River, and past, to the town of Goshen, where the train came through. He ate his lunch at Cozy Corners, the diner where you could buy beer on Sundays. Charlie didn't buy beer, but he ate ham and biscuits, and flirted with the waitresses, girls who'd never been anywhere in their whole lives, even though the train came through every day on its way to Staunton and beyond, places they dreamed about in their girlish way, New York or Chicago, big cities where girls just like them worked in offices and wore lipstick and smoked on the street. But they knew they'd never get to any of these places, and they thought, well, maybe that's just as well.

He drove to Lexington, the county seat, and Natural Bridge, with its old hotel where famous people had come to stay and rock on the porch in the cool evenings, and Collierstown, where the best beef came from. In all of these towns, he never even got out of his truck.

More times than not, he would find himself at the end of the day driving by Boaty Glass's house, looking, always hoping to see her in the yard, and once he did, and he slowed the car down, and rolled down the window, but then he couldn't think of anything to say to her. She turned her whole body to follow him, putting those green eyes on him, and maybe she heard him and maybe she didn't when he finally said a shy "Hey" and gave a small wave that she didn't return and then he drove on. *I'm here,* he wanted to say, would have said if his throat hadn't gone dry at the sight of her. *I'm here. I'm the one.*

It was the beauty of the land that enraptured him, and he drove until it was dark and there was hardly any traffic on the road any more, talking to Jackie Robinson, telling him about the sights, the sparkling river, the stacks of timber in Goshen waiting for the train to come and take them off to all those places the girls would never go. Every now and then he stopped the truck by the side of the road and he got out. Maybe a field of goldenrod caught his eye, or a carpet of yellow swaying in the breeze, a stand of pines or maples, or a little spring where the water was sweet enough to drink.

He went to the old hotel where the auction had been, the remnants of which now filled his own house, and he liked the way it looked, abandoned and melancholy but still proud, something built in the days of a war that was over a half century before he was born, a war that changed everything, a war that people still talked about as though it were still happening at that very minute. Once he even broke into the hotel and wandered the empty halls and imagined the generals and their wives who had come to escape the heat in Richmond or Louisiana, the military posture relaxing just a little in the cool night air, and the long skirts of the ladies, coming and going.

The countryside just stole his heart at every turn of the road. It just broke him down and put him back together. It was wild and it was gentle. It was a comfort to his soul. Sweet Virginia.

◆　◆　◆

AFTER A FEW WEEKS, he had learned to separate the land he liked from the land that truly grabbed hold of his heart, and when he saw something that made his heart beat in a certain way, he would get out, climb through the barbed wire fence, or hike up the hillside, and he would feel the sun on his face and the wind would lift his hair from his forehead, and Jackie Robinson would sniff the air, or run around in circles, or chase wild turkeys, and Charlie would just know that he had to have it.

Sometimes he would take off his clothes and just lie down with the dog in the field or the forest, and sleep for ten minutes with a peace in his heart he had never known.

Buying those places he wanted wasn't hard. There was so much land, and it wasn't worth much.

In the diary he always brought with him, he would write down carefully the location, the county road number, the specifics of what he had seen. Sometimes there would be a farmhouse in view, and he would knock on the door and find out if he had the right owner, and they would agree on a price. Sometimes it was ten acres. Sometimes it was a hundred, once five hundred.

He never paid less than eighteen dollars an acre, and he never paid more than thirty. He gave a good, honest price, and he never left an owner feeling cheated. When the price was agreed, he went to his truck, opened his suitcase, carefully counted out the money and paid every farmer in cash. "The only money that counts," he'd always say, "is cash money."

He wrote it all down in his book, sometimes drawing a crude map, or a sketch of what it was about that particular piece of land that made it so special to him. There was always something in a piece of land that cracked his heart wide open.

On Monday mornings, when business got slow after the morning rush, he went to Bobby Hostetter, the lawyer, and they made it all legal. The owners came in, in their town clothes still smelling of strong laundry soap and the hot iron, and the papers were drawn up and left to be registered at the county courthouse, in Lexington.

He asked Will one day, "Who owns the most land in town?"

"Never thought about it. But it's got to be Boaty Glass. You could look it up."

Everybody knew he was doing it. Land sales were published in the *Rockbridge Gazette*: the acreage, the sale price, the seller, the buyer. People talked about it in quiet voices on Wednesday evenings as they sat on their porches, reading the paper. But nobody talked about it to Charlie. He was a stranger, and strangers do funny things, and he saw something, they figured, in the county land they never gave much thought to.

Charlie Beale had his reasons, but he kept them to himself, the way he did everything else. There was a reason, though, and he knew it in his heart. A reason to build an empire, to make an impression. The reason had a name, and that name, ever since that first day in the butcher shop when she walked into his life in a white linen dress, the reason his travels almost always took him by her house, that name was Sylvan Glass.

CHAPTER TWELVE

He heard her name everywhere. He heard it in the rustle of the trees outside his bedroom window while he slept. He heard it in the ripples of the creeks on his land, in the swish of his tires on the asphalt. He felt it as a sweetness on his skin, a freshness of the air he breathed, a blessing in the sheets that wrapped around his body at night.

Sylvan. He had never had a conversation with her, had heard her child's voice only once. Now he couldn't think of any other thing, and every time he thought about her, it was like a punch in the gut.

He had taken such pleasure in so many things. The shifting of the weather, always unpredictable but expected in the valley, the way the valley fell into scented darkness like the underside of a leaf, mossy, then rose to shimmering morning light, like being born over and over and over again. The easy talk of men about sports or hunting dogs or their troubles at home, the pop of a fastball landing in a glove's weathered palm, all these things he thought had been enough. Enough to fill his heart.

Now the only thing that distracted him from Sylvan was Sam Haislett. Wherever Charlie went, Jackie Robinson went with him, and wherever Jackie went, Sam went. His endless chatter was like the song of a bird, "Beebo, Beebo," and Sam knew far more than he could express, about Prince Valiant and his adventures, which he followed every day in the paper, about baseball, and the gun he was going to get when he was ten, a lifetime away and right around the corner all at once, in his mind, so his thoughts ran away with him sometimes. Charlie reined him in, then egged him on to more and more talk. Sometimes he couldn't think of a word, and Charlie helped him out. Sometimes he had so many thoughts going at once he rattled on like a runaway train, and Charlie had to get him back on track.

Sam was the only one besides Will and Alma who didn't treat him like a foreigner, who just took him as he came. It touched Charlie's heart, the way the boy would reach out to take his hand when they crossed a creek, or climbed a steep slope. It charmed him, the way the boy called him Beebo, no matter how often he told Sam his name.

Charlie had never much seen the charm of children, he had thought it was continuance he sought when he dreamed of his child, not companionship. Charlie had been one of those boys for whom childhood was a kind of prison in which he only longed to be grown, to be a man, but Sam was starting to change his mind. Because Charlie had been a prisoner of his own childhood, he had never really stopped being a child himself. He found he could talk to Sam easily, and tell him everything about where he'd been and the people he'd known, knowing Sam would never pass on the information. He told him that everything he was telling him was private, just between them, and he made sure Sam knew what that word meant.

Childhood is the most dangerous place of all and no one gets past it unscarred. In Charlie's heart there grew a need not to be one of the scars in Sam's life, to help and not to wound this boy.

And Sam, in return, told Charlie everything. He told him about Will and Alma, about baseball stars and places he wanted to see, all the things he'd learned about while his father was reading him the paper.

Maybe because Charlie was younger than Will, and boyish, or closer to his own size, but Sam found he could tell Charlie things he wouldn't tell his mother and father, mostly about how he felt about things. Will was always interested in what Sam was doing, but it never occurred to him to ask how he *felt*, as long as he seemed to be happy, and he did, and he was. Everything seemed new to him, every day, all the time.

When it got into late September, it got to be butchering time. The pigs were getting heavy without getting so overfed their kidneys were lost in fat, the lambs were poised in that delicate stage between being sheep and turning into mutton, and the flies had begun to die off in the cooler valley nights.

Every Wednesday, Charlie drove out to the slaughterhouse to pick up the week's meat, and Sam went with him, as he had always done with Will, even when he was barely able to walk. It never frightened him; he knew what it was, he just didn't seem to pay it much attention. He never saw the actual killing or skinning, never saw the living animal, just the great sides of meat hung up in the cold locker, so maybe he hadn't made the connection yet between the meat he saw and the animals that grazed in the pastures.

As they drove on Wednesday afternoons, Sam would point out to Charlie every house they passed, and tell him the names of the families who lived there, the Hostetters, the Ploggers, the Willards, the Mutispaughs, the names that popped up all over the county, the names of the women who came every morning to buy the meat for the day. He knew all the names, and the names of their dogs, and he recited them all, every time, as though Charlie had never heard of these people.

On the first trip to the slaughterhouse, Sam pointed at a big white farmhouse on a rise just outside of town, that house Charlie already knew so well, her house, its massive solidity and squareness softened by the gingerbread fretwork that hung from its wide, full porch, and he said, "Mr. and Mrs. Glass." He said it like "Miz," the way all the people talked. Charlie slowed the truck down, as he had done so many times before, looking for her, and then he drove on about his business.

On the way home, he slowed the truck down just a little more. There was a blonde woman standing on the porch, in a flowered housedress, common as any in town, but light, blowing open just slightly in the breeze. This time, her eyes didn't follow him as he drove past, and he didn't wave.

"That's Miz Glass," said Sam, and Charlie just nodded without saying a word. But that night, after closing up the shop, he bought a box of Crayons at the general store, and, lying in bed, he filled three pages of his diary, writing her name over and over until he had used up all twenty-four colors in the box.

After one trip to the slaughterhouse, Charlie told Will he wasn't happy with the way the local men cut up the meat, that it wasn't efficient, wasn't focused on separating the good from the less good, and he said he knew how to do it better, and Will told him to give it a try. After that, Charlie took his knives with him, and the trips took most of the afternoon, as Charlie first cut the corpses down the middle with a hacksaw, and then carefully went to work separating out the various cuts of meat.

He also had a problem with the fact that he didn't think Will was hanging the beef long enough. Will resisted, saying it had always been good enough, but Charlie persisted and he gave in, so Charlie turned down the temperature in the locker a few degrees, and they aged it for ten more days, a full sixteen, before they started selling it. The day came when they started selling it to customers, and all the women, black and white, and even Boaty Glass, said it was a miracle, that they'd never tasted such good beef in their whole lives.

Charlie didn't brag about it. He wasn't that kind; but you could tell he was satisfied, even though Will never said a word of thanks.

Sylvan Glass began to come into the store, on her own, after her husband had come and spewed his vulgarisms and gone off to Staunton, buying things they all knew she didn't need or want.

Sometimes she ordered almost the same things as Boaty, and what she did with all that meat was anybody's guess. Two people, even if one of them was Boaty Glass, couldn't possibly eat that much.

On one of these trips, Charlie picked up the package of wrapped steaks and chops and roasts and followed her silently out to the car. She seemed not only to accept his help, she seemed to expect it.

As she was getting into the driver's side of her fancy car, Charlie opened the other door and placed the packages carefully on the seat beside her. "You know, Mrs. Glass," he said, not knowing where either the words or the courage to say them were coming from, just knowing his deep and inexpressible need, "if you weren't married, I'd surely make a run for you. So you be careful now, you hear?" He smiled at her, as open and honest and smitten as a boy.

Sylvan Glass, Mrs. Harrison Glass, turned to him and stared, her hand on the key in the ignition. She started the car, and once it had settled into its expensive purr, she said just loud enough to be heard above the machine, "Mr. Beale, I can't immediately see what difference my being married could possibly make. And I am," she continued, putting the car into gear, "always and ever careful with my heart. You be, too." She put the car in gear.

And then they were quiet, looking at one another, not long enough to cause talk, just long enough to express what needed to be said, to be agreed to between them.

"Take care," he said, closing the door as the car began to inch forward. When she was already moving off, and couldn't possibly have heard him, he said, with a rush of blood to his brain, "See you soon."

On one of his land-buying trips, he heard that one family, the Potters in Collierstown, grew the best beef around, and he started buying the beef over there, even though it was almost an hour's drive away in those days. The Potters killed the meat differently from most farmers in the county. They never shot a steer in front of the rest of the herd. They would lead it gently into another pasture, walking just as slowly as it wanted, never rattling the animal, and then quietly shoot it once in the head, close up, before slitting its throat in one quick, clean swipe of the blade while the heart was still beating, so the cow never panicked, was practically bled out by the time its knees hit the ground, never shot those chemicals into its bloodstream that made the beef taste like fear and death.

Charlie wouldn't let Mr. Potter cut the meat up for him, though. He always drove it back to the slaughterhouse and did the work himself. He always took his knives on Wednesdays.

On Wednesday, November 3, 1948, Charlie and Sam headed out to the slaughterhouse, the way they did every week. Sam still recited the names of all the residents of every house, and named every dog in every yard. When they got to the Glass house, there she was again, and Charlie didn't just slow down, he stopped the truck in the road, outside of the closed gate, just staring up at the woman standing on the porch, smoking a cigarette and leaning against a post. She was dressed this time in one of her fancy movie star outfits, and wearing scarlet lipstick, red even from the road. She wasn't smiling, or even looking their way; just standing, waiting to be seen, waiting for something, maybe even she didn't know what.

After a full two minutes of this, they drove on. Charlie cut up the meat while Sam and Jackie Robinson watched from just outside the door, silhouetted in the bright fall air, behind them the trees the color of honey and amber and copper, even the mountains, so blue in summer, now burnt orange.

Then they loaded up. Charlie's clothes were covered in blood, but he had scrubbed his hands clean as he always did, until they were smooth and clean as a woman's.

On the way back home, when they got to the Glass house, the gate was open. She was still there, or she was there again, in a soft rose-colored dress, shining in the golden late-afternoon light. Charlie stopped the truck.

"Why are we stopping?"

"Just hush, Sam. Just be still for a minute."

He let the truck idle for five minutes, just staring, until finally she turned her eyes to his and held his gaze. Then he drove through the open gate, stopped and got out to close it behind him again. Then he drove up the driveway and around to the back of the house. Sylvan came out of the kitchen door and just stood looking at him, saying nothing, not waving or greeting him in any way, as though both he and she belonged where they were, in that moment, the evening coming on, the fall crisping the air to a breakable brittleness that cried out for warmth and comfort.

He turned to the boy. "Wait here, Sam, Okay? Don't get out of the truck. Just talk to Jackie and wait. I'm going to go in that house and talk to Mrs. Glass for a while. I won't be long." He pulled a pack of wintergreen Life Savers out of his pocket and gave it to Sam, knowing his parents didn't allow it.

"If you bite down real hard, it'll make a spark in your mouth. Don't crack your teeth. Your mother will kill me."

He got out of the truck and walked to the door, speaking out her name softly, over and over, Sylvan, Sylvan, up to the house where she stood waiting, never moving a muscle. They talked for a few minutes, no more than two or three. Charlie put his hand up to her face once, softly, the way Sam's mother would lay her hand on his cheeks some nights when he was saying his prayers. Sam could see their lips moving, although he couldn't hear what they said, the windows were rolled up against the chill.

Then they went into the house. There were no lights on, and Sam could see them only vaguely in the slanting light. They had hardly spoken, but something had been agreed to, had been decided.

The light had gone from gold to silver by the time Charlie came out and got back into the truck. He didn't say anything, didn't even look at the boy beside him. He drove down the drive, opened and then shut the gate, bouncing over the cattle guard, and then he drove slowly back toward Brownsburg.

He stopped the truck at the edge of town, and sat and stared at the road for a couple of minutes, looking at the lights of the known houses, the lives of people, dinners getting started, Brownsburg just coming into night. He turned to Sam.

"Make any sparks?"

"I couldn't see any."

"Give me one." He placed the Life Saver carefully between his teeth. "See?"

He bit down suddenly, and a small flash of light went off against his cheek. "Now you."

Sam put the last Life Saver in his teeth, exactly as Charlie had done, and felt, even if he couldn't see, the quick spark as he bit down, and Charlie smiled. "See? A trick." Then he just stared at the road for a while until he spoke again, and this time it was in a different voice, more serious, talking to Sam for the first time like a distant grownup.

"Sam. Pay attention now, son. We're friends, right?"

"Sure, Beebo."

"You know what a promise is?"

"Yeah, I do."

"A promise is a secret that you keep, that you don't tell anybody, forever and ever. You understand that?"

"Ever and ever."

"Not even your mother and father. Understand?"

"I think about things sometimes and I don't tell them."

"Then don't tell them this. Don't ever tell anybody we ever stopped at that house today. Don't ever say that you saw me talking to Mrs. Glass. It's important, Sam. Promise me."

"Course, Beebo. Promise forever and ever."

"If you ever tell anybody, listen to me, if you ever tell, something really bad is going to happen to me, and maybe to Mrs. Glass."

"Will you go to jail?"

"Maybe. Maybe worse. Just promise."

"I promise."

Charlie started the truck, and they drove back to the shop in silence, while Sam sat and tried to forget the thing he'd promised he'd never tell. By the time he got back into his father's lap, he almost had.

He never did tell, never said a word until it was too late to matter. But in the hour that he sat in the truck, talking to Jackie Robinson, something had happened, something he didn't have a place for in his brain yet, and, in the moments before he went to sleep, he thought about it, and he knew that he would remember everything, in every detail, the cold afternoon, the sparks from the Life Saver in Charlie's mouth, the word *wintergreen*, the way she laughed as Charlie walked up the yard, calling her name softly, like he was calling Jackie off a possum, gently but with a kind of haste, the far-off sound of the screen door closing behind them on its spring as they went into the darkness of the house. And it made him feel both curious and lonely. Something had happened and he had been both a part of it and shut out of it completely, and it disturbed him and roiled his sleep. And he could not ask or tell. That much he knew.

Yes. Childhood is the most dangerous place of all. If we had to live there forever, we wouldn't live very long.

CHAPTER THIRTEEN

THIS IS HERE, he thinks. This is the only thing. This. This violence in the mind, this gentleness in his strong hands, moving slowly over her body, the kindness in her skin, the gratitude in his heart. That she would let him touch her, would open herself for him. Only this, the tremor in his skin, like wind across a pond, silver-scaled, a shimmering of nerve, a reddening of flesh, a slickness everywhere spreading from his shoulders, gathering in the small of his back, where her hands lie, still as a child's.

Sixty years ago this bed, this place, this hour with the sun going down, cresting to redness and fading to lavender and then to blue, but here and now, never changing, never forgotten, never to be recreated. Always a making of something wholly new, always a loss of something valued, built up, kept to be given, a giving beyond money or work, a taking beyond greed or theft.

This chenille bedspread, these pillows beneath her head, encased in flowered cotton, her blonde hair fanning out like golden angels' wings in a white garden, the down on her earlobes, her crimson lipstick smearing his mouth, his shoulder, his chest. Only this, and nothing else.

This secret coupling. These secret hearts and bodies, the child waiting in the truck, with the brindled beagle named Jackie Robinson. That would be the photograph of this moment in time, sixty years ago, if one had been taken, if one existed.

Nothing else. Only this stopping of hearts, and its opposite, that, too, the speed of the having, so waited for, so unexpected when it comes, then this rushing, rushing everywhere. He cannot have enough of her, cannot take enough of her skin at one kiss. His tongue tastes her perfume and her own skin beneath, washed clean, over and over, by his kiss, as she twists and churns beneath him like water, her breath sweet in his ear, choking him with desire, with the urgency of telling her everything, everything about his life and his heart and his memory, telling her not with words but with his body, with every inch of his skin, offered up to her with such hopefulness, with what he hopes is kindness but knows to be a kind of selfishness. Because she is, at this minute, in the chill, the only one, the only woman who ever lived, the only one he has ever touched, has ever told with his body all the secrets that were alive in his heart every day, the things he remembers, the things he has long since forgotten.

But this is here, this is now. This is the only thing, and she is not the first but she is the only, the only one, and every taste of her flesh is something new in his mouth, and every breath from her mouth a kindness he never expected and does not deserve. Right here, in this bed, on this chenille, in this sunset, these flowered pillows and her blonde, blonde body, the wilderness of his general desire becomes specific, the path becoming clear until it leads only to her, to here, to the two of them, wholly wanted and wholly belonging only here and only only now.

He is beautiful, now, like an animal in the wild. She is beautiful and wholly known and wholly foreign, and her voice is a new voice, and her breath is a strong wind that could blow him over, and her mouth is a new thing, her lipstick gone. How her eyes look into his eyes, dark as deep pools, the blue gone black, the depth unknowable, to ask, is this all right? Is this what you want?

Because her desire, her wanting, has waited, too. Because she is what she has always been, since she was a little child in a shack out in that valley, she is what she has been since before she was a woman. She is ready. For this, for him, for her movie star to come riding in the sunset, to her, to here, the smell of his sweat as sweet as rainwater, his hands smelling of blood, the sheen of his skin lit by the red of the sun and by his own blood rushing just under the surface, her Montgomery Clift, her Gable.

Now his arms are around her, his hands on her, his legs pinning her legs and she is Hayworth, she is Grable, the face and body a million boys took to war and dreamed about. She knows who she is, finally, because he knew from the first glance who she was and what he wanted her to be, and so she becomes that thing, here, his hands, his tongue, creating her out of whole cloth, the way Claudie's deft hands made a dress from the flat of the fabric, she becomes something flared and ruffled and flounced and shimmering and feathered and winged, something silken that he can cool his skin against, that trails out behind her like the train of a bridal gown she has never worn, something made only for him and only for now.

All she can say is now, and now again and again, until he comes back from where he was and hears her, and finally allows himself to take what she offers, to take it shyly, to take it with a force that causes no pain, to take it with the kindness and the gratitude he feels in his heart that any woman so beautiful would let him come near her. Each has become for the other, Charlie to Sylvan and Sylvan to Charlie, both the only thing there is and nothing at all. They are joined, they are alone, each needing the other to create that solitude they have lived to find, each needing the war of the other's body to create that wholeness that seems the only place it is possible to live, for now, and now, and for the moment after that.

Every moment would last forever. Every moment would end in a split second. In the end, they wake with a flash to find that they are still who they had always been, that even this now comes to an end, and even this here has a boundary they *cross at breakneck speed, cross with regret, cross with gratitude because the body knows even after the mind forgets that there are some countries in which you cannot live forever, some countries that would kill you if you stayed too long.*

But in the dying, both know for the first time that each will be a citizen in the other's country until the last breath is drawn. The women he had known before her lived in another country, far off. The feeling of being at home in them had been, every time, a lie and a heartbreak, even though he remembered every face, every detail of every body. But this, she, her, here, now, this is the truth he had imagined as a boy, something that, once known, can never be lost.

And for her, for Sylvan, he is Hollywood.

CHAPTER FOURTEEN

IN BROWNSBURG, EVERYBODY went to church, everybody except a few old men and one woman, who were still too drunk on Sunday morning to go much of anywhere. So Alma said Charlie had to go, too. He complained, politely, that Sunday was his day off, that he didn't want to leave Jackie Robinson alone, but in her gentle way Alma won out, saying it was the thing to do, it was expected. And so he agreed, and he went.

There were five churches in town—an Episcopalian church, Presbyterian, Methodist, and Baptist for the white people, and a Colored Methodist Episcopal Church for the black citizens. The CME wasn't actually a church, or at least it didn't look like one. They met—less than two dozen people in all, including babies and a traveling preacher, the Reverend Mr. Shadwell, who only came every other week—in a storefront at the far end of Main Street, right close to where they all lived. They didn't even have to walk into the main part of town to get to it.

Alma and Will were Presbyterians and, while Charlie hadn't been raised one, he figured he might as well go along and worship with the people he knew best. The first Sunday in November, four days after he had first stopped his truck in front of the Glass house, he woke up at dawn, as he always did, and ironed a clean white shirt while he drank his first strong cup of coffee. He didn't know how he felt about going to church; it had been so long he could hardly remember it.

He didn't have a suit or a tie, so he borrowed a tie from Will, but he worried. Alma said it didn't matter, nobody would notice.

But it did matter, at least to Charlie. He was the only man in church who wasn't wearing a suit, even though you could tell nobody else wore one, either, except on Sunday mornings, or to a wedding or a funeral. Most of the suits were brown and old, some shiny; a lot were too small, as though they had been bought before the men gained that last twenty pounds or so. But the women looked nice. Plain, clean dresses, a lot of them made by Claudie Wiley, and every woman wore a hat; Alma even wore short white gloves, which she pulled onto her small hands and buttoned at the wrist as they walked down to the church after Charlie had joined them, waiting on their porch. Even Sam had a suit, and it was brown, like everybody else's.

Of course she was there. When Charlie and the Haisletts walked into the church and took their seats with the assurance of people who sat in the same pew every week, Boaty and Sylvan Glass were already seated three rows in front of them.

Sylvan was the only woman in black, a black wool suit, from

what Charlie could see of her, which was only from the shoulder blades up, her hair swept up tightly under a fitted black hat with a feather on it. She never turned, never greeted another parishioner, and Charlie spent the few minutes before the processional just staring at the back of her head. She wore black jet earrings, the only woman in church who was wearing any jewelry.

George McLaughlin started up the pedal organ, and a boy with a wooden cross led a small, straggly choir up the aisle, followed by Reverend Morgan, all of them staring at their hymnals so intensely they walked like blind people. They sang "Fairest Lord Jesus, Ruler of the Morning," and Charlie was surprised that he knew it, knew the melody, and he sang along, although so softly that even Sam could hardly hear him.

> Fair is the sunshine, fairer still the moonlight,
> and all the twinkling starry host:
> Jesus shines brighter, Jesus shines purer
> than all the angels heaven can boast.

Charlie had thought it wouldn't be so bad, going to church, and it wasn't. Everybody looked so clean and sweet, the men bored, the women attentive, the children squirming but quiet. He stared at the back of Sylvan's head, through the singing, through the morning prayers, praying to the Lord only that she would turn around, look at him, even turn to look at one of the Victorian stained glass windows of the saints, so he could see just the side of her face. But she never moved. He counted the days until Wednesday, the hours, the minutes.

Reverend Morgan was tall and thin, at least seventy-five, and he'd been the preacher there for thirty years, so everybody had heard him say the same prayers every Sunday for hundreds of Sundays, and it gave them comfort, the sameness of it all, every word unchanging, every movement preordained, the kneeling, the standing, the full-sleeved whiteness of the starched cotta against the black of his robe.

So, not so bad. Until the sermon, at least. Before they sat for the sermon, they sang "Lord Jesus Think on Me," and Charlie started to feel uneasy. It reminded him right away of why he didn't go to church any more.

> Lord Jesus think on me
> And purge away my sin;
> From earth-borne passions set me free
> And make me pure within.

Charlie didn't feel impure. And he didn't want to hear about sin. The sight of Sylvan's golden hair was the only brightness in the room.

Nobody seemed to mind. They sang just as heartily as they sang the first hymn, about redeeming themselves from the sin that corrupted their minds and lives, every day, in every action. And, as they sang, they dug into their purses and wallets for coins or bills to put into the passing baskets. Charlie put in a dollar.

> Lord Jesus think on me
> Nor let me go astray;
> Through darkness and perplexity
> Point thou the heavenly way.

They sang as if they believed in going astray more than they believed in the brightness of the morning. They sang as if their lives depended on it, until the verses of the hymn led them finally through the maze of sin and into the arms of redemption and heaven.

Then Reverend Morgan stepped to the pulpit, and you could see the old man trembling—with scorn, with a rage for Jesus, a fury that had never failed him once in half a century's years of preaching.

He had a full, rich voice for a thin man, and you knew from the minute he started speaking that he meant business.

"The Gospel for today's sermon is from John, chapter eight, verse thirty-four. Mark on this, and remember. John said, 'Whosoever commiteth sin is the servant of sin.' He was talking almost two thousand years ago, but he was talking to you, my brother, and to you, my sister. To the old folks and the babies. To every one of you." He stared at them hard, looked into every eye.

Charlie knew he was a sinner. He knew, even as he couldn't turn his eyes away, that even by looking at the back of Sylvan's head, remembering in the back of his throat the taste of her tongue in his mouth, he was committing at least two of the Seven Deadly Sins. But he didn't care. He was fine with that, and with whatever price he would have to pay.

". . . and the sad thing is, dear friends, is that sin is real. As real as the rich man's Cadillac, as real as the poor man's crust of bread. It is as real as your neighbor's wife, your neighbor's land. And it is there *forever*. Forever and ever."

The congregation wasn't stirring now. They were transfixed.

Even the children quieted down at the sound of that rich and terrible voice.

"When you sin . . . and who among us does not, does not sin every day in every way, from the moment we open our eyes until long after we have lost ourselves in lustful dreams? When you sin, God does not abandon you. No. No. It is not in the nature of God to abandon you, no matter how hellish your heart, no matter how sinful your dreams or your covetous desires. No. No. God does not abandon you. When you sin, *you abandon God*, the God who made you for no reason and who loves you beyond *all* reason, you abandon God and turn away into the open, inviting jaws of hell.

"Do you know what hell is? Hell is simply this, dear friends. Hell is the place where God isn't. You may find riches untold there—that Cadillac you dream about, or that woman or that man, that land of riches and jewels and money, always money, that land you dream of at night with lust in your heart—but you will not find God. God waits for you. In heaven. God calls you home. In the midst of your lust and your envy and your sloth and your gluttony and your pride, stop and listen for a sound. And you will hear it, I promise you, God promises you. You will hear it as I have heard it."

His voice grew louder, more commanding, and they sat, obedient to the fear he planted in their hearts and to the power in the old man's voice. Morgan was almost yelling now, his voice was hoarse, rasping, the way you imagine the voice of the devil.

"It is God. He is calling you home. Home to Him. Home to heaven. Sin is real. Hell is real. And God is calling you home.

Which will you choose, on that great day? Which will you choose tonight? Tomorrow? *Forever?*"

He stopped, and stared out over the congregation for a full minute. None of them, not one save for Sylvan, could hold his gaze. They looked at the baby Jesus in the stained-glass windows, they looked at their hands, fumbled in their pockets for a clean handkerchief.

To Charlie, these people around him didn't look like sinners. Sinners wore makeup and drank liquor and bet on horses. Sinners shot people. Sinners lied. They didn't go about their business with the calm and dignity of the people he'd met in the town or around the county. But, apparently, they *felt* like sinners. They needed to think of themselves that way, at least for the twenty minutes a week Morgan harangued them from the pulpit.

He wondered why these people, who worked so hard at doing their best, at going about their daily lives without causing anybody too much trouble, would need that kind of thing—being yelled at week after week, told every week they were going to end up in hell—and in what way it gave them comfort, strength to go on. They didn't covet, or envy, they worked hard and, for the most part, told the truth, because it was a small town, after all. They had to live with themselves, and with each other.

They looked ashamed—of what? he wondered. After the sermon, they said the few remaining prayers as if in a daze, and then they all sang "Alleluia, Sing to Jesus" for the recessional. Their voices rose when they came to the lines, "Alleluia, not as orphans, are we left in sorrow now," and nodded solemnly as Reverend

Morgan passed up the aisle, fixing each of them with his steely gaze. Then they filed out of the church into the chill, bright morning air. In and out in an hour. At least there was that.

Charlie couldn't get out of there fast enough.

In the churchyard, the parishioners stood around talking, as though they hadn't seen each other every day for all of their lives. As they talked to Will and Alma and Charlie, almost every man and woman reached down absently and touched Sam's head, tousled his hair. He was the youngest child there, except for an infant or two, the last fruit of his parents' generation, and the people felt a special fondness for him. Sam liked having his head touched, leaned his forehead into their hands, and smiled up at them, always asking how they were and what they were doing with a genuine interest and concern.

Boaty and Sylvan Glass didn't move around; they just stood in the one shady spot, and every man and woman went up to greet them, but only for a minute. Sylvan smiled, her lips red, her eyes hidden by the shadow of her hat and her dark, dark tortoise-shell sunglasses.

Charlie, when it came their turn to speak to them, couldn't take his eyes off her. He couldn't even pretend to look at Boaty, never heard a word he said. He wanted to see her eyes, her green eyes, he wanted her to look at him and say anything, anything at all, but she never did. She spoke only to Alma, and hardly even that, and nobody noticed how Charlie was staring at her, not even Boaty, who was probably used to it anyway. Nobody noticed except Sam, who also stared at her, but for other reasons, reasons he couldn't quite fathom, as though he had never seen her before, or as though he didn't connect this glamorous woman with the woman he had seen waiting on the porch of a big white farmhouse, just three days before.

Of all the grownups, only Boaty and Sylvan didn't reach out to touch Sam's head, didn't smile at him and ask how he was as though he were grown already, and he stood there wanting to feel her small white hand on his head, feel her fingers with their red nails run through his hair. He felt the wish in his body, his child's body, and it was something he had never felt before. He wanted to be Charlie, to be his height, to stare so intently at her eyes, even if she never looked back. He wanted to know what Charlie saw when he looked at her, what they had talked about that day when the door closed behind them, because they must have talked; that was what grown people did.

Maybe they listened to the radio. Maybe they read the newspaper. He didn't know what they did, but he wanted to know.

He watched her as she talked to his mother while Charlie stared, hunting for her eyes, and Sam knew, all of a sudden, that men were different from women, and that men wanted something from them that he didn't know how to say, something they had that men wanted and wouldn't give up on. It had never occurred to him before.

He knew his mother and father dressed differently, like all mothers and fathers, and that they talked about different things, to him, to each other. But it had always seemed there was no essential difference between them. Now he knew there was. He didn't know what the difference could be, but he knew it was there, and it could be measured in the way Charlie Beale hunted for the glance of Sylvan Glass in the churchyard. He had seen it in the way a beagle would freeze at the scent of a bird, a dog trembling with eagerness in his blood for the animal he knew was there, unseen, frozen in a place of its own.

It lasted no more than a few seconds. His mother took his hand. They moved on — to other families, other men and women and children, all familiar to him. The light went out in Charlie's eyes and a warmer, more pleasant light came on, like the light in Jackie Robinson's eyes after the bird had flown and the scent was lost. But Sam had seen it, and he knew that it was born in Charlie, part of his nature, the way it was born in Jackie Robinson. He also knew he would see it again.

On the walk home, Charlie turned to Alma. "I'm sorry," he said, "but I'm not going there again."

"That Morgan is a tough old bird, that's for sure," Will answered. "But I've been listening to him spew that shit for forty years, and it ain't scared me off yet."

"Will," said Alma. "Not that way. Don't listen to your father, Sam. You're right, Mr. Beale, he's hard to take sometimes. A bit fanatical. But it's good for you, in the end. And, as I said, everybody goes."

"Mrs. Haislett," Charlie answered, "I'm not being disrespectful. I try to be a good man. To do the right thing. But I'm not going to go there once a week and have some old man scream at me about what a bad and terrible person I am. Hellfire and all that. I don't believe it. And I don't need to hear it."

"Then try another church. To me, it doesn't matter where you go, as long as you go. I don't believe in hell, I don't think. I don't know if I even believe in heaven. But I believe in goodness. I think it's the only thing that matters. It's the only thing we'll be remembered for after we're gone. It's the only real money you have in the bank—don't laugh at me, Will—and church is just the place where you go once a week and think, deep down to your bones, whether you're being the kind of person you hoped you'd be, measure the distance between that person and the person you really are. I don't listen much to Morgan any more. I just sit quietly and listen to my own heart, my own thoughts. You can go anywhere you like as long as you go somewhere. The town expects it, and I would consider it a kindness."

So he did. For the next several weeks, he tried other churches, and he said all they talked about was hell. Even the Episcopalians, who were very proper and mostly richer and quieter, and who received him warmly in their small congregation and asked him home to lunch. Even they talked about hell.

"Do you know what hell is?" their minister, Mr. Farrar, asked, the second time he tried them. "Hell is your heart. It is the blood in your veins. It is who you are, if you don't listen to the Word. Hell is you." Farrar didn't yell at them, like Morgan. That wasn't the Episcopalian way.

He spoke in a sad, warm voice, as though he yearned to keep the terrible and inevitable truth from his sheltered congregation. But it was said nevertheless, and the roast beef afterward tasted rancid in Charlie's mouth, even though he had cut it himself and sold it to the Gadsden sisters only two days before. He responded in kind to their girlish, flirtatious chatter, but he felt, the whole time, as he smiled and charmed them in that way he had, that his clothes were too tight, as if he were wearing some other man's underpants.

He tried every church at least once. The Episcopalians got two chances. He told Will and Alma all about it, every Sunday evening, in the kitchen now — it was too cold to sit out on the porch, and the night came on so early.

"Keep going, Mr. Beale. You'll hear it. And, if you don't, just sit quietly and listen to your own heart beat."

In the end, he went past all the white churches and walked through the doors of the Colored Methodist Episcopal Church, where he sat, the only white person who had ever set foot in there, in the far corner, making himself small in the last row of folded chairs. And he knew right away he was home.

He walked in a few minutes late, having paced nervously outside, debating, and everywhere he looked there was color and light and music and joy. The people in the congregation, less than forty including babies, looked at him and froze for a second as he sat down, but then they looked away, they were so focused on prayer and song and rapture. The minister, Reverend Shadwell, spoke in a warm, rich voice. He spoke with the zeal of a missionary, and he talked about heaven and the riches that awaited them there, on that happy day.

Everybody, even the poorest of them, smelled so clean, and their clothes were so bright, reds and purples and pure, blinding whites, the ladies, even the littlest girls, in hats, the men in white shirts so clean and starched they sparkled in the light from the candles.

The words they sang and said seemed brand new, not arbitrary or learned by rote, but fresh and strong and joyful in every single way, as if they sprang directly from the wellspring of their hearts.

Claudie Wiley had made most of the dresses the women wore. Claudie herself never, ever went to church, no matter how often Shadwell knocked on her door.

So he finally heard it, there at the CME, the thing Alma had told him to listen for. He heard the beat of his own heart and, as sure as the gauges in the dashboard of his truck, the beats measured for him the distance between where he was and where he had meant to be. Just as Alma had said.

He thought about the qualities of his own soul, about his many sins that would all be washed away. He thought about God. He thought about heaven, and for all the length of the long service that went on way past lunch, he didn't think for one second about Sylvan Glass.

But as he sat there, he felt in his body exactly the way he felt on Wednesday afternoon, when he was with her. He felt redeemed.

He heard in every word these people uttered, so poor, so maligned and mistreated and overworked and heaped with secret scorn, not even secret, he heard and knew how they went on with their lives. He knew why they did the things they did, the passions that simmered in their souls, still chained by society and law, their hollow, toilsome freedom and their endless fountains of exultation.

They were bonded by blood, both bound and freed because they were the outsiders, as he was, set apart in the towns where they had lived their whole lives, for generations, and they were bound by an unbreakable will, a belief that told them their day was close at hand, even if they had to leave their bodies behind to see it.

"It is close at hand," Shadwell sang to them in exultation in that voice that was later to sing to thousands, millions. "The day of Revelation. The rapture. Freedom. My people, my brothers and sisters, freedom!"

They believed that day would come, no matter what, and that day would be called freedom, would be called Salvation, and it would last until the universe darkened and froze and time stopped still and there was not a breath left in this or any world.

Charlie left the church as the last amens were being shouted. Nobody saw him leave, so lost were they in the wholeness of their revelation.

He walked home, completely at peace. He knew now he would go on doing the things he was doing—going to work, buying up land he didn't understand, seeing Sylvan Glass for reasons he couldn't help. But he also knew it would all be fine, whatever happened. He knew it was the right thing to do. He was in the place he was meant to be. He was home, finally, at the happy and complete end of his long and troubled road.

He was home.

PART TWO

The Prisoner of Sin

CHAPTER FIFTEEN

"MISSED YOU AT Sunday dinner" was all Will said the next morning. Charlie didn't say anything, just went on sharpening his knives.

"Alma missed you, too. And Sam asked about you, didn't you, son?"

"There's a new comic strip in the funny papers," Sam said. "Roy Rodgers. I wanted to show you."

The man and the boy looked at him, but Charlie didn't answer for a long time.

"Had things to do," he finally said. "Chores. Nobody looks after me but me."

"Well, son, we try, you know. Alma and me." Will sounded a little irritated.

"I know that, Will. And I'm grateful. Sometimes I just need to be alone. Private."

"It's not right, you know. There's something not right about it. Those people—"

"It suits me fine."

"—you know they don't want you."

"Then they'll let me know." He hoped they wouldn't. He went for three weeks straight hoping they wouldn't tell him to stop coming, especially because the women from the CME came in Monday morning early, as they always did, and a few even said it was nice to see him yesterday at services. But they did, they let him know.

On the third Sunday, right after Charlie had come home from the service and changed out of his church clothes, he was sitting on the porch, just fixing it all in his mind, when Lewis Shadwell walked up the sidewalk, into the part of town where Negroes never went, except to clean white people's houses, and stepped to the bottom of Charlie's porch. His face still glowed with the joy of preaching to his congregation.

He was twenty-eight years old, dark skinned, a little heavy but strong, you could tell. He wasn't yet the firebrand he was later to become, with the sit-ins, and the marches, and getting his picture in the papers. That Sunday, he was just a nice, devout young man who was born shy and gentle and stayed that way until he found a reason to be otherwise. He wore gold-rimmed eyeglasses, and his clerical collar was white and stiff, and tight against his dark, thick neck, as though it had been issued him when he graduated from seminary, before he gained the weight.

"Afternoon, Reverend Shadwell," said Charlie as he stood up. "Please. Come join me. It's a little cold to sit outside, so come on in."

They walked into the sitting room, and Shadwell sat on the sofa, not taking his coat off, as though he shouldn't really be there, and wouldn't be staying long. He seemed so uncomfortable, with his coat bunched up around his waist and the dog sniffing his feet, but Charlie didn't know what to offer him, so he just sat and waited.

Shadwell cleared his throat. Cleared it again. "The thing is . . ." he said, and then he stopped as though he didn't truly know what the thing was, although both he and Charlie knew well enough. "The thing is, we appreciate it."

"I should have stayed later, longer," said Charlie. "I should have said hello to some folks. I apologize."

"No need. You take what you need and leave the rest, and that's fine. But the thing is, well, we've talked, the elders and I, and we don't think it's a good idea. It just can't be. I'm sorry."

"You know there's no place else I'll go. You know that."

"I've been told. And that's a shame. Every man should have a spiritual life. It has saved me from such . . . degradation. And it could save you, if you need saving, and I'm not making any judgments and I mean no offense . . ."

"None taken."

"But we can't give you what you need. And I want to explain why."

"There's no need."

"But I want to. I want you to know that this is not some unkindness on our part. I need, *we* need for you to know that. The thing is, we're grateful. What you've done, coming to us, is an act of both bravery and kindness. But you're not from around here, and there's things you just don't, can't understand."

Charlie didn't say anything. He just called the dog over, and sat with Jackie Robinson at his feet, and he waited. His heart was beating like thunder. He couldn't say why. It was like being called to the principal's office for some infraction he didn't remember committing.

"We are watched, Mister Beale. Every time we set foot out the door, somebody is looking at everything we do. We are the most watched people on earth. Every step we take, we have to be careful. If we put even one foot wrong, even one of the children, our world could end. And I don't mean that in an imaginary way. It is a true fact.

"These people, my people, have no education except what we can provide for ourselves. Not one family owns, or will ever own, the house they live in. They are mostly owned, the houses, by either Mister Glass or those twin sisters you're so fond of.

"And we go about our business, and we put up with it. Because there is nothing else we can do. Except believe, Mister Beale, except worship in a broken-down storefront we pay the rent on where we worship in peace, because we know that nobody in this town except us would ever set foot in there. Not even Mister Glass, who owns the place. Not even him, as long as he gets his rent every month. And he does. Every eye in this town is on us, even when we sleep.

"And we can't stand it. We hide it, every day, all day, but it is hateful and intolerable. It makes our stomachs hurt. Because the one thing we can't do, no matter how closely we're watched, the one thing we can never do is ever look back. Do you understand what I'm saying, Mister Beale?"

"There's no need to say any more, Mister Shadwell. I won't be coming back."

"I'm so . . ."

"No need to be. Tell the people thanks for having me. It meant something."

"I hope so, Mister Beale. I hope so."

"Tell them for me. Tell them I'll remember."

Then Shadwell, *the* Reverend Lewis Tobias Shadwell, as he came to be known, got up, and the two men shook hands, and he left, leaving Charlie alone in his cooling house with his quiet dog and no religion.

No religion except Sylvan Glass.

That night, lying in bed, he drew a crude portrait of her in his diary. He wasn't an artist, but he tried to get her face and features down the way he remembered them. So he could look at her on the days of the week that weren't Wednesday. So he would always have her near, even when he was very, very old.

And around her head he drew a halo, a perfect circle, and colored it in with gold.

CHAPTER SIXTEEN

I T WAS GETTING too cold. Sam couldn't wait in the truck any more.

So, on the third Wednesday, when they turned in the drive, and parked around back of the house, out of sight, Charlie came around and helped Sam down from the pickup, leaving Jackie Robinson in the cab. They walked over to the house, and the door opened as soon as they stepped on the porch. There was an awkward moment as Sam looked up at Mrs. Glass, wary about going into a house he didn't know.

She was dressed, this time. High-heeled shoes, a navy blue dress with a red rose at the neck, her hair swept up in an impossible tangle of curls and ringlets, like something off a magazine cover. Bright red lips. Scarlet nails. A plastic bracelet on her arm as red as the rose on her neck.

The kitchen was hot, spotless, and it smelled good. Whatever else Boaty Glass spent all his money on, he didn't spend it on extravagant things for his house. The floor was plain speckled linoleum, the kitchen table covered in checked oilcloth. There were straight, tall oak farm chairs, just two of them, as though there were never any guests expected; not a crumb on the floor or counter, covered in Formica the color of the inside of an avocado; frilly, frail curtains at the windows, the only touch of grace or care. On the walls, there were pictures of stern old folks in stiff positions, and sad-looking little girls with painted faces and frozen hands, a framed picture postcard of a big grand house with formal gardens and palm trees around it, behind a big, turquoise swimming pool—a souvenir of Hollywood.

The room opened onto two others, a sitting room filled with drab furniture, and a bright bedroom with an iron bed painted white, plain as dirt, but hung with some kind of filmy curtains all around the head of the bed, tied back with colorful ribbons and bows. Next to the bed was a yellowed photograph, a silver-framed picture of a pretty woman on her wedding day, long ago. A staircase led upstairs, to other rooms and other hallways, just like in Sam's house. Bedrooms, he guessed.

Sam knew right away why it smelled good in the kitchen. She'd made cookies. They were piled on a blue willow plate on the kitchen table, next to two short stacks of magazines.

"Sam, say hello to Mrs. Glass. Be a good boy."

"Hello, ma'am."

"Hello, Sam," she said, and he loved the sound of her voice, so young and sweet and fine. As though she had grown up in a beautiful flower garden far away. "I have some things for you."

He walked toward the table. "I made cookies with nuts," she

said, "And I got you these." She picked up one of the stacks. "Look, funny books."

"I can't read yet. I can almost read. My mama and daddy read to me every night."

"These you can just look at the pictures and make up your own funny stories, out of your own head. Look. Captain America and Captain Marvel, and, look at this one, this is Donald Duck. He's bobbing for apples, like at Halloween, but all he got was this big old mean lobster clamped down on his beak. Isn't that funny?"

Sam laughed, but he really didn't understand. He'd never seen a whole funny book, just the covers at the general store. He'd never seen a lobster, either, and he didn't get the joke. He liked the other little ducks on the cover, wearing witch's hats and riding broomsticks, dressed up for Halloween. But he was drawn right away to Captain Marvel, Jr, a dark-haired, dark-eyed boy like Sam, but older, about fourteen, dressed in blue and gold, with a red cape and strong arms, the kind of boy Sam wanted to be when he grew up, with a lightning bolt across his chest, standing on top of a chest of gold coins that flew everywhere, surrounded by fierce pirates, a masted ship in the harbor.

The books his parents read to him were more serious, *The Wind in the Willows* from his mother, or *Mother Goose,* and *The Hardy Boys* from his father. Sometimes his father would read him a wonderful strange book he had had since he was Sam's age, *Poppy Ott's Pedigreed Pickles.* Sam would follow the words on the page with his fingers while they read to him, and sometimes he would carefully pronounce the words, fixing them in his mind. He liked Frank and

Joe Hardy, their small-town world filled with gangsters and spies and adventures that never seemed to happen in Brownsburg.

But these funny books were different, filled with colorful pictures and strange, exotic, dressed-up animals, and men in capes who looked almost like some of the people he knew. Charlie helped him into a chair, and he turned the pages of the thin-papered magazines, excited to see what would happen next.

"And if you get tired of the comics, you can use these . . ." she showed him a box of crayons and a pad of paper, ". . . and draw us some pretty pictures. Would you like that?"

"Yes, ma'am."

"Sam," Charlie squatted on his haunches by the chair, "Mrs. Glass and I are going to go upstairs for a little while, so you be a good boy, and don't make any noise, and just keep yourself busy and have some cookies. Do you think that'll be OK?"

"I think so. What's a lobster, Beebo?"

"I'll tell you later, on the way home. Just be patient. And don't come in the room."

Charlie and Mrs. Glass went up the stairs, and Sam was alone in the kitchen with his picture books and his cookies. He should have been happy, but he wasn't. He worried about Jackie Robinson in the cold. He didn't like being left in a strange room where something was going on in another room but he didn't know what it was. He found it hard to look at the books or eat the cookies.

It was completely quiet for a little while. Then something like voices, like whispers, came through the floor, but no sounds of feet moving. They must be sitting down, Sam thought, talking very quietly. But what were they talking about? Maybe they were talking about him, and that worried Sam. He'd been polite, he'd laughed at the duck even if he didn't understand what was so funny, and he chewed on a cookie, trying to figure it out.

Then the noises began, tiny, soft noises blunted by the thickness of the floor, and all the more mysterious for that. He heard music playing above him, and a woman's voice singing. It wasn't hillbilly music. It was some other kind, softer, with other instruments playing.

Maybe they were dancing. Dancing slow.

He knew it was part of the secret. And he knew, he felt it in his skin, that he must never tell, about the music, or the funny books with strange pictures his mother wouldn't approve of, or being left alone in the kitchen with the dog in the car, or about the cookies and the milk. He understood he must never say anything about this whole day. He wasn't here. They weren't here, Sam or Charlie or Mrs. Glass. He just knew that.

He stopped reading or eating. He just sat. He just sat and listened.

Sometimes it sounded like Charlie and the woman were laughing. Sometimes it sounded like Charlie was in pain, and his heart raced with fear for Beebo. If Beebo got hurt, how would he get home? He heard what must have been shoes dropping on the floor, and more laughing, giggling from her. Then it was really quiet again.

But only for a little bit. He heard Charlie groan and what sounded almost like a wail from the woman, followed quickly by

Charlie's low voice, different, harder, as he said quickly, "Hush, Sylvan. Hush." Sam heard that. And then she was quiet as church during prayers, silent as his room when his mother turned out the light at night.

Maybe they were dead.

After what seemed like a long time, a door opened, and Charlie came down. He looked different, strange and young and sleepy and excited all at the same time. His shoes were in his hand, and he sat down on the other chair and started putting them on. He wouldn't look at Sam as he laced them up, and the boy pretended to be reading the books and took a few bites of a cookie.

They both looked up, and Mrs. Glass was standing in the doorway. She was barefoot, too. She wasn't wearing her dress any more, just a white, silky slip like his mother wore under her dress. Her face was pale, and all the red was gone from her lips. Her hair was tangled down around her shoulders. She just stood there, in her slip and her bracelet, smoking a cigarette in a short cigarette holder. Her lips looked plump and rounder and pink as a baby's. She didn't say anything to anybody, and nobody spoke to her.

Charlie stood up, tightened his belt, and reached for his coat. "Ready to go, Sam?" His voice was soft and kind, almost like a woman's. "Get your coat on, we're leaving." Charlie kept his eyes on Mrs. Glass the whole time, not even noticing that Sam had never taken his coat off in the first place.

Sam started to put the few crayons back in the box. Charlie looked around briefly, "Don't bother with that now. It's all right. We have to go."

They moved to the door. Sam knew he was supposed to leave the funny books on the table. The woman finished her cigarette and moved back into the next room and they heard her going slowly up the staircase. She never even said good-bye.

In the truck, Charlie held Jackie Robinson to his chest and kissed the top of his head. He put his arm out, gently, and touched Sam's hair.

"If they ask why we're late, just tell them Mr. Potter was late getting to the slaughterhouse with the beef. Okay?"

"Okay, Beebo."

The truck didn't catch at first, but then it did. They backed up and turned around, and headed down the driveway. Charlie turned onto the road without even looking, but there weren't any cars on the road, so nobody got hurt.

There was a scratch on Charlie's neck, no more than the length of Sam's little finger, but a drop of blood had hardened on the end just above his shirt collar. His coat was open, as though he couldn't feel the cold, even though the truck took a while to heat up. Sam shivered and rubbed his hands together. Even after the heat of the kitchen, once he was in the cold of the truck he felt as though he would never ever be warm again.

CHAPTER SEVENTEEN

H E KNEW IT was all part of the promise he'd made to Charlie, part of the secret. He had to forget. It took an effort
every time he sat down with his mother and father, but he could
never mention that he had been with Charlie in the Glass house
and eaten Mrs. Glass's cookies and read her funny books and heard
what he'd heard, not that he knew exactly what it was.

But he couldn't forget. He thought about it all the time. The
warm kitchen, the oilcloth, the sounds from upstairs, sounds
meaning what? No, he couldn't forget, and he couldn't stop being
afraid. Afraid for Charlie.

What if something bad happened, the way Charlie had said it
would? What if Charlie died? Who would take care of Jackie?

At night, after he had said his prayers and his mother had left
him alone in the dark, he saw it all in his mind, happening over
and over again, and he prayed his own prayer to the same Jesus,

that Charlie would not die. If Charlie died, it would be his fault, he knew, because the only thing that could make Charlie die was telling the secret he knew, and knew he could not tell.

And he wanted to go back, he wanted to go back again and again until he knew it all, until he was sure Charlie was safe. So he woke early on Wednesdays, and waited patiently while his father read the papers to him and Charlie served the customers, then they walked home to a lunch his mother threw together, now that school was back on, and then they walked back to the shop, and everything between his father and Charlie was no different, as though this thing Sam knew was going to happen was not going to happen. Charlie didn't rush, he just went about his business and sharpened his rosewood-handled knives on the whetstone and the butcher's steel until the edge was fine as a razor, and then finally he said, "You ready, Sam?" and Sam would answer, as though it wasn't a big thing when it fact it was everything, "Sure, Beebo," and they would take Jackie Robinson and get into the truck, which took longer and longer to start in the cold now, and then they would go do the butchering, a thing Charlie did quickly now, still careful, still expert, but quick; then, on the way back, they would pull into her drive and up and behind the house.

It was always the same, and it was always different. Jackie came in the house with them now, because of the cold. She didn't wear those red lips, after that first time, but she was always dressed in a beautiful dress, none of them the same, none like anything he'd ever seen before, and there were always cookies and milk, and new funny books, and those magazines with the beautiful women on the covers, wrapped in fur or filmy cloth, always the big eyes, the hopeful, waiting mouth. Sometimes, when the door had shut and Charlie and Mrs. Glass had gone upstairs, Sam stared at these women and then he kissed them softly on their lips, their eyes, their powdered cheeks.

Sometimes they were gone a long time, and sometimes it was no more than ten minutes. Sometimes there was a lot of noise, and sometimes there was hardly any. Every time Charlie made a sound, Jackie would stop sniffing around the kitchen and freeze, perking up his ears until the sound had passed and Charlie was quiet again.

Once Charlie came down, shoes in hand, his shirt unbuttoned, and caught Sam kissing the magazine cover. He just laughed and came over, took a look and touched Sam on the head. "That's Ava Gardner," he said. "She comes from right down there in North Carolina. All the women down there, in that county, look like Ava Gardner."

"They do not," said Mrs. Glass, standing in the doorway in her white slip, smoking.

"They sure do," Charlie said, lacing up his shoes. "I've been there, Sylvan. One Ava Gardner after another. They're part Indian down there. I'll take you there one day. You'll see."

"Oh, Charlie," she smiled at him for a long time. "Wouldn't that be fine? Divine?"

He looked up from his shoes, stared at her and said, and he wasn't smiling or laughing any more, "Well, I don't know about you. But it'd be just fine with me."

She stopped smiling.

"I never been anywhere," she said.

"'I've never,'" he corrected her. "Not 'I never.'"

"Thank you. It's true. I've never been anywhere, except for that trip to Hollywood, so I guess that's somewhere. You couldn't see anything, I just saw their stars on some sidewalk in front of that Chinese theater, and I saw plenty of that railroad car with Boaty. Supposed to be so nice. Supposed to be what I'd always wanted. It wasn't anything like that. He grunts like a pig, and he sweats all over you. I mean, it wasn't like it was the first time, but I never knew, until you . . . well, I never knew anything, did I?"

"You learn quick, girl."

"'Quickly,' you mean." She laughed. "See? You do it, too."

Sam always had to be told the excuse, the reason why it was taking so long at the slaughterhouse, in case they asked. After Charlie had cut up the side, and laid it on a clean white sheet and tied it up in another one, even though there weren't any flies anymore, he would get in the cab and start the engine and tell Sam what had taken them so long. Flat tire. Potter was late again. Damn truck broke down, but don't say damn. Sometimes it was over so fast they didn't even have to make any excuses at all. Besides, they never asked, his parents. They looked worried, but they never asked.

They didn't want to know. They knew Charlie wouldn't harm Sam, and they assumed they'd been out hunting, or gotten lost tracking one of Charlie's pieces of land. They didn't know how to ask the things that were on their mind, so there they were, all locked together, complicit, and nobody said anything to anybody.

"Say my name again," she said one day, as Charlie was putting on his shirt.

"Sylvan," he said, looking down, then at her. "Sylvan Glass."

"He never says my name. I made it up, you know."

"I figured. What's your real name?"

"Ha. You'll never know as long as you live, Charlie Beale." And she ran laughing up the stairs, and they left quickly, just leaving everything scattered around the table, for her to clean up later.

Sometimes, if it was quick, Charlie would come down and sit at the table with Sam on his lap, reading to him about Donald Duck or Captain America. He would tickle Sam in the ribs when they came to the funny parts, so Sam would know they were funny, and laugh out loud.

With Captain America, Sam could feel the vibration of Charlie's deep voice against his small, thin back, and the tingle gave him a certain knowledge of the adventures the masked hero was going through, how close the danger, how great the triumph over evil. Mrs. Glass would sit in the other chair, smoking and reading her magazines, and, once in a while, laughing as Charlie read to Sam.

Sam hoped she didn't know that he'd just been kissing the woman on the cover of the magazine she held so loosely in her hand. What if they knew? What if they looked through the floor like magic when it was quiet, and saw him kissing some magazine cover? It scared him. But they never let on; just went on as though they were ignorant, and Sam hoped they were.

"What do you want for your birthday, Sylvan?" Charlie's voice was always so soft and kind when he spoke to her, Sam could feel it like a cat's purr through his back.

"Nothing you can give me, I guess. He'd know. You can't hide anything from him. He never gives me anything. He's got a woman, everybody knows it, twice my age, up in Staunton. Charlotte some-body. He gives her things, I bet. Nice things. A fur coat, maybe. A house. Sometimes he doesn't get home until ten o'clock. Some nights he doesn't come home at all. Couple of times, he said he was going to Washington. Staying in a hotel. I bet he takes her. I bet they have fun. She can have him, for all I care."

Her voice was wistful, girlish when she spoke. "No, I never had anything. Nothing at all that ever belonged to me."

"I'll think of something."

"You don't have to give me anything. You give me enough."

"What do I give you?"

"I shouldn't have to tell you that."

They got so used to Sam, they talked as though the boy weren't even there, as though Sam were as much of a mute, untelling pet as Jackie Robinson. He called her baby, or little girl, and she called him darling in a funny, slow kind of way.

One morning in late winter, Boaty came in the shop and told Will he was going down to Nags Head fishing with some of the boys for the weekend, drinking and fishing for blues, and Charlie looked up sharply, and, at the end of the day, he carefully packed up some meats, chops and steaks and hamburger.

"That's a lot of meat," Will said quietly, with the voice he used when he was telling Sam not to get too close to the woodstove.

"I'm going camping this weekend," Charlie answered quietly, "stay in a tent out down by Natural Bridge." He was out of there and cleaned up before sundown, and his truck was gone until Sunday morning, and, not that it was any mystery where he really was, Sam worried about him, and about Jackie. He could see in his mind the funny books lying on the kitchen table, the magazine pictures of the women unkissed, and he tried to picture in his mind how Sylvan and Charlie were spending their time together.

Charlie pulled up in front of his house that Sunday before the sun was up. Sam was the only one who saw him come in, and then Charlie and Jackie Robinson went into his house, and he didn't come out again until late afternoon. He sat on the porch in a clean white shirt, not even noticing the chill, and he wrote in his diary. He wrote beneath her name: "If she whistled, I would come. If she slapped my face, I would turn the other cheek. I would die for her. I would spend an eternity in hell."

He looked like a boy of eighteen. His heart raced like a man in the full headstrong freefall of love.

CHAPTER EIGHTEEN

H E BOUGHT A house, another house. This one was out past the slaughterhouse, beyond the reach and eyes of the town, an old farmhouse that was set in the middle of a wild thick grove of old maples. Saturdays and Sundays, he would drive out there alone and fix it up, putting in a new woodstove, plumbing a whole bathroom with the help of Carl Hostetter, and putting in a new water heater, and filling it with furniture he bought at the auctions, except this time he went all by himself. Whenever he saw something she might like, he bought it. The fancier it was, the more likely he was to buy it, thinking of her. He didn't care about the price, just kept his hand in the air until everybody else dropped out.

When it was all done, he walked down to the courthouse, and he signed the deed over to her. It was completely secret. You could still do that then. You could just say not to put it in the newspaper, and nobody would ever know. The clerk of the court was an honest spinster with an eternal yearning for handsome young men, and

Charlie wrote "Do Not Publish" on the deed while she watched, and she honored that, as he knew she would. Anybody could have looked it up, but nobody ever did.

He gave her the deed for her birthday. She was twenty by then. He put a blue ribbon around it. He met her there, hidden by the dense grove of trees, and carried her across the threshold on the first Wednesday in May. It was the only floor she ever walked on where every board on which she put her foot was hers.

It was enough, that first time, to walk through the house, room by room, holding hands, while Sam and Jackie Robinson sat on the porch, listening to the birds in the greening trees, and watching them through the windows as they strolled from room to room and Sylvan touched every chair, every table, picked up every piece of china.

It was just an old farmhouse filled with used furniture and bits of other people's lives, but it was hers, the first thing she'd ever owned. She gave the house a name. She called it Pickfair, because she'd been to Mary Pickford and Douglas Fairbanks's house in Hollywood.

They went there every chance they got. Every Wednesday, when he went to the slaughterhouse and did his work, afterward he would find her there, waiting to cook up the pork chops or the steaks he had brought, cornbread cooling on the counter.

And then bed, while the boy sat at the table with his funny books and Jackie Robinson dug holes in the yard. It was always quick, and it was never enough, but it was all they had, and, for a while, all they needed.

Most Saturdays, Boaty would go off on one of his trips, to fish or to hunt in his inept way, never coming home with anything, unless some other man took pity on him and gave him some trout or a rabbit. When Boaty was gone for a whole day, and Charlie had no work, they had more time.

Charlie would wait until he saw Boaty's big car glide out of town, and then he would take the dog and get the boy, fishing rods or gun in hand, and he would drive straight to where he knew she would be waiting. Will and Alma thought the fresh air did Sam good; he always came home tired and red-cheeked. They began to notice more and more, though, that these expeditions produced nothing in the way of a catch.

They never went fishing. They never saw a deer. They saw the inside of Pickfair. Sylvan was always waiting, dressed like a movie star. She met them at the door as though greeting royalty, and her lovely laugh and her strange, rounded accent brought them into the house.

The day passed, Sam in the company of Donald Duck or Captain America, Jackie Robinson at his feet, pacing silently around the kitchen, nosing for bugs, Sylvan and Charlie waited less and less time until they vanished into the darkness of the sitting room and up the stairs, where Sam could hear them moving about as though dancing, but only for a while, and then silence, silence and cookies and comic books.

Charlie and Sylvan enveloped him with their warmth and their breathy voices and something else he couldn't name, something about the way they looked, as though they had been waiting for something, as though the thing they had waited for all along had finally arrived, and then they went upstairs and left him alone, to talk, he figured, about grownup things, things a boy wouldn't know or understand. Sometimes Sam felt that the thing they had been waiting for all along was him, and it made a kind of warmth in his heart.

They left him, and they left him with books and cookies and a dog, but they left him with no instructions, and sometimes he didn't know how to pass the hours. He would try to read, to figure out the words, or he would sit on the porch in one of the rockers, while Jackie ran around the yard and chased squirrels.

He thought of his own mother and father. He thought of how they never left him alone for more than five minutes, how they were always with him to make him laugh or understand one new thing about the world, one thing which suddenly occurred to him as though he had never noticed it before, the hunger to know how something worked, where the voices came from on the radio, who those people were and how they lived. Where the light came from when the night got dark.

And he thought of Charlie and Sylvan. He felt something for them he couldn't name, something beautiful, but he couldn't tell what it was. He felt safe. Nothing bad would ever happen to him when Charlie was around; even if he was in some part of the house to which Sam had never been asked, Charlie was there, his big hand, his sharp, short whistle that he had promised to teach Sam someday calling Jackie in from the yard. He wanted to learn that whistle.

There was so much he wanted to know. He didn't know when it

started, but suddenly everything came into focus, and, at the same time, everything was mysterious. Everything worked, somehow, but he didn't know how, and his mother and father would sit with him, and explain it in ways that he didn't even begin to understand.

Sometimes, it was enough just to know that they knew, even if he didn't understand. He'd ask the same questions over and over, sometimes for days on end, and sometime his father would say, "Damn, Sam, you asked me that yesterday and the day before." But his mother would never do that, not even once, so she'd show him how the bread got all puffy when you left the dough in a warm place on the stove, or she'd sit and watch while that old beetle crawled its way slowly across the porch and tell him how many legs it had and what it ate for dinner when it got home.

"Where did I come from?"

She had him on her lap, her sleepy child.

"I've told you."

"Tell me again. I like hearing it."

"You came from heaven."

"How did I get here?"

"I got all big and fat and puffy and then you popped out."

"Out of where?"

"Out of my stomach."

"Why did you get all fat and puffy?"

"Because I was waiting for you. I was waiting for you for a long time. So was your father."

"Did it hurt?"

"Yes, Sam. It hurt."

"For a long time?"

"No, darling."

"How old was I?"

"You were zero."

"What did you do, when I came out?"

"I sang, 'Happy Birthday to you . . .'"

"How old am I now?"

"You tell me."

"Silly, I'm five. You were at my birthday. But I'll be six soon. You know that, right?"

"Right."

"How many days is five?"

She thought for a minute. "One thousand eight hundred and twenty-five. Twenty-six. Leap year."

"And how many is six?"

Every question opening up to another one. What year leap?

"Three hundred and sixty-five more than five. And you know what happens on every one of those days? You go to bed. And it's time for you to go to bed again."

Sometimes he couldn't go to sleep for a long time. It seemed as though he were climbing a long staircase, each step a question, until he stepped off the last step and into the darkness, surprised, every morning, and glad, that he was in his bed, in his room, his mother's hand on his hair, her kiss on his forehead the minute he opened his eyes. And the minute he saw the light, he couldn't remember the questions that had led him up and up and into the darkness.

Usually, sitting with Captain America, or out in the yard,

watching Jackie Robinson rooting around, he had a million questions, about what made it hot, or cold, or where the long trail of ants led to, where they lived and what they ate. Why was it that, for him, nothing moved in winter but everything moved in summer, but for Jackie Robinson, in any season, there was always something moving, something happening he couldn't see? But he wasn't here to ask questions. He knew that his questions weren't part of it. Not here. Not with them off in the house wherever they were. No, his part in this was to wait, and he did, always, so by the time Charlie reappeared, tucking his shirt into his pants, his shoes in hand, he'd forgotten what he meant to ask.

One day, a slaughter day, so it was getting to be dusk already, about six weeks after they had first started coming to Pickfair, he was in the yard and he forgot that part of the bargain. He forgot he was supposed to stay outside. He forgot that they went up the stairs and into that place where he was not supposed to go.

It was rainy. He was tired. Jackie Robinson had run off after something, a rabbit, a turkey, some one of the thousand scents he was always chasing, and Sam forgot that his end of the bargain was to wait. Just to wait.

He wanted to go home. He suddenly wanted his mother and his father and his own house, more than anything in the world, more than cookies or funny books.

So he went in the house, into the warmth and the light and the just-baked smell of the kitchen, and he wanted to know where they were, so he could tell Charlie, so he could tell him that he was sorry, but he had to go home now.

He listened, but there was no noise. He wandered the rooms of the downstairs of the house, rooms with no lights on, so that he could barely make things out, and they weren't there. They were upstairs, where he'd never been. Then he started to get scared.

He had had a dream, once. It was a bad one, and he woke up, and he wasn't in his own room any more. He was alone in the dark in a strange house and something had happened, something bad. Something bad had happened, his father had died, or his mother, or they had decided they didn't want him any more, and they had wrapped him in blankets in the night and taken him somewhere else, and left him there.

He had started to cry, very softly, because he was so afraid in this new house, afraid of the people he would meet in the morning, new people, people who didn't know him or know how to take care of him. But he didn't make any noise when he cried, because he didn't want to wake the new people, whoever they were, wherever they slept.

So he lay awake all night, until the first gray started to lighten the black of the night, until the frames of the windows, unfamiliar, oddly placed, began to come into view. The gray began to turn a pale pink, and he closed his eyes because he didn't want to know, didn't want it to start. He didn't open his eyes again until he could feel the pink turn to a soft orange and he knew he couldn't put it off any longer, and so he opened his eyes, slowly, slowly, just a crack, so afraid, and saw the windows and the curtains and the wallpaper, and they were strangely familiar and completely different at the same time.

The table by his bed was at his feet, the same lamp with the paper shade, right next to the board where his mother heaped up pillows for his head as she read to him before sleep came.

And then he knew. He was upside down in his bed, backward. In his bad dreaming, he had somehow turned around, so his feet were at the headboard of his bed, it was crazy and backward, but it was his room, his own room in his own house, his own pillows and blankets.

Nothing had happened. Everything would be just the same today as it was yesterday. Nobody had died in the night and he hadn't been bundled up and delivered into the hands of strangers.

But it could have happened. He knew that, and he never forgot it. It could have happened. As safe as he was, he was never completely safe, and never would be, and he felt that now, wandering the neat, empty rooms of a house at twilight, everything there but ghostly, Charlie and Sylvan somewhere and he needed Charlie here, now, and he needed to go home.

So he did something he'd never done, never been asked to do. He climbed the stairs to the second floor, and looked down the hall at the neat rug and the four closed doors and he opened them one by one, each swinging into a neat, spare, empty room, all but the last, which he opened, sure, now, that he would find the same clean emptiness, but he didn't; he found something. He found them.

It was the only room with a light on, a glow from a lamp that was a painted figure of a Japanese lady in a flowing patterned dress that came down to her tiny feet, with a silk lampshade floating above her elaborate black hair, and he saw the lamp and knew that he would never forget it, and he saw that the light from the lamp was shining on the immense skin of two grown people, a man and a woman, Charlie and Sylvan with no clothes on, the only grown people he had ever seen naked, and he knew he would never forget that, either.

Charlie was on top of her, his face buried in the side of her neck, and the skin of his back was glistening with sweat, every muscle tight, his neck, his shoulders, his back, everything taut and strong and the color of a rose, a dusty red rose, and there was hair beneath his arms, dark and tangled with sweat and his forearms were strong, and slick, and even his hands, strong, tight, although they lay with such gentleness on her skin, hardly touching her at all. He was on her, skin to skin, body to body, and still he seemed to be floating, stringing and unstringing like a crossbow on top of her, completely covering without even touching.

She was still as a pond at sunset, and as pale. Her face was turned toward him, her eyes closed, a smile playing across her face, her hair a brilliant yellow fan in the Japanese lamp's light, the soft silk shade of the lamp fringed with golden, like her hair. Her eyes were black slits, like the Japanese lady's and, even though she was here, in the room, in the bed on top of the tangled bedsheets, she seemed to be far away, as though she had been turned inside out, as Sam had himself turned around backward in his bed, sometime, sometime before this, before this time which was the only time that ever existed.

Her white white skin was as thin as the silk of the lampshade. He could see the veins of her body through her skin, and she was all softness, without muscle, no way to move, covered as she was, although she arched her back and rose into Charlie and then fell again against the white sheets.

Sam didn't know what to make of it; he didn't know what was happening, whether he was watching a scene of violence or tenderness, so fine was the line, but he knew he must not, could not move. Whatever was happening, it was happening only to them, happening on their skin and in their bodies.

The noises they made were not speaking, but they were saying something, not even to each other, each was speaking to himself but not with words, with sounds he had never heard, and their bodies, moving together, made noise, a sucking sound like boots in soft mud. Somehow, Sam knew. He knew he wasn't supposed to be seeing this, it was a private thing, like the way he wasn't supposed to open the door when somebody else was in the bathroom. He knew he wasn't supposed to be hearing these sounds, that they were private sounds and that, whatever they were saying, it wasn't meant for him to hear.

But the sounds coming from them were getting stronger, her head moving slowly side to side, the breath coming in short bursts from Charlie, not from his nose, but from his mouth. Somebody was going to get hurt. Somebody was in pain. He could no longer tell which sounds were coming from which person, they seemed to come together from somewhere else in the room, and he wished the Japanese lamp lady would turn her head away, he wished he could leave the spot where he stood in the doorway, but he couldn't.

He wet his pants. He felt the warmth flowing into his jeans and he was suddenly ashamed. And then he started crying, at first without a sound, and then louder, and then howling, and that changed everything, she heard him, only Sylvan, Charlie lost in his own howling breath, and she slapped Charlie on the shoulder, once, quick, hard and flat, red as a flat quick hand on a hot woodstove, screamed, "Charlie! Charlie, the boy!" and Charlie, wild and bucking, looked up, saw the boy and suddenly everything moved, their bodies, their faces, the bedsheets, the Japanese lady toppling off the table and shattering on the floor so that the room was thrown into near darkness, deep violet, but not so dark that Sam could not see Charlie's body, his whole body at once. Charlie covered himself with a sheet, ashamed like Adam in the sight of God as he leapt away from Sylvan, rolled like a cat onto the floor and raced and fell on his knees and clutched Sam in his arms and held his shaking body against his chest, shushing him, whispering in his ear, quick hands smoothing his hair, his back, wiping the tears from his face, kissing his cheek, his neck, something he'd never done before, catching his breath and saying, finally, "It's all right, Sam. It's nothing. It's over now. Please, Sam. Everything's fine."

Just holding him, not caring that Sam's pants were wet and he was afraid and ashamed, just holding him in his arms, relaxed now, not caring that his naked body was pressed against Sam's clothes. "It's all right, Sam. Sam, look at me." — and he did — "It's fine. It's fine, son."

He held him until he stopped crying, Charlie's shoulders slick now with his own sweat and Sam's tears, until Sam was calm and stood back from Charlie, stood on his own, looking over Charlie's shoulders to see Sylvan sitting in the bed, sheets wrapped tightly around her, braiding her hair as though nothing had happened, had just happened in this room, everything different for ever after, the light gone from rose to violet and moving now to black, the Japanese lady and the lightbulb broken forever in a thousand pieces on the floor.

"Okay? Okay now? We'll go home, buddy. We'll go home to your mama and daddy."

"But I don't know where Jackie Robinson is."

"We'll find him. Don't worry. He'll come when we call. He's a good dog. And Sam? Sam? You're good boy. Just wait downstairs. Just wait a minute and I'll be down."

Sam did as he was told. He went downstairs and he waited. Charlie was there almost right away, his shirt open, his shoes in his hand. The kitchen was bright, and Charlie dropped his heavy shoes on the linoleum floor, buttoned and tucked his white shirt in his pants, and sat to lace up. Then he stood, and took Sam by the hand, and they stepped on the porch, and Jackie came almost right away at Charlie's first whistle. Then they were in the truck, back and turning quickly, the cab heating up, and everything was just the way it always was, Charlie telling the jokes, Sam laughing even when he didn't understand, Jackie curled between them, the dog's feet in Charlie's lap, his head in Sam's, and nothing and everything had changed and Sam didn't know how he knew that, but he did, he did know it. He knew it like blood. He knew it like the sound of the Japanese lamp breaking on the floor. He knew it like a dream of turning around in bed, of waking up in a house that was not his house, with people who were not his people.

CHAPTER NINETEEN

S HE HAD ON a green cardigan sweater, worn backward, buttoned up the back. It was exactly the color of her eyes, and she knew it. The lady who sold it to her, at Grossman's, had pointed that out to her — that green, the color of the lichen that grew on the sides of the trees that rose from the side of the river. Her eyes the same, lichen green, almost gray in some lights, at certain times of day, but always with an undercurrent of green. Eyes like bright, quick fish swimming in winter water, they never stopped moving, never gazed at anything for very long, except for Charlie, and except for her own face, which she could look at for hours in the mirror.

She sat on the porch steps at Pickfair, the cool early summer breeze just barely lifting her blonde hair, blonder now, from the nape of her neck, and she pulled her skirt down over her knees and leaned forward, hugging her arms around her legs, her head resting on the turquoise cotton of a billowing skirt.

"I was listening to the radio one time, and something funny happened," she said.

Charlie, hearing her voice, loved her so much at that moment he felt his heart might explode in his chest at any minute. He loved her so much he felt his bones would break. Loving her was like lying in a bed of nettles, and the feel of her skin against his was the only balm, the only time the stinging stopped, while, for her, he was the warm bath she took to stave off the cold waterfall of Boaty's indifference.

"It was my show, you know, *The Romance of Helen Trent.* I just love her. I love the way she stands up for herself, struggles to the top of her profession. But I especially love the way she talks. I wish I could meet her one day.

"Anyway, she and Gil, her boyfriend, was . . ."

"Were." said Charlie. "They were . . ."

"Thank you. *Were* talking, thank you, and Gil was asking her to marry him, the way he always does, even though he knows she'll say no, he asks her because he loves her, and she loves him, too, but she can't, you know, give herself to him because she has to think of her professional career, and all those people who would stab her in the back the first chance they got, just to get to the top before her. So she was saying no, and he kept asking her, and then something really funny happened. You want to know what it was?"

"I want to know why she won't marry him," Charlie said.

"I told you. Her professional career. Her duty to be the best Helen she can be. Like I said. She doesn't want to be dashed against the rocks of despair. They tell you that at the beginning of every show. But you want to know what happened?"

"Sure."

"So Gil was asking, and she was saying no, and then it went real quiet for a minute, and you could her a man's voice, and he said it real loud, he said, 'Ah, for Christ's sake, why don't you just lay the dame and get it over with!' You could hear it clear as a bell." She laughed, clear as music, and hugged her head to her knees, blushing at her own vulgarity. "It was real quiet for a long time, and then they just went right on, as though nothing had happened. Who would have said that?"

Charlie laughed, too, and sat beside her on the porch, and he said to her, "Helen Trent, marry me."

She stopped laughing. She looked at him for a long, long time. "I can't marry you. I don't want to be dashed against the rocks of despair."

Charlie pulled away and stood up.

"This is real life, Sylvan, not some radio show. Did you hear what I said? I said, 'Marry me, Sylvan Glass.'"

They stayed that way, staring at each other a long time.

"Then maybe you should ask me again. Some other time. Maybe you should ask me a hundred times, the way Gil has asked Helen. He knows it's hopeless, but he asks her. He always has faith. You should, too. Please, just not now."

Charlie turned away, watched the boy playing in the yard. Sylvan tugged on his pants leg. He looked down as she spoke, "'Now, for Christ's sake, just lay the dame and get it over with.'"

He laughed, a short, harsh laugh. "I love you, Sylvan, in case you didn't know. In case you hadn't noticed by some chance."

"I'm nothing so great."

"No, sweetheart. You are. You're wonderful. You're wonderful to me. A wonderful girl. To me, Sylvan."

And he showed her how he felt, again and again, and it never seemed enough to him. His words never got to the heart of what he felt in his whole body, exploding inside her. Next to that, he had so little way to tell her, his words seemed small and imprecise and mute. He never worried about getting her pregnant. He hoped sometimes that it would happen. Then it would be over, or then it would begin. Then maybe this ache would go away.

If she touched him by accident as they were walking along, or sitting next to each other in the car, even so much as the tip of her little finger against his as he shifted gears, he felt an electric shock. And then a calm like he'd never known, a complete peace, knowing that this woman had touched him, even accidentally. Such a gift, this girl. What a wonder.

He tried to show her, to make her believe, and he couldn't. It was never enough. So he gave her things. He couldn't give her anything that would be visible or noticeable to Boaty, like a necklace or a silk scarf, couldn't give anything that would have to be explained, and so he gave her what he had. He gave her land.

First, there was the house, Pickfair. Then there were two others. Then there were five farms. He gave them to her with a free hand, in secret. With every deed, his love for her deepened, and his hope expanded. She was no longer a hillbilly nobody from nowhere, sold quickly to the first bidder. She was a woman of property. She owned things. He tried and tried to explain it to her. She could, one day, he said, be free.

Every time he gave away one of the parcels of his land, he felt more owned, as though he had given her another piece of himself, of his heart, of his body. He was enraptured by her entitlement. In love with her ownership of what was his. It enhanced his affections, as the landscape of her body became more and more featured, particular, dotted with waterfalls and ravines and pine groves and a white house in the woods.

He hoped she would leave her husband. He hoped that more and more as each deed was signed. There was no longer any reason for her to stay with him, not that he knew of, and Charlie found it hard to accept her reluctance, her refusal.

"We'll see" was all she would say. "We'll see."

Summer deepened, and still he waited. She was young. She was uncertain of herself. All that would change, he knew. He hoped it would.

Her reluctance aroused him even more, to greater and stronger acts of dominion and submission. Intoxicating, but useless and hopeless, in the end. She lay with him, and he knew he could posses her but never own her. Like a fish in a bowl, she darted this way and that, unknowable, wholly created from her own imagination and the images she watched flickering on the screen, platinum and ebony. Her moods changed like the clouds over the Blue Ridge, and sudden gusts of weather would come across her, chilling or warming their conversation, their lovemaking, but that made no difference to him. Now that he had asked her, told her what his intentions were, he wanted to feel the rush to the conclusion, to consummation. But she ran from freezing to feverish, showing nothing. Her darkening cold was as heated to him as her sudden, inexplicable, and luminous fire.

CHAPTER TWENTY

"CLAUDIE, GO TO the movies with me."

"Why'd I want to do that for, girl?" The black woman gathered the sky-blue linen in her fingers, took a straight pin from a cloth strawberry strapped to her wrist, and pinned down the pleats at Sylvan's hip. It was a new season, and Sylvan had seen new things in the magazines, so they'd gone to Staunton and bought bolts of cloth to make her wardrobe all over again. She was being created like a Hollywood starlet, pleat by pleat. She was a creature of fantasy in a small town in the middle of nowhere that knew too much of how hard reality really was, a town that looked on her and her strange friendship with this odd black woman with a mixture of amusement and violent hatred. Their friendship — there was nothing else like it around. The blacks were there for a reason. Friendship wasn't it.

"Moving pictures are a great thing. They're everything it isn't around here. They're beautiful beautiful. They make you laugh even if you're blue. Everything is different, all the time. And the people, they're so beautiful."

Claudie knew, because Claudie knew everything, exactly who Sylvan was, who her people were, and she knew that friendship with a white woman was a thing that wasn't supposed to be. It just didn't happen. But, like most of the things she didn't care about, which was pretty much everything except her daughter, she didn't care about that, either. She liked the hillbilly girl. Sylvan didn't talk fancy around her, she knew better, so, when she talked to Claudie, you could still hear the lonesomeness of her girlhood in the valley, out there.

Like all white women, Sylvan asked too many questions, as though there were things she thought she had a right to know, even though they weren't any of her business. White people thought black people didn't have lives and business of their own, and maybe that was true for most. But Claudie Wiley didn't belong to anybody, and never had, and never would.

"Where's your little girl?"

"Up the stairs, where she always is." Nobody ever went upstairs, beyond the room where Claudie sewed. Not everybody even got that far. If Claudie didn't feel like answering the door's knock, she just peeked out of the curtain and ignored it.

"Don't she ever go out? I never seen her anywhere."

"She doesn't go out. Not for years."

"Why?"

"It makes her kind of shy to go out on the street. She's grown already. It's her decision. Not one friend in the world. They laughed at her and she don't want to mess with them any more. There's reasons."

"What reasons?"

"If you knew her, you'd know the reasons."

"People say she's . . . she's . . ."

"I know what them people say."

"It must be hard having a daughter like that."

"Like what?" Claudie was getting shaper and stonier with every word.

"Like people say she is. Not right."

"She's fine. People talk too much. We have a life. It's fine. We don't care about them people."

"What's her name?"

"Evelyn. Evelyn Hope Wiley."

"Who's her father? Where is he?"

Claudie shot her a look that stopped conversation. A hard look. She sewed for a while, and at least the girl knew enough to say nothing while Claudie's fingers flew in and out of the linen around her hips.

Finally she spoke, a mouth full of pins.

"He was just a boy. He had a way about him, yes, he did. I didn't want to, I told him no, but he had a way. He was handsome and smart. I have to say that. He was the first. I didn't tell nobody till I got to the point where something had to be said, and, even then,

I wouldn't tell his name. He got killed in the war. His name was Lomax. Nineteen. He didn't even know he had a baby."

She sewed. "You want to see her? Would that end this conversation??"

"I'd love to meet her."

Claudie looked at her with pure hatred. She got up and went to the bottom of the stairs and called out, softly, "Evelyn Hope? Mama needs you. Would you come downstairs?"

Then she turned and stared hard at Sylvan as they listened to the footsteps on the stairs, slow, light. "She ain't no circus animal, you know."

More footsteps, and then there she was.

She was tall, taller than Claudie, and slender and pretty. And she was white.

"Say hello to Mrs. Glass, Evelyn Hope."

"Hello, ma'am," the girl said. "How are you today?"

"I'm fine, Evelyn Hope," said Sylvan. "It's lovely to meet you. You're a lovely girl. You must be very happy."

"I'm fine," said the girl. "Mama? Did you need me for something?"

"I always need you, child. But not now. You can go back upstairs, honey. I'll come up soon."

"Nice to meet you," said Evelyn Hope, and she curtsied to Sylvan who, absurdly, curtsied back. Then she retreated into the shadows and up the stairs.

Claudie turned in a rage. "Now, girl. Is that enough? Her father was white. A white boy. Is that enough? Enough to know?"

"I think so."

"Good. She stays inside. The black people don't want her, and the white people won't have her, even to scrub their floors. You're the last person on God's earth to figure this out."

"Why Evelyn Hope?"

"I just liked the sound. Like music. Evelyn Hope. She sits in her room all day. She listens to the radio. She smokes cigarettes. She hasn't been out of the house since she was five."

"And how old is Evelyn now? Evelyn Hope." She saw the look, quick as a match striking, felt the needle prick her hip.

"She is nineteen years old."

"So you're . . ."

"Older than Jesus was when he died."

"It's hard to tell."

"Most folks around here, they know how old I am to the minute. People round here just know too damned much. They been watching us, you and me. If we go to them movies, they just be watching us harder."

"If you think I care, you're wrong."

"That's because you're rich. And you're white. You don't have to care."

"But we're friends."

"Yes, we are. We are friends. In this room. At this minute."

"I don't have any other friends. Not one."

Sylvan didn't speak for a long time, then she repeated, "Well, I do. I do have one friend."

Claudie adjusted the tucks at the hip. She looked out at the window, didn't even flinch when Claudie pricked her again with a needle. She wondered if Claudie had heard her.

"Yes. Yes I do. I have somebody."

"That make you happy?"

"It's the only thing I've ever known that made me happy. The only thing that's ever belonged to me. Person. Him, I mean. I love him, I do, and the only way I can show it is to not say one word about him, ever. That's what he said. Understand, Claudie? Nobody."

Claudie nodded.

"But he's not, you know, he's not a friend. That's not what I mean."

"I know what you mean. So why don't you be with him?"

"I'm married."

"Get unmarried. White people can do that."

"It's not that easy."

"It never is."

"It is in the movies. Things just happen. It's divine. Go to the movies with me."

And one day they did. Claudie Wiley was the first black woman in Brownsburg to ride in the front seat of a car being driven by a white woman. People, knowing what they already knew and didn't talk about, figured riding with Claudie right beside her was just another example of the hillbilly girl's recklessness, and they knew that when Boaty heard about it, he'd be madder about this than he would be about the other.

The movie was called *On the Town*, and it was about three sailors who had only one day to see New York City and find true love. Sylvan paid for two tickets, but then she and Claudie had to go in different doors to get to the movie theater, and Claudie had to sit upstairs in the balcony, the only person up there, a black woman alone in the dark in the middle of the afternoon. And there was all of New York, in Technicolor, spread out before her, a city she might have seen or even lived in, once upon a time. She wondered why she would want to sit in the dark alone and watch a bunch of white people singing and dancing and kissing in a big town she would never ever see, and she scanned the silvery screen for one single black face and there wasn't one, not a single solitary one, except way in the background.

She sat, with her sketch pad, and she drew the clothes the women wore, the lines quick and deft. She knew exactly which dress Sylvan would want, as soon as she saw it, and then she saw more of it, what it did, how it moved as some woman tap-danced through a museum in it, and she drew faster, capturing every detail, until she was practically sewing it right there in the movies, feeling the cloth in her hands, almost, and the swirl of the skirt floating around the legs of the beautiful Southern girl sitting downstairs with the white people. Not for her, no, never for her, these things, and certainly not for Evelyn Hope, although Claudie did sometimes make party clothes for both of them, things out of *Vogue*. She would make one dress for herself, a fancy ball gown of intricate structure and drape, and an identical one for Evelyn Hope, and even a tiny one just as rich and fine for Eveleyn Hope's doll baby, a little white thing she carried with her everywhere, the fine blonde curls of the doll's hair now a rat's nest of carelessness and age. They wore these dresses at night when she made a roast and a cake for herself and her daughter, dressed like princesses in the tumultuous dark maw of her house, by candlelight, the mice scurrying in the cupboards as they ate stringy lamb and rich chocolate cake. Party clothes, clothes that had nothing to do with their real lives, so that her decrepit house was turned into a kind of palace.

But this dress in the movie, this green dress, she knew without even asking that it was for Sylvan. She even heard Sylvan call out once, during the movie, "Claudie?" and she knew, she knew that she would be making it for her.

It was kelly green, tight in the body and full in the skirt, with buttons from the hem to the collar, a collar that was rolled, and made of a black-and-white tartan silk, all of it silk, and fine. But it was when the woman in the dress moved and started dancing that they both, upstairs and down, saw the magic of the dress. As Ann Miller danced, the dress unbuttoned by degrees, and they saw, both of them, that the dress was lined in the same black-and-white tartan as the collar, the portrait collar that showed off her beautiful collarbones and neck, and set her rather vulgar face aglow with a smile that women had only in the movies.

That's when Sylvan called Claudie's name: when the dress came undone and the lining swirled into the air around the woman's thighs. Silk like a bird's wings, fluttering at her hips, her frantic legs, the skirt graceful and green and billowing with flashes of black and white, all elegant, all moving, in motion. It was the fact that the dress—what made it special—only revealed itself after the initial effect had come and gone that excited both of them, as though the dress held a secret, and only told the secret when the time came. Like their hearts: the two women, both of them, not telling much of what both knew, holding back, keeping still even as they flew through their lives. Sylvan had a lover. Claudie had a daughter, upstairs in that mess, upstairs forever, and little was said and much was accepted as being true.

The sailors and their girls got into all kinds of escapades, and there was kissing and more singing and dancing. But nothing really mattered after the green dress. Even Frank Sinatra, with his boyish charm, or Gene Kelly, with his strong legs and the sexy scar on his cheek, did little to excite their hearts, flush with excitement upstairs and down at the prospect of making that dress for Sylvan to wear.

Sylvan didn't want to kiss any of those men, and she didn't want to dance with them or by herself, and she didn't want to be any of those women. She just wanted the feel of the swirling silk against the skin of her body, and she wanted the daring leg and the pure float of the thing as she twirled, in private, for Charlie Beale, maybe in the woods, barefooted on the spring moss, her dress greener than anything in the forest around her, greener than the newest and lightest leaf.

They went straight from the theater to the one small department store. They didn't stop to eat anything, since there was only the one place, and they couldn't walk in there together, anyway, and even in the store, they pretended that they didn't know each other, just walked through the aisles of material, looking only for the silk they wanted and the tartan that made the whole thing work. They didn't find the exact thing, but, through gestures and glances, they found things that would work, that would do, and they chose these, and Claudie stood by the door while the salesgirl cut the cloth and wrapped the two pieces of material in brown paper bundles and Sylvan paid with money from her pocketbook. They walked out onto the street where it was still daylight and drove back to Brownsburg in the big Buick, happy in their day and the company they had kept, not talking at all until Sylvan finally said, as they pulled into the outskirts of the town, "See, Claudie? Wasn't it wonderful? That's the movies."

CHAPTER TWENTY-ONE

THE BOY WAS always with them. The boy and the dog. They began to forget he was there, forgot to keep an eye how far or near or needy he was, and sometimes, when they made love outdoors, they could feel the boy and the dog in the woods, circling them, catching their scent, their sounds, but they were so lost, so gone, they couldn't take the time to think about that.

They weren't bad people. Charlie wasn't lewd, and she'd been raised up in the country, in a natural kind of way, with natural manners and grace and a sense of what's right. And Charlie loved the boy. He sometimes thought he was the boy's father. He knew he shouldn't think that way, that it was a mistake, bad for him, and bad for the boy, who shouldn't, at his age, have been asked to bear the weight of that kind of confusion.

And he knew that, often, when they were running together in the fields, chasing that dog, or sleeping out in the open, doing the things that Will was too old to do, he knew that Sam sometimes forgot that Charlie wasn't his father. Sam himself never forgot where his true home, where his true heart lay. The infinite and inexorable pull of blood. But, with Charlie Beale, he felt paid attention to, watched and guarded, even as he was given the freedom to be, never scolded, never made to sit up straight, or to hold his fork in the way his mother said polite people did.

Sam still didn't know what Charlie and Sylvan were doing when they lay down together, glimpsed through a window or through the branches of a pine tree, but he knew it was something, and it stirred his heart and his body in ways he couldn't explain to himself.

Sylvan was full where his mother was spare. Her lips a full slash of crimson, high, hot summer, whereas his mother's palette was more mute, more like winter. Still, it was Sylvan who seemed to bring a chill to him, where his mother brought warmth.

When his mother's warmth left him at night, after they had said his prayers and the light had been turned off and the wind was rustling in the trees outside his window, pitch black, it was Sylvan's chill that crept into the sheets and kept him from sleep.

He lay, between sleep and waking, and he would think about all the questions he wanted to ask Charlie, things he noticed in the world, things that struck him as strange, or funny, words he had heard that meant something specific to everybody but him, or just things a boy his age would never in a million years know the answer to; things he knew his father was too busy or too tired to answer. Charlie was never tired. And he knew the answer to everything.

They would lie in the grass in the evening, out by the river, without her, just Charlie and Sam and Jackie Robinson, and the questions would come back to him, and Charlie always knew exactly what to say.

"Beebo?"

"What, son?"

"I've been thinking. Sometimes the moon is really, really big, and sometimes it's little. Why does that happen?"

They watched the moon rising over the river, huge, bigger than an orange in the palm of your hand. Charlie smoked a cigarette while he took a minute to think about it, and stared at the sky, as though he hadn't even heard him. Charlie could blow smoke rings, and Sam knew that, when he was old enough, he'd blow smoke rings, too, just the same way, and that Charlie would teach him how.

"Sam? Have you ever been to a party? A birthday party?"

"Once."

"What did they have there?"

"Cake!"

"What else?"

"Presents. And balloons."

"Thought so. Well, the moon is like a balloon. It starts off little, and then somebody blows into it, and it gets really, really big, and then it pops, yours popped didn't it?"

"Yeah."

"So then somebody gets another balloon and blows it up again."

"Who?"

"Promise you won't tell anybody?"

"Promise." He made a cross over his heart.

"I do."

Sam didn't laugh right away, not until he knew Charlie was teasing. Then he pounded Charlie's chest, as Charlie pulled his head down and tugged on his hair and they rolled over and over in the twilight field, stubble in their backs, Jackie nipping and yapping at their heels.

He believed whatever he was told. He was tired of not knowing. He could read already, he had learned in secret just from watching the words on the page as his mother read to him, he could read the funny books by himself, almost. He didn't see any reason to go to school, as he was supposed to do in the fall, but he was tired of not knowing so many things.

Somehow, in the dark, as he listed and memorized the things he wanted to ask Charlie the next time he saw him, all the questions became one single question, a question he knew he would never ask and never get the answer to: What was it they were doing when they took their clothes off? Why was it a secret? Why did they pretend, when he was back with them and they had their clothes on again, why did they pretend that it had never happened?

It made Sam feel alone in a way he had never felt alone before. In fact, he had never quite known what solitude was, he had never felt it, until the first time he saw them walking out of the door in Boaty Glass's house, when they stood in the kitchen and acted as though nothing had happened. While he had been looking at funny books, they had turned into different people, and he knew somehow that the people they had turned into were what he would turn into, as well, once something happened. He didn't know what that something was, he didn't know how long it would take, he just knew that it would happen, and it made him sad, because he suddenly felt as though anything that happened between now and then wasn't any more important than the silly pictures of ducks in pirate outfits he had been looking at.

He grew suddenly aware of the body he lived in, knowing that it would change in time into something else. He hoped it would change into something like the body Charlie wore, lean, muscular, smooth, not tall, instead of something like his father's. A body like Will's seemed too heavy for him to inhabit, too much to carry around.

His father was all warm rounds and folds; Charlie was like a wooden table, all flat surfaces.

Sam grew not just aware of his body, he also became afraid of it. It seemed so fragile to him, so small, so transitory. Things went on inside it he didn't understand. Things moved in him. He heard noises, the noises of his body working, a tiny train running smooth on flat track. He didn't know how these things happened. He didn't even know what were the right questions to ask, and he didn't know who to ask. Not his mother. Not his father. And, even though he knew Charlie would tell him anything, he didn't know what to ask.

But he couldn't sleep. So he fought. He was tired, and that made him angry most of the day, and he fought with his mother and father, acted like a baby, and got into wrestling matches with the other boys on the street. He bullied the younger ones, and he pushed the older boys to their limits. He would come home with scraped knees and a bloodied nose, and his mother would clean him up and bandage him and worry and console, and his father would tell him always to give better than he got. It made Alma sad that he fought, but it seemed to please Will in some way, as though the boy had put on the cloak of a man, heavy on his tiny frame, but carried with energy and purpose.

Sam didn't know why, but he felt mad all the time. Mad and alone, even though he was surrounded by love. But he knew one thing: He wanted to see Charlie and Sylvan again and again and again. He wanted to be near them, to smell their smells and hear the sounds they made when they touched, when they took their clothes off.

Sometimes, he wished it would all go back to the way it was, when he and Charlie were alone in the world. Sometimes he wished they had never stopped at Sylvan Glass's house, but not often. Now, when he saw them lying on a quilt down near the riverbank, or watched them, sweat on his forehead, Jackie Robinson tied up and yowling in the yard, through the keyhole of the locked bedroom upstairs, he wanted to be them, to lie in the infinitely small sliver of space between their undulating bodies, to feel their skin smooth against his own, to melt into them, until he was nothing and they were, as they were, everything.

CHAPTER TWENTY-TWO

I N THE END, she owned everything he had and all he was. Every
piece of Charlie's land, except for the house in town where he
lived and the flatland out by the river, was in her full legal possession. He gave it to her with an open hand and an open heart. He
didn't know any other way to say what was in his mute heart. He
gave without hope of return, except that he hoped, so secretly that
he couldn't even say it to himself or even write it in his diary, that
she would one day leave Boaty Glass and be his wife. He wanted
her, and, once she had all of what he owned, he was glad and free.
Now, when she walked on her land she was inhabiting his heart,
living in his house, her joy in her fields and creeks and woods a joy,
also, in him.

Sylvan didn't understand the magnitude of it. She didn't grasp
that she was, by almost any measure, the richest woman in the
county. Owning almost four thousand acres was to her just another

simple pleasure, like wearing an armful of sparkling bangles he had given her. As he might have, if he could.

Presents from a lover. Simple things. Dirt and streams and magnolia and dogwood, it was all the same to her, and when she pulled back the floorboard in the attic and looked at the deeds to her land she'd hidden there, she was seeing the sparkle of a secret lover's secret trinkets. The land of Sylvan. More than four thousand acres, no heavier than a cheap bracelet on her arm.

"Thank you," she would say, say it often, and he would always answer, "It's nothing," and he meant it. It *was* nothing, nothing to him compared to the ache and storm of his love for her, nothing compared to what lay inside her eyes when she looked up at him in a certain kind of way, a way that said that things would be, were, all right, and he believed her, the way we always believe the things that are said to us by the people we love.

But, lying in his narrow bed at night, fresh from making love to her, or, worse, on the nights he had not seen her and knew he would not for days, he knew it wasn't enough. There wasn't enough land in the world to say what he felt, to make her believe, so he drew her picture, again and again, and none of the drawings looked like her. There was no crayon in the box for the lichen color of her eyes, the amber glint of her hair as she fell into him in the pines at sunset, no color for the rush of it, the breathlessness, the haste of her love, his need, knowing what they knew, that it ended at sunset's peak, and that she would be home and unattainable by dark.

In the margins of his diary, he would write scraps of poetry he remembered from school. "In Xanadu did Kubla Khan a stately pleasure dome decree." Take my heart, he would think. It is your Xanadu. Build it here.

And even Scripture: "Set me as a seal upon thine arm, as a seal upon thy heart; for love is strong as death," snatches of memory that had nothing to do with her, except that everything, every word, had everything to do with her. She was everywhere in his life.

He drew a picture of himself, frozen in midair, the edge of the cliff behind him, like Wile E. Coyote in the cartoon strip, one step away from solid ground, just before the plunge, the instant fall that left plumes of disaster in the air where his body once had been. That was Charlie, in those times, everything the same, everything changed, everything lost, the world gained, because she was not, for him, a woman but the world.

He thought of her, as he drew her picture and wrote her name, thought of the panic and peace that came in the second, the split hair, before the plunge. The peace and the panic.

I want you. I love you. He couldn't even say these things. They weren't allowed. Words like that belonged to other people. Those words belonged to ordinary people who led ordinary lives.

It amazed him every moment that he, too, led an ordinary life. He was amazed he could get up in the morning and make a pot of coffee and put his pants on, the way he'd always done. When he got out of his bath in the morning, and shaved the night stubble from his face, he could see his body, and he saw it the way she saw it, and he liked what he saw, flat edges and smooth skin, still and calm and firm, his body as not just the box he carried his soul around in, but as something made of flesh and muscle and blood that somebody else wanted, his body as wholly owned by her as the rest of the things that used to belong to him.

He would die for her, just as he lived, now, for Sylvan and Sylvan alone. He would be a better person on her behalf, and he would be patient as Job, saying nothing, applying no pressure, wanting everything and expecting nothing. But it was hard for him, it was hard to pay attention to anything else, to focus on anything that didn't have to do with her.

Everybody in town began to notice the change in him, the distance. What he did with his body began to show in his face. They could sense, dimly at first and then more clearly, that his enthusiasms had become particular, and they knew they had become particular for a particular woman.

Charlie Carter saw it first. He saw, in the late light of a Wednesday evening, Charlie Beale driving his truck down the drive and out of Boaty Glass's gate, a beagle dog and Will Haislett's boy on the seat beside him. He saw Charlie get out and close and latch the gate with a practiced assurance, then turn again to wave to Sylvan, who stood on the porch in her slip, and all that care and all that planning went up the chimney. Carter told his wife, who was a talker, and by the next afternoon, the whole town knew that the glow in Charlie Beale's face was there because he was the lover of Mrs. Harrison Boatwright Glass, and the people of the town just shook their heads, amazed it had taken them so long to figure it out.

And they were, if you had asked them, they were glad for Charlie.

Towns like that, nothing is secret, and so Charlie became the subject of everyday gossip. Even Will and Alma heard about it, as they were bound to. They knew Charlie would do nothing to hurt the boy, but they also knew that love makes people careless and reckless, and they began to question, in their conversations in bed at night, whether Sam should still go out with Charlie so much. They talked about it, and they worried, but they waited. They didn't know what they were waiting for. Sam was starting school in the fall. Maybe they were waiting for that, just to avoid any kind of confrontation.

There wasn't any evidence. The boy had said nothing. Maybe the talk was just talk.

The Misses Allie knew. They knew something, anyway, even if they weren't quite sure what it was. His name was *up*, as people used to say. They stopped him on the street one day as he was walking home at noon to eat his dinner.

"It's baseball season, Mister Beale," said Miss Allie, one or the other. They were both wearing red suits, thin women in expensive clothes, each wearing a heavy gold charm bracelet, one on the right arm, the other on the left, dozens of charms on each, heavy, jangling things. They always wore them so that everybody knew they were coming before they even saw them, as he did now. "You have to teach the boys."

"And some of the girls, if they want to, Mister Beale," said the other Miss Allie.

"Yes. Some of the girls. Maybe even some of the old spinster girls." They laughed identical laughs, blue-white teeth thin as milk in their ancient mouths. When they smiled, they looked to be either a hundred or eighteen, their faces breaking into a thousand lines that spoke of delight, decades of pleasure in each other's company.

"We'd need a field. There's no place to play, Miss Allie, Miss Allie," he said, glancing back and forth between the two eager faces, not knowing where to land his gaze, both faces being the same.

"Well, we have it figured out. There's a field . . ."

". . . behind our house. Flat as a board."

"And Cousin Little Walton Mercer is all set to come and grade it down and put in baselines and even some bleacher seats, if you'll just agree to take it on."

"Say yes, Mister Beale. The boys . . ."

". . . and girls need it, something to do, somewhere to go."

"Something to do, Mister Beale, and Cousin Little Walton can have it done in three days. Say yes, Mister Beale."

"Please do, Mister Beale."

"Of course, ladies. That would be a pleasure."

"That's the ticket!" Miss Allie shook his hand firmly, a symphony of gold charms erupting around him. "We'll put an announcement in the paper, and you'll see, it'll be the new thing."

"Be good to do something fun with the boys . . . and girls."

"Well, we've thought about this all winter. Something has to be done. This town is as sleepy as a tick mattress. Needs some life."

"And it's going to be right in our backyard. Thank you, Mister Beale, thank you again. I'll be the Happy Chandler of Brownsburg, Virginia, Elinor." She glanced at her sister, then turned to Charlie, explaining, "He's a Kentucky cousin of ours, you know."

"And I'll be the Casey Stengel, Ansolette."

"Well, we'll see, ladies. We'll see. Now, I have to get on home and have my dinner. Nice day, ladies."

As he walked away, one of them — Ansolette? Elinor? — stopped him with a gentle call. "Mister Beale?"

He turned. "Yes?"

"Is everything all right? All right with you?"

He felt his cheeks flush with shame. He felt as he always felt, as though he had just been stopped for committing a crime he couldn't remember. Except, in this case, he remembered every detail. Everything in him wanted to tell the old ladies the truth, at least as he understood it. It is, and it isn't, he wanted to say. It is now, and it never will be. Some things you don't say. Some things you just carry.

The wonder of her body, he wanted to say, the way she looks at me, sometimes, only sometimes, but then, that way. Between the twins and where he stood, stood Sylvan; he could see her, a full young woman in a yellow dress from the movies, smiling in that way that made his heart explode in his chest, every single time. Explode.

"Fine," he said. "Right as rain" — and, in his smile and his shrug, there was all of the rightness and none of the wrongness in the world.

"Well, we think of you, Mister Beale."

"We think of you often, and sometimes talk about you."

"Nothing bad, I hope."

Taken seriously. Answered fully. "No, Mister Beale. Not at all."

"In fact, the opposite."

"We have the kindest feelings for you."

"Everybody does."

"Everybody in town."

So he went on slaughtering cows, not caring any more to wait until they were calm and accepting of their fate, knowing that his haste made them panic, made their fear creep into the taste of the meat; he slaughtered cows in haste and cut meat and coached baseball and made what he hoped was love to Sylvan Glass, and that was his life, his whole life. And the boy. The boy he loved and he needed, because none of it worked without him, his fantasy son.

He was the cigarette hitting the blacktop at fifty miles an hour, reckless, except for the one thing about which he had to be more than careful, and he was, silent and perfectly careful. He never said her name in public one time, not ever. He never meant harm. He had meant never to hurt another living thing. And perhaps the boy was not hurt, he thought, perhaps, but he knew better.

The boy who now kicked and screamed when he had to go to bed, the boy who fought everything that moved. The boy who wouldn't eat or say much, who did not say ma'am and sir, who smacked Jackie Robinson when he did not come when called, so that the dog now alternately snarled at and doted on the boy, looked at the boy with a mixture of fear and adoration. This was the boy he had made, had raised, they, he and Sylvan, in the world they had made for no one but themselves. Their little family. This was Sam, the apple of his father's eye, the first, last, and only fruit of his tree, who was five and was now about to be six, and Charlie loved him and did not know what to do, lost in the way he was lost, trying to be ordinary, finding any conversation with the boy impossible now, but needing him, needing him because he was part of the secret, and to lose him now, he felt, might be chancing everything.

He tried to be kind to him. He tried to pay attention to Sam as he had once done, to listen to the endless questions and invent answers when he did not know the answer. Why was the moon big sometimes and small at others? He was confounded by this, and by the many things a boy's mind can invent to ask about. A deer can die of fright, a hummingbird in his sleep, for no reason? Is forever a long time? He wanted to hold him, but the boy was not his child, was not even really his responsibility, although he felt contained within the bounds of his care of and for the boy.

Once it had occurred to him to make a will and to leave everything to the boy, but that was when he still owned things, enough to give a boy a life, a place in the world. That was what he had wanted to do, also in secret, to be found out only when he died, but now he could not do that, that one thing he had wanted to do out of simple kindness.

Again and again Alma and Will had discussed how the boy should not go with him any more, on the afternoons to the slaughterhouse, the days by the river, the house in the woods, because they knew, as everybody knew now, that the boy languished alone while Charlie spent his hours with Boaty Glass's wife, not fishing at all, slaughtering in haste, laying waste, laying waste around him without meaning to and ultimately without being able to care, to stop himself. They had discussed it and done nothing to stop it.

So when Charlie came to them and asked what he asked, how

could they not say yes? How could they not go along, thinking, as Charlie thought, that it might do the boy some good, might bring the boy around again, home to himself, to his childhood, home to them, his mother and father?

"It's his birthday soon," Charlie had said. "I want to give a party for him. I want to show him, maybe it'll do some good. Maybe it'll stop the fighting."

And how could they say no, knowing what they knew, wanting what they wanted, some kind of salvation, some kind of return of their boy back to them, and Charlie whole again, his old self, laughing in the crowd, generous, kind, a man whose arms were wide open even when his hands were in his pockets.

A party. A carnival for Sam, in the meadow out by the river, just for him, because he was six, because he had lived that long and had much longer still to live and some peace had to be made with that, some equanimity created with the whole life that lay waiting, man and boy.

"It'll be just the thing," said Charlie. "Good for the boy.

"I want to do it," he said. "Leave everything to me."

And of course they did. Of course they already had.

CHAPTER TWENTY-THREE

Aᴜɢᴜsᴛ 4, 1949. Sam Haislett's sixth birthday. August in the Valley of Virginia, hot as holy hell, hotter than you would think for a place where people used to flock after the Civil War to escape the heat of the cities, everything dry now, gold gray, second cutting come and gone, the willows hanging limply into the still rippling water, lower now than in the spring, but still lively, still heading for the sea and freedom. The sun white-hot against a hot white sky. The river water, the sweet Maury, so fresh and clear, still leaping greenly, the water that flows from the eye of Jesus into the heart of God.

In Pittsburgh, at Forbes Field that afternoon, the man Jackie Robinson went 0 for 4, even though his team got fourteen hits and beat the Pirates 11−3. They went on to win the pennant, and then to lose the Series to the Yankees. On that day, the people of Brownsburg worried about the fact that the Russians were about to explode an atomic bomb, and, in fact, they did it three weeks later. Happy Chandler, the commissioner of baseball and a cousin to the twins, even if it was so distant, so convoluted he wasn't aware of it, spent the day at home in Versailles, Kentucky, quietly reviewing some legal papers in the Danny Gardella case, a case that ultimately changed baseball forever.

It was a Thursday. A fire started in the Mann Gulch near Helena, Montana, and by the next day it had killed thirteen people. Montgomery Clift and Olivia de Havilland were on the cover of *Movie Story*. Big things happened. Little things happened. It was a busy day on the planet and in the county. But people around here still talk about that day for one simple reason. August 4, 1949 was also the day on which six-year-old Sam Haislett died and was brought back to life again by a single kiss from Charlie Beale.

It was after that day that everybody who knew him, and everybody who didn't, called Charlie Beale by the name Beebo. They called him that because that was the first thing the child said when he opened his eyes, saved by a single kiss from Charlie Beale, alive again, after the doctor had failed.

To save one life is to save the whole entire world. That's what the Jews say. Just one single life, among the billions being lived. It changes everything. And not just for the one who got saved.

The day before the day, the day that changed everything, Charlie took Sam out to the field by the river where he had first lived when he came to town, to make sure it had been mowed and raked, that the tables had been set up, long planks on sawhorses that could seat fourteen. He had planned a feast, and had slaughtered two baby pigs on Tuesday, and spent the afternoon digging a giant pit to roast them over a wood fire. He split logs, and Sam stacked the wood for him. As they were getting ready to leave, he showed Sam a magic trick, or the first part of it.

He asked Sam to pick out his favorite tree, and when Sam had found it at the edge of the water, a young willow with branches trailing among the minnows, Charlie had pulled from his pocket a piece of Bazooka gum, and carefully and soberly planted it in the soft dirt at the tree's roots. Then, when it was covered over and the dirt stomped down with their boots, he promised Sam a surprise on his birthday.

Sam didn't sleep much that night, he spent his time lying in the dark, pressing his fingers against his closed eyes to watch the fireworks in the dark, but at some point he fell, flying in the iridescent dark with Captain America, and then he woke into joy, so when he headed out the door that morning, his sixth birthday, over two thousand days on the planet, all spent in the streets of the same small town, he was heading out to wonderful. He was heading out to Charlie Beale.

Everything is different on a boy's birthday. Every moment is blessed with a kind of luminosity of self, an awareness that every gesture, every word, is a birthday word or gesture. People know who you are, on your birthday.

At breakfast, his mother recited: "'But now I am six and I'm clever as clever, so I think I'll be six forever and ever.'" And then she kissed him, and said, "Happy birthday Darling," as Will led him, eyes closed, to the back porch where a brand new bike waited for him. His birthday, his poem, his bike.

As soon as he could, he got over to Charlie's. He couldn't wait to find out what the next surprise was. "Morning, Sam," said Charlie. "You ready to dig?"

When they got out to Charlie's field, it wasn't any later than eight o'clock, hot already, and there was his birthday surprise. The willow tree had sprouted hundreds of pieces of Bazooka overnight, from the tendrils that trailed in the water to the highest branches. A bubblegum tree, just out of nowhere, overnight. And Sam knew that Bazooka cost a penny apiece, so he was awed by the fortune his one piece of gum, planted the day before, had yielded in a single night. He picked and picked from the branches, and filled his pockets, but there was still more, higher up, hundreds of pieces he couldn't reach, each one with bubblegum inside, and a joke, and maybe an offer for a free whistle.

"Sam," said Charlie, slowing him down. "Sam. You've got a life-time. This bubblegum is forever. It's your birthday present. One piece at a time. Just one. It'll last you forever. Later, we'll harvest them all and put them in a secret place. Okay? This is your birthday, Sam, and you've got a whole life of Bazooka ahead of you. Imagine that."

Sam threw his arms around Charlie's neck, his cheeks puffed with gum, and just held him like that, smelling the morning, Charlie's soap, the river, his birthday.

Then Charlie led him to the truck and gave him one more

present, his first baseball glove, a Wilson, stiff and taut, a boy's glove, too big now, something to grow into. Charlie told him they'd put Wesson oil in the glove that night, oil it down, and in time it would grow supple, and grow to fit exactly as his hand grew, smooth and supple as a second skin. Sam was in heaven. He had died and gone to heaven.

"Now we dig, son," said Charlie, gently taking the boy's arms from around his neck. "Get you a shovel out of the truck." He'd started to talk like a country man, by then.

Sam helped for half an hour, then wandered by the river with his new glove, tossing a ball and letting it bounce off the tight new surface of the glove that smelled so sweet to him, while Charlie dug the pit for another three hours, until the hole was three feet wide and five feet deep, like a child's grave.

Once the pit was dug, they filled it with kindling and logs and set it on fire, the blaze so hot you couldn't get within five feet of it, so hot that any log thrown on it hissed like a snake, popped like summer fireworks, and then burst into flames immediately. The fire started, fresh wood stacked over Charlie's head, they went back to the butcher shop to get the pigs, which had been soaking in brine in the meat locker. Charlie knew nothing about what he was doing, not really, but old man Tolley, who had sold him the three week-old piglets, who had been fattening them up for Charlie from the day they were born, had taught him carefully, step by step, about the brining, the pit, the basting with melted butter and cider, how long, how hot, how high. The old man had been doing it since he was a boy, and his father before him, so being taught how to roast a pig by old man Tolley was like being taught how to paint by da Vinci.

"Are they babies?" asked Sam, staring down at the two grayish pink carcasses floating in tubs.

"Well, they're not getting any older, not any more," said Will, "but that is some of the finest pig you will ever eat in your life."

"I wish they weren't babies."

"If you're going to eat it, son, you ought to know where it comes from. You're six now. You have to pay attention. It shows respect. Always remember that. You don't get a full belly out of nowhere.

"Can't live on air," said Charlie.

"I don't need food," said Sam.

"Everybody needs food."

"I don't. I've got Bazooka!" shouted Sam, spilling the pieces out of his pocket onto the floor.

"Where'd you get that, boy?" asked Will, gathering them up and holding out his hands.

"The tree. The magic tree."

"I did it, Will. I gave them to the boy."

"Wish you hadn't done that, Charlie. Alma won't like it, you know."

"Sam?" Charlie knelt on the floor in front of the boy. "Whenever we pick a piece off the tree, you'll ask your mother first, right?"

"Well. Okay."

"Just think. That way, it'll last longer. It'll last forever, your whole life."

"And how long will that be?"

"At least a hundred years. One hundred and ninety-seven years."

"That's a long time."

"It's a very very long time."

"Do some pigs live that long?"

"No, Sam. Just boys. Just some boys."

"Will you? Will Daddy?"

"I have every hope."

While they talked, the sky outside had turned from white to black, the air had thickened, and there was a sudden crack and a flash and the sky opened up and poured rain, so thick you couldn't see across the street and Will had to turn on the lights in the shop, at midday, it was that dark.

It lasted five minutes, and when it was over, it was fifteen degrees cooler, and the sky was the color of a baby's eyes. A perfect Virginia August day. And a day like that, well, you'd be blessed to see it, just once in your life.

The storm, in its five minutes, created both destruction and perfection. Limbs and lines were down. Susie Hostetter, the telephone operator, packed up and went home for the day.

The storm didn't put out the fire in Charlie's pit, although there was volcanic steam rising from it by the time he got back there, and the pigs were on the spit by one o'clock, turned by him by hand every fifteen minutes with a makeshift iron crank made by the blacksmith in Lexington. The fat from the slowly turning carcasses dripped into the fire, explosions of flame shooting up around the flesh. Charlie kept buckets of water from the river handy, to splash on the coals, so the skin wouldn't burn before the meat cooked.

He brushed them every twenty minute with a paintbrush dipped in melted fat and cider.

People started coming in around two. He'd invited more than a hundred, even some of the town's black people, knowing they wouldn't come, and they didn't. They knew, just as they knew that Charlie's invitation was genuine and heartfelt and gracious, that they wouldn't be in the right place if they were in that field on that afternoon. The Reverend Lewis Shadwell considered going, even got dressed to go, with a present for Sam wrapped and sitting on his bureau, but he wavered at the last minute, then hung his clothes carefully back in his closet and lay down in his undershirt and took a nap in the fresh afternoon air. By the time he woke up, what happened out by the river had already happened.

There was a sense of lightness, after the storm, a brightness in the air and in people's hearts. There was music in the air from a band Charlie had hired all the way from Fincastle, a bluegrass band that played all the songs the people of the town had grown up on but didn't listen to much anymore, songs like "The Knoxville Girl," with its sad tale of murder and grieving. "She fell down on her bended knees, for mercy she did cry, 'Oh, Willie dear, don't kill me here, I'm unprepared to die.'" The singer was an old man. He sang the songs his grandfather had taught him, and played the fiddle without ever changing his expression or looking up, while two other men played banjo and guitar, their faces as flat and sharp as their instruments.

People heard the songs, the music of the mountains and hollows they came down from, first love and murder and hard dirt and the hard, hard life of sorrow, heard the old man, and heard the flat country voices of their own grandmothers and grandfathers, the songs they had heard on the wide wooden porches of their childhoods.

And then Sylvan came, Sylvan and Boaty, stepping out of their vulgar fancy car, Sylvan wearing the green dress from the movie. She'd tried to get Claudie to come. She figured Claudie was the only black person brave and careless enough to go, but even Claudie had begged off, saying she couldn't leave Evelyn Hope alone all afternoon. Instead, Claudie left Evelyn Hope after all and went out and sat on the other side of the river, where they could all see her, making drawings of the goings on, and of Sylvan in particular.

Sylvan was luminous in the full bloom of her twenty years, as bright and fluid as the air. She greeted Charlie delicately, without either distance or familiarity, and she and Boaty moved into the crowd as though she and Charlie had never lain skin on skin and body to body, in full view of a boy who was not yet six years old.

There were presents for Sam, of course, everybody had bought some little thing, and he was drunk with the treasure. Whistles and yo-yos, and bullwhips and cap pistols, everybody brought what they thought he would like, because they genuinely liked and admired Will, and particularly Alma. And, too, they hoped their generosity to Sam might bring better grades to their own struggling youngsters, or even a leaner pound of hamburger. Alma wrote down every present in a little ruled book, and wondered how long it would take for Sam to thank everybody personally with a card.

Charlie saw Claudie across the river, everybody did. He walked down to the edge of the stream and waved and called and motioned for her to come over, but she didn't even acknowledge his greeting. She didn't even look up from her drawing when Sylvan broke away and called her name, twirling in the green dress so it rose up and everybody could see the tartan lining.

People did not know what to make of that dress. It was so exotic, so far beyond the realm of anything the women themselves could purchase or even sew. It was like looking at some wild African animal, or a penguin from the South Pole. They didn't see its prettiness, or how it brought the life into Sylvan's rich body; they looked on it as though she were trying to trick them into taking her for something other than she was, a hillbilly from some desolate valley most of them had never even seen. They were used to her shenanigans, to her putting on airs, but somehow this green dress in this field, in those shoes, on this afternoon, it was just too much.

Who did she think she was, and who, in fact, was she? And how long would it be before Boaty found out? The easiest way to find out something secret is to ask somebody who doesn't like whoever the secret is about, and a lot of people didn't like Sylvan Glass, at least they didn't like her at that minute. Things would change, though, when what happened happened, when she did what she did, because she did the first part, the brave part, not the miracle, but the first part, the right thing. For a brief time, she would mean a great deal to them, and they would look at her with a kind of graciousness, but only for a short time, only until she did what she did after that.

And what happened was this: About three o'clock, when Charlie and Will were about to take the pigs off the spit and lay them out to rest on slabs of marble borrowed from Coffey's place that cut gravestones, Sam saw a piece of gum high up on the tree he just had to have. People weren't paying attention to him any more, the presents were opened and their stomachs were empty. They were watching the pig on the spit, and listening to the old man sing in a high falsetto, "It was on a moonlight night, stars shining bright, whispers on high, love said good-bye . . ."

It was a mistake a man who was not a father would make, to hang so much bubblegum so high up on the tree. There were a lot of children there, and the lower branches had been pretty much stripped bare. Talking, hungry, nobody saw Sam crawling out on the limb, over the river, but they heard the sharp shiver and split of the willow branch breaking, dry now in the late summer, and, even if they didn't see him fall, they saw the splash, and heard the thud as the broken branch hit Sam on the head as he hit the water, and they saw the plume of blood where the boy went down. So quickly such tragedy can happen. While you're looking away. Just a glance and then something, something wrong out of the corner of your eye. The dog and the car. The blade and your finger. In a breath. A blink.

They all ran, even though they hadn't seen the boy fall, only heard the snap of the branch. Some of the women screamed. The music abruptly stopped. Charlie ran, and he could run the fastest, but Sylvan was already there, in the water and gone under, leaving Charlie helpless, darting in the shallows, trying to spot the boy, uselessly calling his name, as everybody was doing. The current here was strong, everybody knew it, and the boy was already moving downstream in the rushing current, banged against rocks, dragged to the bottom.

No, it was Sylvan who dove in, this twenty-year-old girl in a green silk movie costume with a tartan lining, her body a blade into the water. A quick green slash in the tossing, tumbling blue-green water, and then they both were gone.

She couldn't see through the green water, the light hazy, filtered, shadowed by leaf and cloud above. She followed the current, let herself be carried on it, pushing through it, knowing that the boy had been carried the same way. There was only one direction to go, and the river would decide where they would end up. She pulled through the water in front of her, her arms in butterfly sweeps, reaching for the tail of a shirt, a shoe, a hand trailing behind.

One minute. Two minutes. She darted to the surface for air and plunged back in, to find him right below her, caught on the spring of an old mattress, limp, lifeless. She pulled; he wouldn't come loose. She pulled again, then turned herself around in the water, and put her foot against the mattress, quick green short snakes slithering out and up around her. Grabbing his shoulders and pushing herself off, freeing him, one sneaker left behind, its laces floating in the water, ghostly streamers.

The mud was soft at the bank, like the icing on a cake. Her feet couldn't find purchase. She could not get a foot free, couldn't get his head above the water. He seemed to weigh a thousand pounds. Then Charlie got to them, pulled at her billowing hair, reeled her in, the mud sucking the shoes from her feet, and the boy, the boy in her arms, now in Charlie's, now lifted up and out and into other hands, Raidy Tate, Charlie Howard, then his father, who laid him on the ground, as Doctor Brush kneeled over him and then they all fell silent while the doctor felt, and listened and turned the boy over and thumped, and back again and pushed, and put his head to the boy's chest and listened and finally looked up at Will and Alma and almost imperceptibly shook his head. But that said all there was to be said. *Dead.*

Alma howled and Will fell to his knees sobbing, his only child, the light of his life, now dead, rough hands pushing the hair back from Sam's face, as though the sun could warm the boy back to life, and Alma screaming, falling into the arms of keening women, her arms reaching out for the body her legs could not carry her to, fighting for freedom from the women who locked her into her instant, her eternal grief.

Charlie's face was wet with tears and sweat. Guilt. This was what had come from his foolish birthday trick for Sam—this tiny body, dead, one shoe off, one sock, dead. Sylvan turned away, grateful for the first time for the arms of her fat husband, his heavy shoulder, so that she did not see what happened next, did not see as Charlie pushed Will back and stood above the boy and then fell to his knees, straddling the small body, picking it up and grasping it to his chest, then gently lowering him again, the imprint of the boy's wet body dark and damp on his shirt.

Sylvan didn't see as Charlie leaned forward and whispered something in the boy's ear, something that took a while and nobody heard what it was, although people spent a lot of time afterward guessing what it might have been, a prayer, a poem, an apology, a verse from the Bible.

Sylvan didn't see as Charlie then put his face to the boy's and kissed him for a long time. Mouth to mouth, he held his lips against the boy's for a full thirty seconds, the women howling, Will kneeling, head bowed, his breath heavy and wet against his chest, his streaming eyes closed.

She didn't see as the boy's eyes opened, as water shot from his mouth, but she heard what everybody heard, the boy's small voice, a mixture of alarm and wonder, as he said the first word of his new life.

"Beebo?" he said, looking up at Charlie, and then, turning away, "Mama? Mama?" And he was alive again, the pink of his blood pushing the blue from his skin, from the tips of his fingers. He was alive where he had been dead, and the crowd parted as the women released Alma and she rushed forward as Charlie stood and ran into the shadows of the willow, pulling the pieces of bubblegum from the branches and throwing them into the water. The crowd stood silent, the boy alive, the men and women knowing that whatever happened after this, it would forever and always be after what they had witnessed on this day. This thing that nobody knew the name of, but some people thought and were afraid, ever, to say what it was, but would just say, and still do, that they were there, that they saw it, the whisper and the kiss and the coming back to life—and then just pausing in the telling to shake their heads, dumb with the wonder of it.

Everything in this town, in this county, in history and in the lives of those people who were there and those that weren't, everything was before that kiss — the music, the Knoxville Girl, the graceful, awkward dancing to the sad laments, the heat of the morning and the thunderclap of noon, the pig burned and forgotten, their hungers that were suddenly gone — these things were before, unremembered, their hearts now full, and everything else was after.

And after, for a short space of time, whatever happened and wherever he went, Charlie Beale walked on water in their eyes, and he could do no wrong.

CHAPTER TWENTY-FOUR

EVERYBODY, MAN, WOMAN, and child in Brownsburg, loved Charlie Beale. Everyone, except one man. From that minute, Boaty Glass hated him. He had looked the other way when Charlie Beale started buying up land, even swallowed his pride when he heard talk that Charlie had surpassed him in terms of acreage held, and the quality of that acreage. He had even turned a deaf ear to the rumors flying around about what Charlie Beale was doing with his wife, even though he knew in his heart that all rumors are eventually true. He didn't care much for his wife and her full body and her fancy ways. Didn't care much at all, as long as she kept on being his wife.

He had wanted a glorious hood ornament for the car of his life. Sparkling, finely made, isolated and virtuous. He had wanted to be an object of envy. But, most of all, he had wanted to be loved, because, with a magnificent wife, he would be seen as someone who was himself adored. He had put on a wedding ring because then, if he walked the streets of Brownsburg or Timbuktu, any stranger passing could glance at his hand and know that he was loved.

But the idea that Charlie was now held in such exalted regard, the regard he had longed for since the moment his mother died, scratched at his throat as though he had swallowed barbed wire. When Boaty got riled, he heard a constant, high-pitched whine in his ear, and felt the bitter tides of the bile churning in his stomach. It took Boaty a long time to get mad, but when he did, he stayed mad and waited patiently, hands folded across his expansive stomach, for his revenge.

Even Sylvan didn't seem like part of his holdings any more, ever since she pulled that boy from the water. She no longer belonged to him in the way she had. People who normally nodded politely or avoided her altogether, looking on her only as an extension of his property, began to stop her on the street, to pay her compliments on those foolish getups, those things she dreamed up with that crazy woman. They treated her as though she were some kind of a great lady, instead of the back-hollow trash she was born and would always be.

He made it clear to her one night, quite casually, who she was and who she belonged to and what she was supposed to do and say in her situation. He made it so clear that she wasn't able to leave the house for a week, except to sneak off to that colored woman's house and sob over her piece of pie, or whatever those women shared when they spent their afternoons together.

He'd never hit a woman before. Never had one to hit, and he

took a liking to it right away, wondered why it had taken him so long. If you want to produce an effect in this world, make an impact, it's a pretty easy way to do it, and it didn't take much skill.

After all, what was she going to do about it? Leave him? If she left him, she also left her own family homeless. The contract said so. And then where would she go? If she told Claudie, who was Claudie Wiley going to tell? That idiot daughter?

No. Like a good farmer checks his fences in the spring before letting the cattle and the calves out to pasture, Boaty made sure his property was securely kept in, kept at hand.

He knew instinctively not to hit her in the face. That first week she spent at home, swollen and blotched, made him realize that, if people knew he was beating her, they'd never look at him in the way he wanted them to. While a lot of men around here hit their wives, those men were not Boaty Glass and those wives were not Sylvan. So his punishments of her became more secret and more humiliating. Her legs. Her back, her breasts.

He even drove her out there one day, all the way to Arnold's Valley, to the home place. Her family looked at her like she'd come from Mars, and they only stayed long enough to make it clear to Sylvan, as though it wasn't clear already, that her family didn't want her and she didn't want them.

Charlie saw the bruises, the welts. Charlie knew everything. He wanted to kill Boaty, told Sylvan he'd do it, but she talked him out of it over and over. He made love to her, wounded, careful not to hurt her any more than she had been already, not to cause her the slightest discomfort. He felt that she was a damaged child in his arms. He touched her bruises with his lips, as though that would heal them, make her skin pure again. He wept as he came inside her, cried for her pain and her sorrow and her humiliation. He understood nothing of what kept her from leaving her husband.

She understood less. "Leave him," said Claudie. "You've got a good man, a holy man, a man who loves you and will take care of you. Why bother with that old fool?"

"Can't" was all the girl would say. "Wouldn't never do that. There's reasons."

"Tell me. Tell me the truth."

"If I ever leave Boaty, he gets the old home place back and throws my family out. They have nowhere to go. It would kill them."

"They could come live with you and Charlie. He'd provide."

"He couldn't. You don't understand. My mama has never been anywhere in this world, never set foot outside that valley. My father hardly, either. That place, that valley—you're born there and you die there. You leave it, for them, and life is over. Like a fish out of the bowl. They couldn't breathe the air. Their feet couldn't find purchase."

"You left."

"I left a long time before I left. I left when I started listening to the radio at five years old. I never really lived there after that. Just pretended to."

"You're still walking around. You don't owe them anything. They're grown. You got to think about you. And the only thing you need is him. Let Glass have whatever he wants."

"I don't need anything," said Sylvan. "I don't even need Charlie

Beale. I have . . ." but she couldn't say what she had, because she wasn't quite sure what it was. Some papers in an envelope underneath a floorboard in the attic of Boaty Glass's house? What was that? What did they mean, really?

They meant she owned things, Charlie had told her. The papers under the attic floorboard meant she was free. But she obviously wasn't. She'd never owned anything. The land she grew up on, the land her father worked every day, she did, too—did they even own it? She never knew. And even if those papers did mean she owned the land, what was she supposed to do with it? Become a farmer?

She didn't trust anybody, except Claudie. When she was with Charlie, she understood that she meant the world to him, the whole world, in that hour, during that sunset. But after? There was a life he lived, separate from hers. What did he do when he wasn't with her? Did she even cross his mind?

She thought of him all the time, but it was his body she thought of, his physical self, the way he held her and moved above and inside her. She didn't think about *him*. She didn't really know who he was or what he might do to her if she were his.

Because if Boaty, who had for her a complete lack of feeling, other than his sense of ownership, his right to walk and live on the property he had bought, if he could do this to her, what might a man in love do?

Charlie was a saint, people said. He brought that boy back to life. People said he was blessed. Even Claudie said it. She'd had made a drawing of the moment the boy had risen from the dead, and it hung on the wall of the room where she sewed Sylvan's dresses and put balm on her bruises, and Sylvan looked at it and thought, Who is that man? What is he to me?

He was the man who said, "I'm so sorry, baby," through his tears, the man who fell to his knees at the sight of a welt across her flesh. He was the only one in the world who had ever said her name as though it meant something, something that was larger than her body, finer than her clothes, something that had meaning and place in the world. SYLVAN. He carved her name in a tree, next to his, and carved a heart around it, and so, when she thought about it, she knew that's where her heart was.

He wanted to marry her. He asked her again and again. She was rich, he said. She could be free. They could be together. But every time she was about to say yes, she saw her mother's face, her father's face, homeless, displaced, dying on some alien porch somewhere, away from the farm where their mothers and fathers were buried, and she couldn't do it.

In the third week of September, on a night so warm that Charlie Beale had left his bed and driven out to the river, where he threw himself on the ground and slept without quilt or cover next to his dog, Sylvan Glass was driven to Sheriff Ricky Straub's house by her husband, where she woke him up in the middle of the night and spoke to Straub and said that she was Mrs. Harrison Glass—a name he didn't even recognize at first, as sleepy as he was, he hadn't heard it in so long—and that she had been raped by Charlie Beale.

You may wonder why, and I'm telling you that I don't know.

Nobody knows what she told Boaty or when she told it, and nobody knows what things a husband like him in that situation might do or say to a wife like Sylvan, a woman who had pieces of paper that showed she was the richest woman in the county, papers that she didn't understand except insofar as they were a secret, never to be shared, and that, instead of being a ticket to freedom, they had become another lock around her spirit, put there by another man. A better man than her husband, absolutely, but nevertheless a man whose ownership of her consisted of giving her power over everything he had in this world, so that he had nothing, nothing at all except her, and was there to be caught and captured and done to as she wished, at whatever command or whim, it didn't matter.

Let's say that Sylvan told Boaty what she told him not because she volunteered the information, but because he demanded to be told the thing he already knew. Let's say that he said he'd kill Charlie Beale, the one everybody adored, that he'd kill her, a woman who had no sense of her self or her worth or her place in the world.

Certainly he would have sat her down at the kitchen table and shown her for the hundredth time the marriage contract, the one that left her mother and father, her whole family, without any place in the world to go or to be. And that it struck her as odd to see her own name in the legal document that made her his, her name in the same sentence as a sum of money and a tractor. Let's say that she finally understood the burden of that, couldn't bear the thought of the guilt over the misery, even death, her own potential happiness would cause.

Let's say he put bullets in his gun and put that gun in her mouth, his fat, strong hand strangling her throat, but then stopped, realizing that in killing her he would lose his best piece of property, and that, in killing Charlie, he would instead be seen as protecting what he already owned, doing his duty, assuming a kind of manhood that had eluded him. Let's say he was heading out the door with the gun in his hand when she blurted something out to him that stopped him, and that she then sat beside him in the car while he drove her over to Sherriff Straub's place.

A rock and a hard place. We hear people say it. But when the rock was the eviction and slow, dwindling death of her whole family, and the hard place the sudden quick death of her lover, maybe Sylvan had to make a choice, and she made it, and it broke her heart and put out the light in her, but her choice would have done that either way.

Straub later said in court that, as soon as he had put on his badge and pulled himself together, she stood before him and repeated without hesitation, "I'm Mrs. Harrison Glass and Charlie Beale raped me." And then she stood her ground and never blinked or blushed or stammered when Straub asked her all the questions he asked her, questions that had never been asked in Brownsburg before. She told him where, and when, and how many times. Sheriff Straub had heard what everybody had heard about Charlie and Sylvan, and he doubted that her account, however well acted, was in any way factual. But he saw that Sylvan Glass was very, very afraid of something. And he also knew that Harrison Glass was Harrison Glass and so therefore her story must be held to be in some way true and he also knew that something then would necessarily have to be done about it.

CHAPTER TWENTY-FIVE

CHARLIE'S BROTHER APPEARED out of nowhere. Ned Beale was a twenty-one-year-old carpenter, a gawky, on-his-way-to-handsome kid with a head of stiff blond hair, even though his beard was as soft as the hair on the nape of a woman's neck. He couldn't have been less like Charlie in height or weight. He nevertheless had his brother's steeliness, his workman's hands, and his tendency, as it turned out, to rush headlong into disaster.

Charlie sent a telegram at Western Union and that's how people in those days got to know that other people were in trouble or need, and often they came, and Ned did. From where, exactly, like his brother, nobody really knew.

It's a terrible thing to see a man whose heart is broken, whose spirit has been irrevocably shattered. We turn away. We look for a happier face. But not Ned. Ned came to Brownsburg, and settled into the little house that was all Charlie had left, and he cooked the meals he didn't eat, and he picked up the dirty clothes Charlie couldn't bring himself to put away.

Every day, in the butcher shop, Charlie Beale was the same, the same man, kind and helpful and expert with the knife, sending all the women home with what he always told them cheerfully was the best meal they would ever have. But you could see what it cost him, going on when nothing, nothing at all, really mattered any more.

If your heart is broken and there is no visible wound, no sign of sickness, what else is there to do but go on, act the way you're supposed to, do what has to be done? No use to say it hurts. Everybody knows that already, everybody can see it, and they know as well that they could never in a million years touch or soothe the place where the hurt begins.

Ned hardly knew his brother. He was a baby when Charlie left home. But he was the only one who could touch that place in Charlie's heart that Sylvan Glass had sown with salt. Ned kept Charlie presentable, made him shave his face, change his clothes, eat a bite of supper. They tried once to share the table with the Haisletts, but it was awkward and awful, even the boy was fractious, and they didn't repeat the experiment, just ate sandwiches alone at the table at night, not speaking. What was there to say, what other topic was there, could there possibly be?, and they didn't talk about that. Charlie wouldn't, and the boy knew there was no use in trying.

Instead of talking, Ned went to the lumberyard, got supplies, and began to fix up Charlie's house. A warped board on the stairs. A rickety rail on the porch. He moved from room to room, and whatever needed putting right, he did it over. And the work was fine and careful and meant to last for a long time. Nothing has been done to the house since that time, and it's still sound.

It was his way of saying to his brother there was a future. Ned had nobody, and he needed Charlie, needed a brother, and so he believed and did what he could to see that things turned out all right. Charlie would come home, and he would come back to a house meant to last a long time.

People noticed him coming and going, and he did odd jobs for them, too, good work. Solid structure to give safety and comfort. When he wasn't working, and Charlie was at the butcher shop, he drank whiskey at the kitchen table and shivered with fear.

When he was at home, Charlie never talked about Sylvan at all. From the day Sheriff Straub appeared and read him the charges, putting him in handcuffs at the ball field where he was coaching boys and girls in the art of baseball, while the twins looked on, then leading him away to spend a night in jail until bail could be set and Will had paid it, he never once mentioned her name.

But in his dreams she devoured him. Night after night she picked at his flesh like a hawk on a deer dead at the side of the road, picking the bones clean. His diary was scrawled still with her name, Sylvan, Sylvan, again and again, but the pictures were no longer of angels descending, but of a vampire who drew his blood, her lovely mouth fanged, dripping crimson, taking him piece by piece until he was a skeletal remembrance of his own body. Gone were the rose and violet he had used to paint her loveliness, the gentle line and the fine hand. Now the drawings were the color of dried blood.

"You have to get a lawyer."

"I didn't do anything, Ned."

"What's the truth? What really happened?"

"What happened is private. And that means that nobody will ever hear it from me. No matter what, I owe her that. But the thing she says I did, I didn't do, and that's the only fact anybody needs to know."

Charlie had loved her with a violence that had electrified his whole body, and now that love had been flicked off, like a light switch, and he didn't know what to do with all the love he felt in his heart, and there was nothing to do with the hatred he felt for her. So, he just kept his head down and his mouth shut. He had lost the one true belief he had ever had, that belief that had come to him by the river, so long ago — that the only enduring thing was goodness — and now there was nothing left in him or of him.

Nobody believed her, of course. Behind their doors, where they talked about little else, they said only that it was the biggest lie they'd ever heard, probably cooked up by Boaty, that she wasn't a bad girl, how could she be, after she'd risked her life pulling that child from the river? She was just a naïve country girl who'd gone funny in the head, running around with that Claudie, her life turned into some movie only she was watching. Maybe she had been unfaithful, but there was a general sense that, if you were married to Boaty Glass, infidelity wasn't the worst sin in the world.

Until the Sunday when both the Baptist and the Methodist preachers spoke from the pulpit, and told them exactly what they were facing. " 'He has become a prisoner of sin,' " said one, quoting Scripture. "He has defiled us all," said the other.

"Let the law do whatever it wants, he will burn in hell," they said it at almost the same time. "He will burn in hell forever.

"Any man or woman who keeps company with him will go to hell with him. Do not let him into your houses and put him from your heart and from your mind. No man can defile you unless you are ready to be defiled.

"And even if you do it in secret, take him into your house or into your heart, if you give aid or comfort in even the smallest way, the rack and the wrath will be yours, and you will live among the filthy and the degraded and the vile for eternity."

The two ministers spoke as though they had met and decided what it was they were going to tell their flocks, and they had, and their flocks believed their ministers, even though it broke their hearts to shut their doors and close their hearts to Charlie Beale. Still, they did just that. These were religious people, and they had not forgotten the duties they owed their faith and their pastors.

The husbands said that Charlie Beale had done no more than was natural, and hellfire had nothing to do with it. But the wives were adamant. Their hearts, always soft for Charlie, turned hard and bitter, and their fear ungovernable. The superstitions and moral rigor of their mountain grandmothers ran through their veins, and now it beat in their hearts and in their minds every moment of the day.

Some of the men approached Charlie at the filling station, while he was putting gas in the truck he didn't have anyplace to drive to any more. "We don't know how to tell you this," one of the men began, taking Charlie's hand in a handshake that was more goodbye than hello.

"No need," said Charlie, "I heard. You know who I am. You know how I feel."

And they all shook his hand and then stood for an awkward minute until Charlie's tank was full, looking anywhere but at him, and then it was over. Charlie screwed the cap back on, got in the cab of his truck, and drove slowly off, raising one open hand out the open window in farewell.

He left them all alone, then, after that. He didn't offer to rake their leaves, or help fix their roofs, or wash their cars, or teach their children how to drive or throw a curveball. He loved these people. He didn't want to embarrass them. He didn't believe in hell, but he didn't want them to go there.

"They sure don't seem to like you much any more," said Ned one night, when Charlie was trying to explain it.

"Not the point. You're not seeing it. They don't have to love me back. Sometimes it's just important to remember that you can feel something for other people, even if they don't feel anything for you."

"Seems like a waste of time," said his brother. "And a world of heartache."

"It's that anyway, isn't it? A world of heartbreak, I mean. A whole wide world."

So he walked around the town from then on as he did before, in the days when he first arrived: alone, talked about, stared at but not spoken to. The only way he could show his affection for the people of Brownsburg was to leave them completely alone, and to accept the same in return.

For a few days after the ministers spoke, the women stayed away from the butcher shop, eating chickens out of their own backyards, until their husbands began to complain and ask for a steak, and then they came back to Will's, but there was a silent understanding that Will would wait on them, that any exchange would be with him, even though they still expected Charlie to be the one who did the actual carving and weighing. His attentions, his extra weight and his fancy butcher's bows, the way he made every package look like a birthday present, went unremarked, as though he weren't there. They just could not see him any more. Now he knew what the colored people in the town felt like.

The Reverend Lewis Shadwell came to see him, sitting in the same stiff way, careful, immaculate, and filled with an anger that rippled across the calm surface of his face.

"We know the truth," he said.

"Who is we, and what truth?" asked Charlie, sitting as stiffly as the preacher, and this time with the same sense of indignation just behind the cool manner.

"I could answer that in several ways, Mister Beale. I could say that we know that the woman is lying. Or we could say that the town is full of hypocrites. Or we could just say that the world is filled with a meanness of spirit which in no way reflects God's love for us."

"The world is what it is."

"A year ago, I told you you weren't welcome to come to us on Sundays. That was a meanness on my part, and I apologize. You would be welcome now."

"I don't want to come any more. But thank you."

"Will you pray with me now? Get down on your knees?"

"No. Thank you."

"Why don't you leave this place?"

"You forget there's a trial. I could go to jail. I could be sent to prison in Harrisonburg for a long time. That's a funny one. Harrison. Burg. Just thought of that."

"You didn't do anything."

"As much as anybody, you should know that a lot of people go to jail who didn't do anything."

"People will speak up for you."

"Trial's in Lexington, you know that. Nobody knows me there. Besides, the only person who has to say anything has said it already, and, for all you know, it's the truth. All kinds of people do all kinds of things."

"Not your kind of people, Mister Beale."

"Kind of you to say. I'm truly grateful."

But the truth is, for Charlie, he wasn't sure that he wasn't that kind of people. Maybe what she said was true. He took her that first time because he had to have her, because there was a fire in his blood, and she had said no before she said yes, and she stayed around because she had nowhere else to go. And so maybe it was true, some time, a while back. And maybe some things you don't get beyond, even if you get to like them later on, live for them, even.

Even after what had happened, she was still the only thing in his life that meant anything to him, really. He would still die for her, and he wouldn't die for anybody else, no matter how much they might touch his heart. Even the boy. Even his own brother. So, inside of him, where the object of his love should have lived, there was nobody at home, and so a void was created, and a terrible stillness descended on Charlie Beale, a stillness in which only he could live, in which he couldn't sleep and felt he could make no sound when he opened his mouth.

"Reverend, thank you for coming. It's my dinner time now."

"I didn't want to come, Mister Beale. Now I don't want to leave. I don't want to leave you alone."

"My brother is here. He keeps me company."

"I save souls, Mister Beale. I've been doing it since I was ten, in a tent in Memphis. I've looked into a thousand eyes, and seen both the grace and the filth that lives behind them. I am looking into your eyes now, Mister Beale. Yours is a clean house."

"Not everybody gets saved, Reverend. Even you . . ."

"Yes. I know, Mister Beale. Even me."

"So."

"So then we're done."

"Afraid so. But I am grateful to you." Charlie held out his hand, and they shook.

"You will rise above, brother. You will rise. So shall we all."

Charlie looked into the reverend's eyes and saw the future of something there, and the reverend looked back into Charlie's and saw the history of the whole world up to that point.

CHAPTER TWENTY-SIX

NED WORRIED. HE was a fretful boy.

He had come all this way to help Charlie, because Charlie had said he needed help, but there was nothing to do for him. Charlie wouldn't get a lawyer, he wouldn't confess or deny, he just held himself, his body and his talking, in a steel blue stillness that could not be broken. Ned smoked the first quarter of eighty cigarettes a day. He emptied ashtrays and swept butts off the porch from the time he got up to the time he went to bed. Lucky Strikes. They cost fifteen cents a pack. He washed Charlie's clothes, left wherever they fell when he took them off. Made him change them when they were dirty. He cooked for him, because Charlie didn't want to burden Will and Alma with his presence any more than he had to.

Everything irritated Charlie. There was not one thing that didn't irritate him. The way hot foods burned his tongue and cold drinks made his teeth hurt. The way his clothes fit, the way the cotton lay against his back, the denim on his legs. The way his pillow held his head at night, not sleeping, tossing, until he finally got up and put on his miserable clothes and went out to the river, to his last piece of property, in the dead of night to stare at the voluptuous moon and wait for the first bird song, irritated, enraged.

But nothing irritated him as much as Jackie Robinson, who brought stinging tears of love to Charlie's eyes, followed by an immediate urge for cruelty. He hated the way the dog looked at him with such pathetic faith, gave himself wholly to Charlie, even in Charlie's neglect of him. There's something about helplessness that makes us despise the helpless. There's something about despair that makes us unable to abide affection. When Charlie paced from room to room, the dog followed him everywhere, nose at his heel, sometimes touching, the hard clack of Charlie's heels on the wood floor, the soft pad of Jackie Robinson. Irritating, relentless.

Sometimes, he would hold the dog in his arms, softly, gently, and lay his head on Jackie's back, just resting there, knowing that the dog would cradle him. And, almost immediately, he would want nothing more than to be rid of him, just because Jackie squirmed, because Jackie wanted to lick his face, to take his wrist gently in his mouth, to love him, for god's sake, and that could not be allowed to happen. He thought that dog would make him crazy.

Jackie Robinson, frightened now, confused by signals he did not grasp, misbehaved, barked, raised his leg in the house, until Charlie got up, grabbed him, and smacked him on the head, something he'd never done before, something he regretted immediately, and saw at that moment that it had gone too far, that whatever had gone wrong between him and the dog was irreversible and would get worse. He grabbed a length of rope, and tied it to Jackie's neck, and led him down the street and forced Alma and Will to take him. He said, "I can't do this. I can't have him any more," and they knew he was telling the truth, and took him in, in the night, not knowing how they were going to keep him, with them gone all day. They could see from Charlie's face that it had become an impossibility.

They took the dog's rope from his hand, and stood with Jackie and watched Charlie walk sadly back up the street and get in his truck to go out to the river and spend the night alone in the chilling air on the hard ground.

He woke up the next morning and everything hurt, stiff, chilled and sweating, as though he had been drunk all night. He saw the river, grasped its beauty, and thought that he could wade in and bathe, but he didn't. It was too far. Everything was too much trouble.

"Have some coffee," Ned said as Charlie walked into the house. "Shave. Change your clothes. One foot in front of the other, that's all."

"Fuck you," said Charlie. "Fuck you, fuck you, fuck you." And the brother just took it, stood there holding out a hot cup of coffee, staring at him the way the dog had, and Charlie felt a wave of love and regret for this brother he didn't know, a blush of shame at his own behavior.

"Get me a lawyer," Charlie said, "Could you figure that out for me?"

"Already have," Ned said. "Just say the word, it's all set."

It was closing in around him, all of it, but he changed his shirt the way Ned asked and went off to work, cutting steaks and roasts and chops all day for women who wouldn't look at him, except for Claudie Wiley, who looked him in the eye and said, as though she knew what the answer might be, "How you doing, Mister Beale." And "Just fine, Miss Wiley" was all he could think of to say, although he knew that she knew that he was lying and would have said more, would have told her everything, knowing that she knew most of it anyway, but there were limits and laws and "just fine" would have to do for all that there was unspoken and felt between them.

She would tell that woman she had seen him, that woman who never came in the store anymore, or the husband either. They had retreated into wherever couples go when they don't want the world to see the bruise of their marriage, and they sent Claudie Wiley into the store to get their meat for them, and she would tell the woman that he was fine and that he had on a clean shirt but that he had not shaved his face, and that would be enough of a message. Everything that was going to be done was almost done, and no message from him through her would change any of that. Claudie had seen it all, made drawings in the night she showed Evelyn Hope and nobody else. The drawings frightened her, but a lot of things frightened Evelyn Hope.

Charlie Beale drove out to the slaughterhouse every Wednesday afternoon, as he always did, most often taking the boy, driving past her house without looking or stopping, wanting to say to Sam, don't ever let this happen to you. Every week, Sam would look out the window and wave, shouting, "Look, Beebo. There's Mrs. Glass. Look, Beebo." But Charlie never turned his head to see her there, perfectly dressed, made up, staring down the hill into the road from her wide porch.

Instead, they talked about the World Series just past. The Yankees had won, breaking Sam's heart, because if the Dodgers lost that meant Jackie Robinson lost personally, although, even if he was listening on the radio, the prospect of the first baseball game played under lights thrilled him and Charlie, both; they could picture the grass lit up to an incandescent green, the white men and Jackie, a black man, now moving in stride with other black men, Newcombe, Campanella, all the men as though in slow motion, shielding their eyes from the unfamiliar glare, the brightness of baseball made brighter by its stark silhouette against the Brooklyn evening. The Fireman, Joe Page, had been named MVP, and Jackie Robinson had gone home to his wife. They had all just gone home, the way they did every October, winners or losers. Sam took this personally.

Charlie and Ned drove over to Lexington after one of those afternoons. Ned had to drive because Charlie was shaking so bad, smoking, drinking a beer in the truck, his shirt still blotched with the blood of animals. They went to see Charlie's new lawyer, Cully Blake, lean and preened and red-faced, already drunk, having been drunk since ten in the morning, as he always was. Cully Blake was white, clean-shaven, with buffed nails, immaculately starched shirts and drunk to the gills from ten a.m. on every day, which did not put him in an unusual position among Southern men of his time and station, and which didn't interfere in any way with the performance of his job, which would have been slack under any conditions. Cully was a lazy, well-bred man of intelligence but no consequence, looking at two oddly matched brothers sitting in his office at day's end and already wondering if his bill would be paid.

Anticipating that, Charlie pulled five hundred dollars in cash from his pocket and laid it on the table. "Think that'll be enough, Mr. Blake?" he asked, and Cully knew it would, without even counting it. He'd seen piles of money before.

"Tell me what happened, Charlie. You don't mind if I call you Charlie?"

"I do. That's my money on the table, Mr. Blake."

"Mr. Beale. Then. Sir. Tell me what happened."

"I didn't do it."

"What did you do? Usually in this kind of case, a man has done something, even if he hasn't done what the woman says he's done."

"I didn't do anything. And I'm not going to talk about it."

"Mrs. Glass says . . ."

"Don't ever mention her name to me again."

"That's going to be a little difficult."

"Hard or easy, that's the way it is."

"She'll say things in court. Things you don't want to have said in public."

"Whatever she says, that's what happened."

"You look guilty, Mister Beale." Blake said, thinking now only of his next drink of whiskey. "You have the look of a guilty man."

"That could be. Every man has done something. I've done things. Plenty of things. I just didn't do this. I didn't do this thing. Good evening, Mister Blake. Let me know when to be in court."

They drove home in the autumn dark without talking. Charlie, drinking another beer, thought, How can you give so much of yourself without love? How can you do that thing with your body, your lips and breasts and tongue, and not feel some trace of love in your heart? Confused, troubled, and not less confused as he drank beer after beer, he who rarely touched alcohol, now on his way to being solidly drunk for the first time in a long time.

They sat up late, drinking in the near dark of Charlie's kitchen, Ned talking softly from time to time. Charlie crying, sometimes just tears running down his face in horrible, flowing silence, sometimes huge, heaving sobs.

And all he said, with the vehement enunciation of the totally drunk, before he lurched up to bed, was, "I dint do anything. Did. Dent."

CHAPTER TWENTY-SEVEN

N O SIR."

A six-year-old boy in a scratchy new wool suit and an immaculate white shirt to which is affixed a clip-on bow tie, all of it from Mr. Swink's in Lexington, this little boy sits on a hard wooden chair in an almost empty courtroom in Lexington, the county seat of Rockbridge County in the Commonwealth of Virginia, and he perjures himself, he lies and lies over and over again until they just stop asking him questions, knowing that he is going to hell for telling a lie, and knowing that telling twenty is no worse than telling one, he lies because he knows that the thing they're asking is part of the bargain he made with Charlie long ago never to speak to anybody of certain things, and knowing that if he does speak of these things, that something terrible will happen to Charlie that is far worse than the fires of the hell he knows are waiting for him.

Be a good boy, his mother had told him; just tell the truth. But he knew he couldn't do that, he didn't know what it was that would happen if he did tell, Charlie had never told him, but he knew it would be something worse than any pain he had known, worse than gasping for breath in the gray river water, losing his sight, his breath, until he finally gave in and just sank. Worse than that.

When he made his promise to Charlie, in the truck on that cold fall day a year ago, it really hadn't occurred to him to question what such a promise might mean, or how he was to carry it out when the time came. He had been raised to tell the truth, and he did, and he answered the questions that came at him in the same way. Yes, he threw the rock that broke the window. No, he hadn't done his homework. His mother said that it was so much easier telling the truth because then you didn't have to remember what you said; if the question was asked again, you'd naturally answer in the same way.

The first lie was the hardest, because it was his mother who was doing the asking, and he loved her, and he knew she didn't want to see him in hell, and he knew that she didn't deserve this, not from him or from anybody, and he understood instantly that she knew he was lying, that every time he lied, the lie would be as clear and hard as a glass windowpane before the rock went through it.

Things are so easily shattered, and once they're broken, certain things are broken forever. They don't heal. They don't come back.

"No, ma'am," he said, he had never seen Charlie and Mrs. Glass together, and his mother looked at him in a certain way, with a slight hesitation before her eyes blinked again, and he knew that she would never look at him again any other way but that, never look at him as she always had. She looked sad, broken, somehow, broken in a way that she would have to go on living with.

"Are you sure? Never?"

"No, ma'am. Never. I'm sure."

"Not once?"

"She came into Daddy's store. I guess . . ." He looked her straight in the eye. It was horrible, and it hurt his heart like a knife. It was a pain in his blood.

"I mean, outside the store. Alone."

"No, ma'am. Never alone."

Which was almost true. Because, except for that first time, when he waited in the truck, he was always there, he was with them, and so they couldn't have been alone in the way she meant. Jackie Robinson had been there, too, and even a dog counted for something, didn't he?

"Remember something, Sam. Always remember this. If you behave badly, or make a mistake, you can act better or do it over and nobody will mind. But if you tell one lie, just one, you will be a liar forever. Do you understand that?"

"Yes, ma'am."

Every lie like a stab in his heart, but easier every time, the pain lessening, his brain hardening around the fact that he had become a person who did not, who would not, tell the truth.

He didn't tell Beebo about the lies, about the questions. Beebo knew, and he seemed to treat the boy with a new respect, a greater kindness than ever before. There was no need for them to talk about it. It was just a fact, and now everybody was keeping secrets, and everybody was lying. Lying about what they knew. Lying about who they were.

They went fishing again, just the two of them, with the dog. They went to look for eagles on the top of House Mountain. Sam had never seen the world from so high up. The carpet of the valley lay spread out far beneath him, and he asked a thousand questions, and Charlie answered every one of them, patiently, and with such enormous gentleness, pointing out where their town lay, Sam's house, a tiny dot among a thousand other tiny dots. Charlie pointed out, as well, the farms and rivers and waterfall that had once belonged to him.

Their companionship was closer and more constant than ever, but there was a kind of farewell feeling in it, too. Sam learned for the first time that you didn't say everything that came into your mind, that most things that came into your mind, in fact, went unsaid, unremarked, left there to wonder at and be troubled by. He didn't even know what it was Charlie was supposed to have done, but he knew enough not to ask.

In the weeks before the trial, Charlie seemed nervous all the time. He tried to make Sam feel better, even though they never discussed what it was that was making Sam feel bad. He just knew, and he seemed sometimes to be close to crying about it, but they never talked about that, just other things, but those other things in such a way that Sam knew Charlie was trying to give him all his strength and courage.

Charlie drove the boy all the way into Lexington to have soft ice cream, and to see a movie, just the two of them. They saw *Red River*, and even Sam could see that Charlie looked like that actor in the picture. One night, Charlie pointed to the sky and named a star after Sam Haislett, but the boy couldn't find it the next night or the next, or ever.

Now, on a very warm October day with all the courtroom windows wide open, Sam was doing the thing he knew was right, even if he also knew it was wrong. He was saying nothing.

There were very few people in the courtroom, other than the judge, the lawyers, and the officers of the court. There was a policeman who never took his eyes off Sam. His mother and father. Claudie Wiley. The man who was asking him questions. Charlie and his lawyer, Charlie dressed in a brand new suit from J. Ed Deaver's on Main Street, the tie knotted too tight at his neck. His brother, Ned, was there, looking like death warmed over. The only people from the town who had come were the twins, and they sat right behind Charlie. They were too old to care about what their minister said about not going to the trial, they figured they were so old they were either going to hell or they weren't, probably weren't, and one day in court just to sit and show Charlie Beale that he did have a friend in the world wasn't going to make a damned bit of difference in their fate for eternity.

And, of course, sitting at the other table was Mrs. Glass, all in black, with a hat and white short gloves, and, behind her, her husband, smooth as silk, so calm you might have thought he was asleep, except that his black Boatwright eyes stared at Sam, and even he knew Sam was lying every time he opened his mouth.

"Do you know what lying is, Sam?" the tall, ugly prosecutor asked.

"Yes," said Sam. He surely did know that one thing, if nothing else.

"What is lying, Sam?"

"It's when you don't tell the truth."

"And what happens to little boys who lie?"

"They go to hell," Sam said, in a voice so soft the judge asked him to repeat his answer.

"They go to hell," Sam almost yelled.

"Yes!" the lawyer yelled back. "But first you know where they go before they go to hell? They go to jail. They go to jail, Sam, and they don't ever go to school, or see their mama and daddy ever again, and, if they live, *if* they live, they grow up to be as mean and ignorant as the coloreds. Is that what you want, Sam, because I'm pretty sure you're lying right now."

"Your Honor." Cully Blake rose unsteadily from his seat. "The prosecutor is badgering and unmercifully threatening a six-year-old boy. He's said what he knows, and what he knows is nothing. For shame, sir." He turned to the prosecutor with a magisterial turn of his neck in its white collar, so starched you could hear the rasp of the cloth against his red neck.

"Please stick to the facts, sir," said the judge.

"He's lying, Your Honor," said the prosecutor.

"Well, then either catch him at it, or leave him alone. That's an order."

"Okay, then." The prosecutor turned to Sam. "Let's try this another way. You say they were never alone together?"

"No, sir."

"You didn't say it, or they weren't alone?"

What was the right answer? Sam spoke out of confusion. "I think they weren't not ever alone."

"Well, then, when they weren't alone together, did they ever talk to one another?"

"No, sir."

"Did they ever touch each other, when they weren't alone together?"

"Objection." Blake rose again to his feet.

"Overruled," the judge said. "Sit down, Mister Blake. I'll allow it, for now."

"And when they weren't alone together, did Charlie ever kiss Mrs. Glass?"

"No, sir."

"Take their clothes off?"

He had seen her. He had seen all of her, and the picture of her body in his mind was so sharp and bright, it was almost as if he had touched her himself. She had made him cookies and given him funny books, and then they had gone into another room and she had taken her clothes off and he knew what it sounded like more than he knew what it looked like, and he understood the sounds better than he understood the picture of her, so bending, so everywhere, so blonde.

"No, sir."

"Damn it. I give up. You're lying, Sam. You know it. I know it. Everybody knows it, including the God who will put you in hell and the judge who will put you . . ."

"Objection."

"Sustained."

". . . in prison for a long time. Sorry, Your Honor. I have one more question. Sam. When you were alone with Charlie, did he ever say anything about Mrs. Glass?"

Sam just sat for a long time. Jail, one night in jail away from his mother and father, frightened him almost to tears, and hell was forever, that much he knew.

"Sam?"

"Yes, sir," he replied, in a tiny voice.

"Speak up, Sam. Speak up. What did Charlie say?"

"Beebo said . . . he said he would die for her."

"What?"

"Die for her. He said he would die for her."

"Thank you, Sam. He just might do that."

Blake said he had no questions, speaking with a flourish about the child's age and the tenderness of his youth and so on, and Sam just sat there until they told him it was time to go, that he could go back and sit with his parents. His mother took his hand and squeezed it tight, and he knew that it wasn't over like they said. It was far from over.

Next came Claudie Wiley, dressed, fantastically, as though for a Negro Baptist wedding in New York City, bright in fuschia, cut from a pattern she had found in the back of *Vogue* magazine, and adapted to suit her figure, with a hat to match, and a veil, and shoes, all the same intense color, the color of sunset, the last burst of color before the darkness falls.

She swore on the Bible, and she did mean, in fact, to tell the

truth, because, even though she hated what she had to say, her fear
of white men and courtrooms was so great, she felt compelled, lest
she lose her freedom, her daughter, her hope. White men would do
you in, she knew that for sure, and not even think twice about it.
Send a six-year-old white boy to prison? It would not ever happen.
But a black woman who kept her own and minded little else? They
would leave her in the darkness and her daughter would go to char-
ity and that would kill them both.

"Now, Claudie," said the prosecutor, whom she hated immediately.

"Aren't you supposed to call me Miz Wiley, or something?" she
asked.

"I can call you anything I want, but if you want Mrs. Wiley,
then I'll call you that. In fact, are you Mrs. Wiley? I mean, is there
a Mr. Wiley?"

"Not anymore."

"Ever, was there ever?"

"Not exactly."

"Well, have it your way. Mrs. Wiley," he almost spat at her,
"how well do you know Mrs. Harrison Glass?"

"Right well, Your Honor."

"I'm not the judge. The judge, who is sitting there, is called
'Your Honor.'"

"Excuse me. She's my only friend, just about."

"And did Mrs. Glass ever talk to you about Charlie Beale?"

"All the time. That's hardly all she ever talks about any more."

"And what does she say?"

"She say how cute he is, how he looks like some actor in the movies. We saw him in a movie last week. He didn't seem like a very nice man, that actor, in that movie."

"In real life, is Charlie Beale a nice man?"

"I guess. He has the power. He has the gift."

"What gift, Mrs. Wiley?"

"The healing gift. I saw it."

"Did she say anything specific to you, anything particular, about Charlie Beale in the first week of September?"

She was a queen, Claudie. She sat alone in the witness box, trembling with terror and excitement both, reveling in the attention and fighting for her life.

"She said he raped her. She said he raped her three times."

"Three times?"

"Yes, sir. She was very particular. She made me write it down." She pulled a piece of paper out of her handbag. "He raped her on November eighteenth, 1948, April twelfth, 1949, and then just the last week in August, right after he saved that boy, on the twenty-fourth."

"May I see that piece of paper?" Claudie handed it to the prosecutor, and he showed it to the judge, then to Blake, and then he entered it into evidence.

"Did she say how he did it?"

"He did it the usual way, I guess. He would bring that boy to see her, and, while she was playing with the boy, he would just up and grab her and rape her with the boy right there."

"And how many times?"

"Asked and answered," objected Blake.

"Three. Three times."

The prosecutor seemed much nicer to her now. "Thank you, Mrs. Wiley. You have been very helpful. Your witness," he said to Blake, and then he sat down, smugly.

Mr. Blake got up. He didn't get too close to her, like the prosecutor did. He didn't like to stand close to people, in case they could smell the whiskey on his breath.

"Mrs. Wiley, that is a very beautiful dress you have on."

"Thank you."

"You also make dresses for Mrs. Glass, don't you?"

"Yes, sir."

"And you're friends as well, yes?"

"I guess so. I guess she's about the only friend I have."

"How many times have you seen Mrs. Glass in the last year?"

"A lot of times. 'Bout once or twice a week."

"A hundred times?"

"Maybe could be."

"And in all that time, did Mrs. Glass ever mention these alleged rapes before that one time?"

"No, sir, she did not."

"Not on November nineteenth, right after it happened the first time?"

"No, sir."

"Or on April thirteenth, the second time?"

"No, sir."

Claudie's rehearsals with Sylvan hadn't gone this far. Sylvan had thought just the statement of the dates would be enough, the specific times, the hour, the setting, all these had been gone over, but they didn't seem to be of any interest now, and Claudie knew that her friend was expecting her to lie for her, but friendship with any white woman didn't go that far. Claudie wasn't going to be caught out and sent to jail just because a white woman asked her to.

"Not even the day after August twenty-fourth? The last time?"

"No, sir, she never said a word."

"When did she first tell you about these alleged rapes?"

"About two weeks ago, sir."

"And when you finally heard her confession, her story of these brutal rapes that had been going on for a year, almost, how did you feel?"

"At first I felt sorry. She cares for him. I believe she does."

"And then?"

"I didn't believe her."

"Objection, Your Honor. Speculation."

"Overruled."

"And then, Mrs. Wiley?"

"I didn't and I don't. I don't believe her."

"Objection. This is pure speculation."

The judge ignored the prosecutor's protests and excused Claudie, who left the chair as though leaving the throne, a queen deposed, but with her head held high.

The bailiff called Mrs. Harrison Glass, and the two women, so close as to be sisters only moments before, passed each other without a glance.

As Sylvan walked through the swinging gate that led to the witness stand, Charlie stood slightly, and turned to look at her, and he spoke in a voice so hushed and breathy that only Elinor and Ansolette, sitting directly behind him, could hear.

"Sylvan," he said. She stopped, but didn't turn to him. "Girl, what's done is done. Don't do this thing, don't say it. Not to my face. Not in front of the boy."

Sylvan stepped into the witness box and stood, looking around, as though she didn't know what she was supposed to do. The jury looked at her, her posture, her black dress copied from a movie, the white gloves, which she removed with agonizing care.

A Bible was placed in front of her, and she was asked to place her left hand on it, and she did, shyly, not sure at all of what was supposed to happen.

"Do you solemnly swear to tell the truth, the whole truth, and nothing but the truth?"

And then they just waited. She was frozen in her stiff posture, her black dress and her veiled hat, her golden hair, like some statue of elegance and mourning.

"Mrs. Glass?"

"Can you repeat that?"

"Do you solemnly swear to tell the truth, the whole truth, and nothing but the truth?"

She coughed, she cleared her throat, and then she spoke in a small, elegant voice, the voice she had learned so patiently and so carefully on so many afternoons in the dark, her voice that came to her twenty-five cents at a time, in the dark, from the mouths of women she would never meet and never ever be, no matter how she might dream.

"No. I don't believe I will. I don't believe I will do that. You must excuse me."

And then she calmly put her gloves back on, the left and then the right, lowered the black veil of her hat to shield her eyes, and she stepped from the witness box and walked slowly through the courtroom, then through the door and down the steep marble steps, wiping the lipstick from her mouth with a white lace hand-kerchief, and moving into the fall sun. And then it was over.

It was the last moment of full possession she was ever to have. Just twenty years old, and she had, at the same moment, finally become most completely a self she would never be again.

She had had her closeup.

Whatever she did, she was not a bad girl. Whatever you think, she was not a bad girl.

Life had been hard on her, and now she had been hard back.

CHAPTER TWENTY-EIGHT

S HE LAY IN bed for two weeks, and did nothing but weep. She wept so hard, so convulsively, that her body hurt. When she got up, finally, he beat her so badly she was in bed for another week. There was, for her, no longer anything to hold on to, nothing to let go of. Except one thing: She still had her secret, the pieces of paper locked beneath the floorboards of the attic.

When she got up, it was to be Mrs. Harrison Glass, nothing more than that. Her Hollywood finery, all her fancy things, stayed shut away, and she passed her days in house dresses that hid her shape and showed her station. Until one day, five days after she could get out of bed and the swelling had gone down, she took all that stuff, those dresses that Claudie had spent hours and hours making, the green dress she had worn when she pulled the boy from the water, all that dressing up for Charlie, for show, for pretend, she took it all out into the backyard and poured gasoline all over her clothes and set it all on fire, watching as the person she had tried to be went up in flames. She cried as she watched them burn up. Her clothes. Her self. If she was not to be the thing she had dreamed of being, what, then, was she to be? Who was she?

Why wasn't everything the way it was in the movies? Why had the screen gone dark? When she made up the character she had played, her face flickering with the luminosity of the silver screen in her shining eyes, who was it she was supposed to be? The flames told her nothing. She was an unschooled country girl who had learned everything she knew from people who were not real, and she had loved Charlie Beale, that much was sure. And she had known, briefly, blindly, the moment she had waited for, in the dark.

There ain't nothing after this, she thought. There is no after.

He had been her whole movie, her movie star, but had she loved him? She had loved the way he looked, his posture, the way he moved, the way he laughed quietly with the boy over some man's foolishness, fish or bird or rock, she had loved him before he ever came to her that first time, but then he had come, and he was no longer the flickering brightness she saw behind her lids when she closed her eyes at night and let in the dark, let him in to steal her heart and her soul, in the dark, in her dreams. When he had come, he had been smells, and skin, and a mouth that was all over her, and his weight scared her, his hands, his body, so real, so tight and muscled, smaller than her own, but coiled with power and need, need of her and for her, an endless need that was not a dream, that did not flicker, that was never-ending, and she couldn't have that, couldn't accept it, couldn't endure it, and so she had shut the door in his face, had turned out the lights and sat in the dark, every inch of her skin wanting every inch of his skin, just like in the movie, shutting him out, the only natural man she'd ever known, the fullest, richest being who had ever come to her, and she just couldn't take it.

She told herself that she had acted to save her parents the misery of loss, to pay back a debt of care that was owed. She told herself that she did it because Boaty would have killed him. But she dimly knew somehow that she did it because she preferred the fantasy of the movie in her mind to the reality of Charlie Beale.

So now she wandered her husband's property in her plain housecoat, widowed but still married, in mourning for a man she had never really known. She crawled into thickets and lay down in the cool damp of the autumn woods and touched herself, remembering his hands on her, feeling the waves of pleasure, imagining him again, but this time as a shadow without weight or breath, without smell or sound or a hunger that surpassed her own.

She knew that she had ruined his life. She was not unaware. But men recover. They go on. He was forty years old, and filled with a desire and a craziness for love that was too big, too desperate. She was pretty sure that his heart had been broken before, and hadn't he come to her anyway?

The leaves fell around her in the woods, the birds flew south, as she sat with her skirt hiked up around her waist and tried to play in her head the movie in which she could live out the rest of her life, the never-ending reel of her fantasy.

She called Boaty Mister Glass, now, when she was with him. He called her nothing, slept apart, wouldn't touch her or come near her. He seemed to be figuring out what to do with her. Throw her out, yes, but she'd cost a lot of money, and you don't throw good equipment away. She made his supper, and behaved herself, as far as he could tell, and she'd taken down those foolish pictures and burned up her embarrassing clothes, and stopped her damned talk of Hedy Lamarr and such, so, for now, he'd just wait and see how she turned out.

He was older. He'd never been attractive. He just didn't have the taste for the hunt right now. Besides, the horse was already out of the barn. He saw the looks in people's faces, felt their eyes on his back when he walked away. A man whose wife had cheated on him. They'd been snickering at him all his grown life, so what if they snickered now?

Besides, now that the truth was out, or whatever version of it people took to be the truth, he was freed from the awful burden of having to touch her, visit her in the night, and all that mess was behind him. No more romancing. Better his own hands, his magazines, in his mother's bed, in the dark, and breakfast on the table.

He couldn't stand her now, couldn't take the sight of her for very long, but, as long as his house was clean and his food was on the table, why look for more trouble? She belonged to him, bought with good money, and he didn't feel much like throwing out good property.

No, he would keep her, keep her like Rapunzel in her tower, knowing that no prince would come near her, ever again. He would put up with the stares and the snide grins, knowing that they'd go

away, in time. He'd even put up with having to see Charlie Beale
every now and then, as long as the man didn't open his mouth or
look at him in any way. Truth is, Boaty was both lazy and a cow-
ard, and he knew that confronting Charlie would take a whole lot
of doing, and that Charlie would probably kill him if he tried any
funny stuff on him. If the man had any sense, he'd just go away,
the same way he'd come, back to wherever he came from, or onto
the next new place and the next man's wife.

One day Sylvan took the car keys from where she knew Boaty
had hidden them—he wasn't that complicated—and she drove
into town to see Claudie Wiley, but Claudie, even though her car
was parked right in front of her house, wouldn't open the door
when she knocked, again and again. Finally she drew back the blind
on the glass-paned door—because she was in business and maybe
it was a customer with a hem or an alteration—and stared straight
at Sylvan for a full minute, before she let the curtain drop and disappeared back into the silence of her house, her life measured out
in stitches. Claudie would never open the door to her again. She'd
open it to any other woman with a bolt of cloth and a dream, but
not to her.

Sylvan drove into Lexington and walked into the State Theater one more time, not even looking up to see what was on the
marquee. She sat herself down in her usual seat, thinking for a
second of Claudie upstairs in the Negro balcony with her sketch
pad, thinking of the days when that had been good and possible,
and then she drew a breath as the lights went down and the picture
began to roll on the screen. The same silver light, the same bright

faces with their handsome, big features that seemed to throw off light into a darkened world, but there was nothing there for her. Not any more. She left the theater, walking out into the blinding fall sunshine of Nelson Street, searching for her car keys in her purse, trying to see her way through the blinding, chilly brightness, back to her car, back to her life, back to her self. Back to being a country girl she did not know and had never known.

CHAPTER TWENTY-NINE

THE FIRST WEDNESDAY in December that year came on the seventh. It was Pearl Harbor Day and the flags were out, there would be services in every church in the afternoon to honor the almost five thousand who were killed or injured on that awful day only eight years before, every man and woman in town wore a little rosette to mourn the tragedy, so fresh in their minds, that day of infamy, as they all thought. But it was getting on toward Christmas, so there were also Christmas decorations hanging along with the flags, and there was a lot of butchering and planning to be done. Things went on in the world; Chiang Kai-shek fled China for Taiwan, but hardly anybody in Brownsburg noticed. The fate of millions of Chinese people didn't matter nearly as much as the fate of the souls they lived beside every day. The rich soil of the undulating, stony county lay still and mute, cold but not frozen yet. The land, rocky as it was, had been kind to its people, and they were pretty generally kind to one another in return. Maybe that was something that the land whispered, maybe that was the message — there is kindness. There is kindness everywhere. Hard won, long remembered and rarely noticed, but there. There forever.

Charlie Beale woke up in despair, as he did, as he did every morning now. At least he woke up in his bed this time, and not on the sofa or the kitchen floor, where he had found himself too many mornings since that morning, that morning she had walked from the court and out of his life, changing the course of that life beyond recognition.

Even though he looked the same to the people he passed, the people who now both loved and shunned him, he was unrecognizable to himself. It took an hour every morning for him to take a familiar shape again, eyewash to clear his eyes, a hot bath to wash away the night sweats, the slick sheen of fear and rage that covered his body in the night. His body, thinner now but somehow stronger still, lay inert in the bath, and all the night terrors gradually were rinsed away, dissipated in the water as the water cooled, and when he felt, even for a moment, at peace, he rose dripping from the water as he had from the river — so long ago, that — and he dressed, and crept past the door to the room where his brother slept, whiskey and sawdust, that wiry boy who had come and showed no signs of leaving, as though he knew beyond knowing that Charlie Beale could not live alone now, could not feed himself or ask for the help he needed, had to get it from somewhere and that somewhere might as well be his own flesh and blood, at least that comfort.

It was hard for Charlie, now, to face Alma. It was her warmth he couldn't take, because he knew it was a warmth mixed with disapproval, and rightly so—her disapproval of what his lust had led him to. She was never less than kind, but now she was afraid, too, afraid for him and, of course, afraid for her boy. She and Will had talked the night before. The outings had to stop, they agreed, some way had to be found to separate the man from the boy, even though Sam seemed to be Charlie's only comfort now, and it broke Alma's heart even to think it, but it had to be done. Sam spent half the day in school now, and he should be playing with boys his own age, other first-graders. At least that was the reason she gave, while Sam listened from the top step.

She was just putting on the coffee pot when she saw Charlie pass on his way to open the shop. He wasn't wearing a coat, and his cuffs were unbuttoned. Alma thought that both of these things were a sure sign of mental disturbance. Crazy people didn't wear enough clothes in the winter, and they wore too many in the summer. He seemed, to her, not to know where he was, although he walked steadily and directly toward the butcher shop. Before—when it was before—he might have stopped in for a cup of her coffee and one of her biscuits. He hadn't done that since then, since that day in October. A man who was innocent, but who had sinned. Now a prisoner of sin, as the good book said. She measured out the coffee and wondered what to do. So much happens, she thought, when you've got biscuits in the oven. Her heart went out to him, but she didn't call out or wave. She didn't know what she would have said if he had come in, which he wouldn't have done anyway. Not now.

Charlie made his way down the street in the new light of a

December day, and opened the shop and flipped on the lights. He went through the familiar routines of sweeping the floor, checking the freezer, washing down the butcher block. Everything seemed tender to him, everything fragile. The sad, cold beef in the locker, the coarse salt and steel brush on the wood, the bleach on the marble counter. His own hands doing these things, sweeping, scrubbing, making ready for the day, the day he could not envision or enter, although he was there, he was doing these things, he was making do. Just don't ask any questions, he silently begged Will, who was still at the breakfast table. At the last, he raised the flag on the pole outside the shop, to honor the dead and the day.

When Will came in at nine, everything was in perfect order, the slicer and the grinder shining, the knives whetted into razor sharpness, the goods, the chops and ground meat laid out in the case. "Pearl Harbor Day," said Will, handing Charlie a brown paper bag that had, he knew, an egg and bacon sandwich that they both knew he would not eat. "Sad."

"Yes, sir," said Charlie.

"Lose anybody?"

"Not there."

"No. Me neither. Still."

"Yes."

"A lot of boys."

The morning began, the black women coming in first, as always, counting out their money in quarters and nickels, speaking little. Then came the parade of white women, all of them talking only to

Will while Charlie waited on them, each wishing in her heart that she might be the one to save the man who had saved the boy, and each knowing that it was not she, if any such person existed, with the power to bring him back into the fold. Once done, it was done forever, beyond amelioration or exoneration, or even acceptance. If they ever forgot that fact for a moment, their preachers had reminded them every Sunday, and their faith kept that truth in their hearts, as much as it saddened them.

If he knelt among them and begged for salvation, as Sylvan had done, if the preacher laid on the hands and made him whole, it might be different. But that, Charlie wouldn't do, and so it was the way it was.

They all wished something else, something they could not say even to themselves. Each wished she had been the one, the woman. There was not one among them who would not have gone to hell with him, just like that Glass girl did, not one who would not have opened her door to him, whatever the ferocity of her belief.

But they just told Will what they needed for the day, and took the packages from Charlie without a word, noticing, as they did, how thin he'd grown, how sad, how marked by his own infamous sin. Yes, he had saved the boy, but, still, the mighty are often fallen and even the divine are sometimes damned. They were kind, or thought themselves so, but they were not forgiving. Perhaps God would be — they were certain of it — but not them.

By noon, most of the ladies had come and gone, and Sam ran in from school. A boy had peed on the floor and the teacher had called him a baby and made him sit in a high chair for the rest of the day. That was the most exciting thing pretty much ever at school, and Sam was just glad it wasn't him.

They had pork chops for lunch, fried in a black cast-iron skillet. Ned joined them, hungover, looking like he couldn't find his way to the door even if you left it open. Alma tried not to let her sadness show, the loss of respect, the anger she felt in her heart toward this man who had brought her own, her only boy, back from the dead in what she still believed was a miracle. The men ate well. She ate little.

"Sam? You ready to go see the cows?" Charlie turned to him.

"Will?" asked Alma, looking at her husband. They had talked, hadn't they?

"Oh, let the boy go, Alma. It's a beautiful cold day, he could use the fresh air, now that he's cooped up all morning at school."

Alma rushed back to her classes, the dishes still in the sink, where, by nightfall, they would bring such a rush of tears to her eyes that she would have to grab the counter to stop herself from falling.

By nightfall, she could only think of all the things she had meant to say, about forgiveness, about her gratitude that the life of her boy would continue, the continuance making everything else possible, almost all else bearable, except this, her own neglect. By nightfall, she could only wonder, staring at the dishes, trying to think of how people were to be fed, how they were to go on, one supper after the next. She could only think, There are no fires of hell. There is only mercy.

But that was later. After lunch, Ned walked back home to read his mysteries and replace a rotted board on the back porch, and Will went back to the shop to wait for the customers who never came, whittling the afternoon away, talking to other shop owners, knowing he'd close up the shop at three thirty to join Alma for services for the dead boys.

Charlie gathered his knives from the shop, Sam got the baseball glove he took everywhere now, except to school, where it was not allowed. Then Charlie hoisted the boy into the cab of the truck, and waited for Jackie to jump into the front seat. They drove out of town about one thirty, listening to the radio.

"Beebo, why are there flags everywhere?"

"Something bad happened on this day, Sam."

"What happened?"

How to explain the awfulness of that cataclysm, that grinding of metal under bomb, those men sitting there like ducks in a pond, the bombers coming out of nowhere and raining fire? How to explain the death toll, the mothers and fathers bereft, the president on the radio? How to explain the size of it to a six-year-old boy?

"It was in the war, before you were born. Some planes came and dropped bombs and a lot of people died."

Suddenly, their favorite song came on the radio, and its magic lightened their hearts, and Charlie and Sam laughed and sang along with the Count Basie Orchestra.

> Did you see Jackie Robinson hit that ball?
> It went zoomin cross the left field wall.
> Yeah boy, yes, yes. Jackie hit that ball.

Young again, young and free and completely at ease, Charlie sang at the top of his lungs, and pulled on his Lucky Strike and threw the butt out the window, but the sparks were invisible in the bright rushing sun.

Yes, yes, yes. . . Jackie's a real gone guy.

The song ended as they passed her house, as they always did, except this time she was standing on the porch, and this time Charlie did look up and over, and he saw her, a simple girl on a plain, whitewashed porch, his girl once. No, this time he saw her clearly, not a movie starlet anymore, those days were gone and would not return, but he saw her as she was, as God had made her, and he saw also his fields and his houses, the house in the woods, and he wanted her beyond belief. He drove on with only the slightest hesitation, the tiniest slowing of the black truck. He tousled the boy's hair, sang, "Yes, yes, yes, Jackie's a real gone guy," even though some other song had come on the radio, and it seemed as though they had never done more than look, had not stopped that first time on the road, then driven through the gate and hidden the truck behind the house.

CHARLIE SEEMED SUDDENLY FREE at last, as though the charges had finally been dismissed just this minute. He was free of guilt, free of property, and he laughed with the boy and talked about exactly how long it was until spring training, and what Sam supposed the real Jackie Robinson was doing right that very minute, up there in Connecticut where he lived. Playing with his kids, Sam guessed. Taking a nap, as Sam had to do, still, every day except Wednesday, when he went to the slaughterhouse with Charlie. On those days he had to go to bed early to make up for it, even though he stayed awake, as he always did now, until the whole street was asleep and dark, in case he missed anything, in case somebody decided to creep into the house and murder his whole family, his mother and father, whom he guarded fiercely in the dark.

THE SLAUGHTERING WENT QUICKLY. Sam waited outside with Jackie, messing around. There weren't flies, this time of year, not much for Jackie to chase, so Sam and Jackie played ball, the thud of the ball in his glove, the racing of the dog and the return of the ball, all slimed up, until the palm of his mitt was dark with the dog's spit; Charlie inside, cutting, carving, doing his work, during which he didn't like to be interrupted, couldn't play catch with a boy.

DONE AND WASHED, THE sides of beef hanging in the coolers, the back of the truck filled with steaks and chops and rumps and legs, covered with a clean white cloth, Charlie came out, his sharpest knife in its leather case hanging from his belt, and he looked at the boy, and he looked like a boy himself again, fresh and ready and rested, and he and Sam threw the ball back and forth while Jackie raced in and out of their legs, trying to steal it. Charlie caught the ball, and jumped and spun in the air like a shortstop, magic in the fluidity and grace of his motion, and threw gently, more gently than his arm motion would suggest, and landed the ball smack in Sam's glove.

"Out! Out at first!" Sam yelled, and threw the ball over his head, so high he could barely see it, and felt the wonder as Charlie ran forward and caught the falling ball, catching Sam up in his arms at the same time, swinging him around, racing for home, a graceful, continuing motion that landed Sam in the truck, the ball in his mitt in his lap, and Jackie beside him, the truck gunning to life, a Lucky lit, the radio back on, country songs now, the high twang of the mountains, the lonely fiddle and chattering banjo.

On the road, Charlie drove faster than ever, until they rounded the corner and there was her house, and she was still on the porch, and even Sam could tell from her face that she was sad, like her dog had just been run over. A flowered housecoat was open at the knees, her feet bare even in December, barely twenty-one years old and alone in her grief, but Charlie drove on past, looking, swiveling his head, drove about fifty yards past the house, then slammed on the brakes, throwing the boy and the dog against the dash, the ball rolling onto the floor. He stopped and backed up as fast as he had gone by, and then he just sat and the two of them, Charlie and Sylvan, just stared at each other for a minute.

Then Charlie threw his Lucky Strike out the open window, and turned to Sam. "I'll be back in a minute. There's something I have to do. Be a good boy, Sam. Take care of Jackie." He touched the boy on the head, and looked in his eyes, and kissed him for only the second time, this time on his head. He tousled the boy's hair and then he was out of the truck and through the gate and up the hill, roaring her name, walking fast, head down. He had one hand up, but Sam couldn't tell whether he was waving hello to the woman whose name he called out or good-bye to him. Charlie and Sylvan met, and stood staring at each other without a word, then she abruptly turned and he followed her into the house.

On the radio, Doc Watson was singing, "Go with me little Omie, and away we will go, we'll go and get married and no one will know." Then Sam heard the first noise, her scream, the first of seven that afternoon, and he got out of the truck, Jackie at his heels, and he ran up to the yard, and stood in front of the house, and listened, trying to tell where the noises came from, first downstairs, then upstairs. They were terrible noises, Charlie bellowing, Sylvan's screams punctuating the roar, the clatter of breaking dishes and chairs, everything upside down.

Hadn't they been singing just a minute before, Charlie and Sam? Hadn't Charlie swiveled in the air like a boy, and kissed him on his head where his hair still felt warm?

These were not the noises they usually made. Sam was frightened, and thought of climbing the porch steps and looking through the window, but he was too afraid. Whatever was happening was only between the two of them, and he didn't want to see it, was frightened to know what it was.

They were in the attic now, he could tell from the noise, and everything was ripping and turning over and breaking. And then it was quiet for about ten minutes, not a sound, then back down the stairs with more noise, and Sam backed away, backed away from what he knew was coming toward him, seeking air, a witness, and he didn't want to be a witness, didn't want to know what had been happening. He usually did, he usually did want to know what happened, to know what things meant, their secret reason for being, but this thing he wanted to back away from and not have the knowing, not have the memory that would be in his head forever. Then there was another long period of silence, another ten, fifteen minutes, no sound except Charlie barking short, blunt orders, and those were even more frightening.

But it started again, the screams, her name bellowed, the name Charlie hadn't said once since that day, not even spoken to her except that once, in court, and that so low that it couldn't be heard—but it was, by the twins, they heard and they told.

Then Sylvan came out of the door, and Sam knew what it was.

Sylvan came out of the door, and across her chest like a constellation of red stars were seven stab wounds, blood everywhere, seeping and spurting, a savage show of blood across the gaudy flowers of her country housedress and then she fell dead, her last scream ending in a lowing, keening sigh that came only at the end, as she fell on her face, down the steps, sliding, bouncing until she lay dead, half on the steps, her face in the yard, the blood flowing downhill to drip from the stairs and pool in the yard around her face, Charlie following after, the knife in one hand, bloodied, in the other a manila envelope, also crimson, everything red and slick with blood.

Charlie stepped over Sylvan's body, looking down, seeing what he had done, making Sam afraid for a minute that he was going to bend over and carve her up. But he straightened and howled one last time, a howl of grief at the ending of things, of everything, then he just looked and walked to where Sam stood, crying now. "Beebo. Beebo," the boy said, almost in a whisper, a pleading for it to stop, for it not to have happened, because he understood what had happened, didn't even have to be grown to be familiar with the sharp steel smell of dying.

Charlie stood above the boy, the boy he had brought back from the dead, and he dropped the envelope on the ground and reached out to place his hand on the boy's head.

His hand is covered with blood, and now there is blood in the boy's hair as well, and there are scratches on Charlie's face, and there is fear in Charlie's eyes, the fear of the animal in the second before the trigger is pulled, before the buckling of the knees, the toppling, the meat of his beautiful body going rotten with the fear, but in Charlie's eyes, it is not there for a second, it is there for an eternity, bright, his eyes filmed with blood and tears as he looks out of the vast sea of blood and regret into which he has launched himself, and the envelope lies on the ground, and the knife in Charlie's hand is slick with blood, the crimson sheen on steel. Charlie touches the boy's face, and hair, and speaks in a voice that he has used once before, in the courtroom where he pleaded for mercy from a woman who had betrayed him, and he speaks and he says, "Remember this, Sam. Remember. Take up that envelope and don't lose it ever. It's yours. It's what I'm giving to you for your birthday every year for years and years. Try to be a good boy. Please don't forget me," as though Sam would or ever could anyway. And then Charlie lifts his head and he looks at the late afternoon sky, and now it's time for services for the dead war dead in town, and the bells start to toll, one bell for each soul lost, and Charlie puts his hand beneath his own chin and stretches his neck back and takes the knife and slits his throat cleanly and deftly and deeply from ear to ear, and the bells are tolling and the radio in the truck is still playing, "Go down go down you Knoxville girl with the dark and roving eye," and the bells are ringing and the bombs eight years before are raining down again on the innocent boys and his mother and father are kneeling on the bench now, far away, not here to tell him what to do, far away in prayer but, if he had known, both thinking of him, of their own child engulfed in Japanese flames, and Charlie falls almost immediately, his head just barely still attached to his neck, and he falls on the boy, the weight and smell of him, the blood, the laundry soap of his shirt, sprayed now with the blood from his neck, the boy sprayed, too, and trapped under the weight of Charlie's body and the gush of his blood, until he can wiggle free, until he can stand, Jackie already nosing in the blood of the man who had fed him all those mornings and evenings, Jackie skittish, knowing something is wrong, and looking to the boy for guidance, for a command, and then the boy says, "Get, Jackie," screams it, "Get. Away!" and Jackie backs off, looking up at Sam with those eyes, those eyes that say what, What is happening, what am I to do?

Sam snatches up the envelope and runs, the truck still idling in the road, useless because he doesn't know how to drive, his feet don't even touch the pedals, and so he runs along the road, a mile from town, a long way for a boy, followed by the dog whose nose is dipped in the blood of his master, "Go down go down you Knoxville girl," and Sam knows a shortcut, and so he takes it, the envelope clutched to his heart sticky with Charlie's blood, his present, Charlie had said, but he doesn't know what it is, just that he is not to lose it and he is to remember, not even to tell maybe but to remember, and what is he to do with one more secret?, knowing that he will tell because he has to, because he doesn't understand and somebody is going to have to explain it to him.

Sam is running now off the road and into the woods, which are filled with autumn's thicket, and he loses a shoe in the brambles, but he runs on anyway, scratched by blackberry and raspberry and scrub pine. He is crying, truly scared, *but racing toward the only place he knows and the only people who will take him in, Jackie at his heels.*

The bells aren't ringing any more when they reach the town and Sam races home and sits on his own porch. He is howling hysterically and his legs are covered with cuts and scratches and his face, too, and there is blood in his hair, and when his mother sees him, hears him and then sees him, she thinks that an accident has happened, that the truck lies mangled somewhere in a ditch with Charlie and beef strewn over the road and Sam can't speak, can't tell where it hurts or what happened, can only howl, the dog howling, now, too, and the neighbors gathering at the end of the walk, their own prayers put away for the night, and where is his baseball mitt that Charlie gave him for his birthday and his mother is asking where it hurts, feeling his thin arms and legs to see if anything is broken, asking if there was an accident, and Sam shaking his head no, no, no again, no nothing had happened but Charlie is hurt, he is hurt real bad, and they wouldn't have believed him except that there is no Charlie and there is blood everywhere on the boy, and something, something must have happened, and so they get in the car, and Sam, howling, points the way, the headlights on now, until they come to Charlie's truck in front of her house, the radio still playing in the idling truck, and they see it for themselves, the young girl, the handsome man, face down and dead, and then it is official, the only crime that ever happened in Brownsburg, Virginia is over, is done, the ballad ended, the string broken, the last note played. Yes, yes, yes, Jackie's real gone. Jackie is a real gone guy.

CHAPTER THIRTY

I T TOOK FOUR hours to bury him. In the end, there was only the
brother to do it. The preachers had railed about sin and hellfire,
and said that anybody who touched or went near Charlie Beale's
body would go to hell as surely as he was bound there. Will would
have helped, he offered, but, at the last, the brother knew that it was
something he had to do alone, was something that he had, without
knowing it, come all this way to get done.

Sylvan had been swept up at once, headlights ringing her dead
body with men in uniform circling in the dark, while Boaty Glass
sat on his porch, mute and unmoving, watching as the dead body
of his wife was first examined by the coroner and then carted off
to Kenneth Harrison's to be made ready for the funeral. When the
coroner told him that Sylvan was pregnant when she died, not a
muscle in his face twitched. He figured he knew whose child it was,
figured everybody knew as well, but he just didn't care any more.

He was going to bury her in some old housecoat he found in the closet, but then that nigger woman showed up with some getup she'd made for her, never worn. It was ludicrous, but it might as well be that as anything else. But no shoes. She might as well go out of this world like the barefooted hillbilly she was, he figured.

Boaty wanted her buried the next day, no viewing of her body, mangled anyway, her face bruised from the fall on the stairs, and he wanted her shut in the ground and out of his life by nightfall the next day. He wanted her put down in the town cemetery, but nowhere near his family, and since her own people were not buried there—god, where *were* they buried?, some field out in Arnold's Valley somewhere—she was to be put off to the side, alone, to spend eternity apart, away from her betters. He didn't go down there in the dark to pick a spot. He just didn't care.

He didn't intend to hang around her grave anyway, ever, so it didn't matter to him. Any free spot would do.

Charlie's body, they left out all night. First frost. Not even anybody to watch over him, who was there? Alma, in bed, grieving; Will, sitting by his boy Sam, who was mad with night terrors, Will saying what he could, doing what he could think of, but nothing worked, the terrors wouldn't be ameliorated by touch or word or prayer; Jackie, jumping at every sound, the scent of blood still in his nostrils; the whole town, worked up, sad but somehow thrilled, touched with the enormity of the tragedy that had happened right there in their own backyard; Ned, drunk and weeping as he would weep for pretty much the rest of his life. Even the coroner wouldn't touch him. Defiled, the ministers said. *Damned.*

The preachers reminded their flocks in hastily called prayer meetings that Sylvan was murdered and, in the eyes of God, an innocent victim, and so she could be buried in sacred ground. Charlie was both a murderer and a suicide, two things that made him both damned to hell and inadmissible in the town cemetery. No, he wouldn't be buried with the holy and the heaven-bound, and no faithful person would touch him without risking following him to the fire. The women believed, and the men at least listened, and did as they were told.

So there was only Ned, and nobody was sure except him that he could do it by himself. Some things you just know how to do, even if you don't know you know it. How to bury your own flesh and blood is one of those things. And Ned was a carpenter, so he knew it not just in his heart but to the board foot and the last nail.

He went down to the lumberyard and ordered what he was going to need. Charlie Austin got it all together and just gave it to him, free, no charge, at least he could do that, no threat of hellfire in giving away some of his stock to this helpless boy whose grief was like an anvil dragging him down. The boy drove back to the house and got the only suit Charlie owned, the one he'd worn in court. He got it out of the armoire Alma had picked out at a country estate sale the year before, when everything was just starting, before anything really had begun, when everything was empty rooms and full hearts and bright hopes and a limitless future, and he pulled out the black tie, the only one, and he wrapped these things in a clean quilt from the bed and got back into the truck and didn't remember until halfway out there that there were some good shoes, too, and there should have been socks, and maybe even some underwear, this was what his own brother was going to wear until time ran out, but he wasn't going to go back, not now, not until it was done. He drove up to the house and got out to unlatch the gate and bounced the truck over the cowcatcher, then got out to latch the gate again, carefully — even though Boaty hadn't kept cattle for years, there was nothing to get out, get away — and that done, he was alone with it, ready and not ready for the task and the grief that confronted him now, naked in the face in the cold late morning.

And it staggered him, buckled his knees to the ground, wracked him with the sobs of a child. Things you cannot bear are borne; the breath comes into your body on its own. Things don't stop. They just don't.

First he built some sawhorses, then he started to measure and cut the boards. He warmed up in the sawing, and he took off his jacket and worked in his shirtsleeves. Last night's liquor began to run from his skin, mixed with the tears that wouldn't stop coming. He built a plain pine box, bigger than his brother's body, because in his mind his brother was bigger than he was in life, and he stopped when he heard the bells start to ring, signaling the start of that other funeral, and he could picture it, just for a minute, the dutiful town dutifully lining up to pay their respects, not even so much to her as to Boaty, to Harrison Boatwright Glass, the preacher saying what Boaty told him to say and nobody believed, the men imagining the coupling of the two of them even in death, the women trying to picture, inside the box, the dress they'd heard about; the men had told them, when they came back in the dark to supper, about the dress that Claudie had held in her hands, the dress that Sylvan Glass would wear, barefoot, when she got to the gates of Heaven.

As the boards came together, the beat of hammer on nail, the procession moved from the church to the cemetery, Boaty walking alone, behind the hearse, and in the graveyard, the words were said, and Sylvan Glass, aged twenty-one, went into the ground forever.

When the box was built, Ned stripped his brother naked and tried to wash him as best he could with water drawn from the spring in an old bucket he found there, with bits of an old blanket he found in the back of the truck. Even he could see the beauty of that body, the grace, the correctness of the way everything met everything else. He washed the body, and there was nothing gentle about it, not even the sounds of the brother weeping, not even the silence of death in the body of Charlie Beale, not even that—even in that there was a roughness and rage at the doing of things that were not wished but had to be done anyway—and the brother then dried him off with the blanket, and dressed him awkwardly in the shirt and suit, and tried to tie the tie around his neck, but the tears would not stop, they would not stop, and so he gave up, and wrapped the black wool tie around the slash of his brother's throat, hoping it would be all right. His body was wracked with sobs for the man he barely knew except in his blood, but loved because of that. He cried for what they might have been to one another, for things that were not able to be saved, not any more, for crimes of his own that his brother didn't even know about, for the crimes of his brother that were already famous and would not die with him.

He hoisted his brother by the shoulders, the heavy suit, the light but still body of the man, the bare feet, and he tried to get him in the box straight, and then he realized that his brother's eyes were still open and he tried, but they would not close, and he had no pennies, and so, as he nailed the boards above him one by one, Charlie Beale would stare into the approaching darkness with the same look of startled fear, the fear of the animal before the trigger is pulled, forever and ever amen.

The sun was getting long over the mountains to the west, and he dragged the box to the truck and he somehow got it into the flat-bed, and he drove to town, and as he drove through it, the people of the town, home from the funeral of a woman they had not loved, shut their curtains and their blinds and their shutters on the body of a man they had loved, lest the spirit come into their house and dwell among them, still living, still asking in its gentle way for their forgiveness, which they could give, but not now, not tonight, could not under orders from the men in the pulpits.

Ned drove to the cemetery, not fast, not slow, just drove, and he parked in front of the gate, locked for the night, and looked into the cemetery to see if he could spot the place where they had buried Sylvan Glass, and he found it, marked by a single spray of roses from the Kiwanis Club, "With Deepest Sympathy, Our Sister in Heaven," and he banged his fists against the gates until his hands bled, rattled the rusted steel but they did not open and no one came, no one listened, although everyone heard. He pulled the box from the flatbed, dropping it on the ground, mad now, crazy mad and struck dumb with his grief and his solitude in all this, alone, a boy, a carpenter boy who had not even done his best work in burying his brother, but done what he could.

He dragged the box around the high wall of the cemetery, until he came to a narrow open place on the side of the road that was nearest to the place where Sylvan lay, and then he said "fuck" out loud and went back to the truck and got a shovel and started digging close to the wall that separated Charlie Beale from Sylvan Glass, and it took a long time. He stopped, thinking it was enough, but he saw as the light began to fade that it wasn't enough, and so he jumped back down into the hole and dug until it was dark and that would have to do, feeling the chill of the cold walls of his brother's grave, and he slid the box in, and started shoveling the dirt, jumping at the thudding sound of every shovelful as though he were being smacked repeatedly in the face.

When the dirt was up to his waist over the body of his brother, he threw the shovel in the road, and began to climb the mound, tamping down the dirt with his feet, like he had just planted a row of potatoes, and kept thumping with his feet until there was only a gentle mound, no higher than his shin, and he paused, and tried to think of some words to say, some words that would be different and more true than the words that had been said over the body of Sylvan. He spoke of blood, the bond of blood, and he spoke of the dirt and the animals, and the beating heart, the beating heart, the beating heart of brothers.

And then he was done, and it was over, and Charlie was laid to as much rest as he was going to get, and Ned picked the shovel up out of the road, careful even now, of his tools, and he drove home, back to the only house Charlie still owned, and he sat on the porch, the porch light on, tilted back in an old cane chair, and he drank whiskey until he was unconscious, with everybody watching, waking from sleep and watching, and when he woke up and it was still dark and he was still drunk but not drunk enough, he went in the house and got more whiskey and he drank that until he passed out again, and this was to be how he spent his days, in public agony, a cacophony of grief and inebriation. Day after day and night after night, he sat there drunk and drinking and nothing would stop him, and they all knew it, and the women began to bring him food, and the men liquor, and sometimes the twins came and sat with him, just sat, knowing there was no comfort to be given, so profound was this grief, so reckless was this sweet youth with the sympathies of his heart, and there was no diverting what was happening, and so they abetted, believing they shouldn't but knowing there was nothing else that they, as Christians, could do, and within seven weeks the boy had drunk himself to death on an open porch in the middle of town while everybody watched, and, by that time, Harrison Boatwright Glass had gone out into the country and bought himself a new bride, a true redhead, who walked into a situation she knew nothing of, inherited a place she tried to make the best of, the second wife, the redneck beauty who couldn't do the simplest figures in her head, and she was the new wife and the brother Ned was dead and it was winter and the snow fell on the graves of Sylvan Glass and Charlie Beale, the places where nobody would go and stand witness, not ever again and that was the end of the story. That was almost the end of the story.

CHAPTER THIRTY-ONE

WE CAME HERE this morning . . ." the man said.

"You came here because, like everybody who comes here, you were having your hair cut at the barbershop, or you were buying some lavender sachets over there at the Herb Farm, and the barber or the butcher said his son was a real Beebo, and you had never heard that before, and you wanted to know what it meant, and they told you to ask me. They told you I was there. They told you I knew him."

"Yes," the man said. "The barbershop."

They sit across from me, the lawyer and his lawyer wife, and they've been sitting there all day and it's late and the coffee is all gone, I can smell the burning of the scorched pot, and there wasn't any skimmed milk anyway, and they want to know. They all want to know. Such a simple thing, or so they thought when they came in the door. But they can't know, they can't understand without the whole story.

"I didn't sleep all night, that night. Nobody did. Before it was light, I got out of bed, and the only light on was up the street, where the brother sat drinking in the dark.

"I dressed, it was cold by then, the winter was on us, so I put on a coat and I crept down the stairs so my parents wouldn't hear, and I ran through the town toward the cemetery, past the houses where the curtains and the shutters were still drawn, because I wanted to see. I had to know where he was.

"I got down to the cemetery, and it was getting light, and I could see through the bars of the gate, across the graves to where the one new grave lay, and that had to be hers, but I had to know. I had to know where Charlie was. There was only the one grave in the cemetery, and he had to be somewhere.

"I circled the wall, hugging it close, feeling the cold of the stone, and it was a long way around. It was an old cemetery and people had been being buried there for two hundred years, so it was big, and it seemed a long way around.

"Then I saw it. I saw it, and her at the same time. Claudie, standing in the dark, in black, no coat, a veil over her face. Beside her was a young white girl I'd never seen before, and never saw again. They were holding rolls of material—linen and silk and cotton, and they were unfurling these over the mound where Charlie Beale lay.

"They were standing there, and where they stood was a mountain of flowers. The most beautiful flowers. The flowers rose up over my head, over Claudie's head, even, every flower, must have been, in Lexington and Staunton, white flowers and red roses, and lilies, every flower from every cooler. Planted here and there were those kind of arrangements they make for funerals, sprays of mourning, with satin ribbons that said, Dear Friend and Sadly Missed and Our Prayers Are with You and Farewell, and the people of this town, they had driven, singly, secretly, each of them, to every flower shop and they had laid the flowers on the grave. And it was all wrapped and beribboned by the fabrics from all the dresses Claudie would never make for Sylvan.

"Claudie walked over to me, and she took my hand, and we stood there as the sun was coming up, and we could see the frost on the flowers, and there was nothing to say, we knew, we knew everything so there was no need to speak. We were glad that, from behind their drawn curtains and shutters, the people of the town, in the night, had come out, and would not let him lie unmourned, unmarked, unloved.

"We stood, the black woman and I and the strange young woman, until it was fully light, and the frost had dissipated until there was no more sparkle left. Charlie Beale had not gone into the dark without notice.

"Woman, girl, and boy. Black and white. The sun coming up on an event that was already yesterday, the day before yesterday, the past. But it wasn't past, and it wasn't over, and we both knew it, although we didn't say anything then, or ever. It was enough to know, to know the story, to have been in the story, a part of these lives, touched by them, the bearers of their witness, their truth, what was to be their legend. Which is why you're here."

"And the envelope . . . ?"

". . . was of course the deeds, the deed to every single piece of property, dozens of them, rocky lots and fertile fields and waterfalls and river bottomland, and it was a source of great anguish and disquiet to Boaty Glass, who even filed a lawsuit, but the law looked the other way on Boaty Glass this time, and that is how I became, at the age of six, the richest landowner in Rockbridge County."

"Yes," said the man.

"Yes. And you want to buy a piece of it, Pickfair, the old place, and I'm going to sell it to you, because it's time. I'm not young and I have no wife or children, never had, which is maybe what some psychiatrist would say is the product, the result of all this, this life I've led, apart from the start, alone by nature and habit, not liking it much but living with it. Living in this house, Charlie Beale's house. Not the house of my mother and father, but this one, where he lived, where the brother drank himself to death on the porch in the freezing cold, fed and liquored by kindly neighbors.

"It's a harsh story. It is, as gentle as it looks from the air, not an easy county. But you can't live on the land without knowing the land, you can't walk on it without knowing that your footsteps are not the first.

"Claudie Wiley and I stood there that morning, and we knew that we were to keep the story, to keep it to ourselves, but keep it. The dead were owed some respect, but it wasn't long before the first barber or butcher watched his son jump in the air, catch a ball and swivel his hips to throw to first, and turned to his neighbor, awed by the grace and splendor of it, to say, 'That's my boy. He's a real Beebo.' And, since that day, whenever any boy excels at baseball or football or lacrosse, they call him a Beebo, and that boy wears that name with pride, not even knowing the story, but knowing that there is no better thing for a boy to be."

"And no girls?" says the wife.

"No, ma'am," I say. "Incorrect, I know, but that's the way it is. You might say, not every boy is a Beebo, but every Beebo is a boy."

We discuss a price, and water, and easements, and all those sad modern ways we have of trying to keep the land from being consumed by vulgarity, and they're good people, I guess, they need some dirt under their nails, but they'll do all right. They get up to go. We shake hands. It has been a long day.

"Now it's your land. But it's important, at least to me, that you remember that it's not *just* your land. There is a history. Now you're part of it. Good night."

And off they go.

I RINSE OUT THE coffee pot, make the coffee for the morning so all I have to do is flip the switch. I put out one cup, one saucer, one silver spoon balanced on the rim, my mother's wedding china and her wedding silver, used every day because every day is all there is, and I move silently through Charlie's house, turning off the lights one by one, until the rooms are ghostly in the lamplight from the street. The breeze outside rattles the gutters once or twice, but everything's stable, everything fixed in this house where I have lived for almost fifty years, this house whose rooms I know, the rooms in which nothing, not one single thing, has ever happened since, and not one thing has been moved, or torn down, or even changed.

EPILOGUE

I LIE IN BED, and I think about those eager young people who will come with their money and take over Pickfair, and knock down some walls to make a great room, as they call it, and put in a pool, and raise their children, and I wonder if they will remember, if they will feel it in their hearts, or if what there is will begin to be lost. I tried. I tried to keep everything. It can't be done. It can't be done.

As I told them, I'm not young, and it's time to let go. I wish I didn't have to let go to strangers, but that's the way it is. There is no one else. The world I live in is filled with strangers, now, the old ones dead, the new ones careless with the past.

No, there is only me, now. Only me.

I turn out the light, and I lie in the dark and smoke a Lucky Strike by the light of the streetlamp. In Charlie Beale's house, in Beebo's bed. Make of it what you will. And suddenly I think of what I had meant to tell them, and I tell them now, before I sleep:

There is in this valley a beating heart. It is always and ever there. And when I am gone, it will beat for you, and when you are gone, it will beat for your children, and theirs, forever. Forever. Until there is no water, no air, no green in the spring or gold in the autumn, no stars in the sky or wind from the north.

And when you cannot speak, it will speak for you. When you cannot see, it will be your eyes. When you cannot remember, it will be your memory. It will never forget you.

And when you cannot be faithful, it will save a place for your return. This is a gift to you. It cannot be taken away. It is yours forever.

It is the narrative of this world, and the scrapbook of your own small life, and, when you are gone into ash and darkness and the grave, it will tell your story.

ACKNOWLEDGMENTS

I am the luckiest writer in America. Lynn Nesbit is my agent and my friend, Chuck Adams is my editor, and Algonquin chooses to publish my books. No writer makes a book alone and no writer could have a stronger team. To all the people at Algonquin—Chuck, Robert Miller and Michael Taeckens, Ina Stern, Elisabeth Scharlatt, Kelly Bowen and Brunson Hoole, Craig Popelars and Lauren Mosely, as well as the extraordinary Kendra Poster, I give special thanks with all my heart.

Some people have a genius for friendship. Guy Trebay is one of them. His support and constancy and advice are a godsend. Liz Wright is another, the best cheerleader a writer could have. In Dana Martin Davis I have found a new sister to my soul, and her kindness and friendship lift me every day.

I am also grateful to Beckett Rosset, who gave Charlie a body, James Whiteside, who gave him his heart and soul, and Robert

Hoyt, who gave him his passionate and reckless nature. These men, who don't know each other, are bonded by kindness and intelligence and strength, and they have brought Charlie to life in this book, and I thank them. I am beholden to Eugene Orza as well, for letting me draw on his vast store of baseball knowledge, and for his friendship.

Mitchell Kaplan and Cristina Nosti, of Books & Books, did an extraordinary thing for me: they gave me a paradise of space and light and time to finish this book, and without them, it would never have gotten done.

Stephen and Julie Perkins have been a constant source of friendship and delight and affection, and if they didn't live down the road, I'd move.

Ellen Goldsmith-Vein and Luke Sandler have become more than associates. They are my friends, and their support and enthusiasm sustains me every day.

Finally, to all my friends and colleagues who run and work in the country's independent bookstores, big and little, metropolitan and far-flung, you are my heroes. Your intelligence and bravery astound and humble me.

Heading Out to Wonderful

The Passion of Place, the Place of Passion:
A Note from the Author

✻

The Constancy of Goodness:
Author Robert Goolrick Talks with *Chapter 16*

✻

Questions for Discussion

THE PASSION OF PLACE, THE PLACE OF PASSION

A Note from the Author

Thirty years ago, a friend of mine sat down and told me a story, a long story, about something that had happened to him as a child. It took him an hour to tell it, and it was the best story I have ever heard. The story, told over and over through the years, had taken on an element of myth, and in the days that followed, my friend took me to many of the places in which the events of the story had taken place, walked me through the countryside of his personal mythology, the defining moment of his life, which had happened decades before.

In those places, I could see my friend as a child; I could look through his eyes, feel what it must have been like to stand in his shoes and witness events that continued, after all the years, to mystify him, events that still created the boundaries of the country in which he lived and worked.

The town where the story took place is in a foreign country, and the qualities of the landscape and the light are very particular to that place. The particulars of that place are very different from those of the country in which I spent my own childhood, but in the vivacity of his telling, I knew completely what it was like to be him, at that age, in that place.

Over the years, I've told the story many times to many people. They've all agreed that the story is a magnificent one, and I knew that eventually I would have to write it down and tell it to as many people as I could. It is a mysterious story, and it has taken me many years to begin to understand the motives of the people involved, why they did what they did, and how all of these events must have profoundly affected the course of my friend's life.

Heading Out to Wonderful is the result of three decades of meditation on these events, on this one story. It is, in its essential elements, a true story. Of course, as the opening sentence of the novel states, all memory is fiction. We have to fill in details and make the story real for ourselves in order to bring to it a deeper understanding.

I have set the story not in the foreign country where my friend lives but in Virginia, where I spent my own childhood. It is a story of passion and place, because the place is so dear to me, for one thing, but also because the big things that happen in our lives don't happen in a vacuum. Our memory of them is colored and enhanced by the marriage of event and countryside, event and weather or season.

I wish everybody could have grown up in the Shenandoah Valley of Virginia as I did. Southerners are born into and tied forever to two things: time and place. We are our history, for good or ill, the history of our family, the history of our lovely and tragic land. We are born into both beauty and guilt, and we live with a sense of loss that never abates. The ground on which we walk; on which so many died, so many were bound into slavery; on which so much devotion and dereliction have been lavished, give our own little knot in the string of time a beauty and a benediction that we cannot escape.

The passions we feel are inextricably linked to the place in which we feel them, and I hope that this novel conveys the importance of that fact. In *A Reliable Wife*, the setting was austere and bitter cold. In this one, it is lush and effulgent, and the complexities of the story echo that. It is about the homes we build on the ground we are born to, homes we are too often forced to leave too soon. Childhood, for me, is one such home. Love is another. We come and go, events occur, but the land abides. The land endures forever.

And, every now and then, the best story you've ever heard comes along, and you are blessed to live with it, and the people in it, in the country in which it dwells. I hope I have done justice to the story, and I hope, in telling it, that I have made some measure of peace with the land that has nurtured me and torn out my heart for every day of my life.

So, here it is: *Heading Out to Wonderful.* A man arrives in Brownsburg, Virginia, in the summer of 1948. He brings with him two suitcases. In the first are his clothes and a fine set of butcher knives. The second suitcase is filled with money. A lot of money. He sets foot on the ground of Virginia, in the countryside where I live now, and the story that I first heard thirty years ago begins to breathe.

THE CONSTANCY OF GOODNESS

Author Robert Goolrick Talks with Chapter 16
about Writing as the Path to Something Resembling Peace

by Tina LoTufo

Robert Goolrick grew up in the 1950s in a small college town in Virginia, where he lived with his charismatic father, a college professor; his beautiful mother, a homemaker; and two siblings. When Goolrick lost his job as an advertising copywriter, he turned to writing memoir. *The End of the World as We Know It* (Algonguin, 2007) shines a searing spotlight on the excesses and failures of both the social underpinnings of the time and his own parents' inevitable alcohol-fueled decline, culminating in a devastating portrayal of the sexual abuse he suffered as a child.

Three years later, Goolrick's first novel, *A Reliable Wife* (Algonquin, 2010), quickly garnered both critical and popular acclaim, became a favorite book-club selection, and hit the top spot on the *New York Times* bestseller list. In *A Reliable Wife,* Goolrick spins a web of mystery and suspense around deceitful lovers in a bleak, early twentieth-century Wisconsin town in the dead of winter.

Goolrick's second novel, *Heading Out to Wonderful,* begins with the arrival of a mysterious stranger, Charlie Beale, in a quiet Virginia town during the summer of 1948: "It was a town where people expected to live calmly and die and go to heaven in due time." Beale brings with him two suitcases—the first filled with knives and the second with money—and a powerful desire that "things would finally turn out better, and that this would be the place he could feel at home."

You began your writing career at age fifty-three, after losing your job in advertising. Has literary success changed your life? Is pursuing a new career at midlife a course you recommend?

I changed careers because I had no choice. It was agonizing and not easy, but looking at the results, it's the best thing that ever happened to me. People had always told me I should be a writer; now I am.

Explaining the impetus to write a memoir, you have said, "My clothes were immaculate, my house charming, and my dinner parties a success, yet inside I felt completely dead. I found that writing about my life was a way of saving what's left." Are you willing to elaborate on that point at all?

Adults who were abused as children often function at a very high level. It's the mechanism we develop to conceal and manage the fear that governs our lives. People often ask me if writing the memoir was cathartic. It wasn't, because I was only recording what I already knew. But what was extremely redemptive was seeing it on a shelf in a bookstore. I had made my experience into an object that was entirely separate from me, and that gave me an enormous sense of both vindication and pride.

Some reviewers of *A Reliable Wife* used descriptions such as "Gothic potboiler" in the context of generally positive reviews. How do you react to descriptions of that kind, and how would you characterize the book?

I have to confess I have never read any of the great Gothic novels—*Jane Eyre*, for instance. It's a genre of which I am almost totally ignorant. And I don't read potboilers. It doesn't bother me to be included in that bunch, but I think in many ways that *A Reliable Wife* was misread by many of its readers. Those who expected a stereotypical bodice-ripper are generally disappointed, I think. *A Reliable Wife* is not actually a historical novel; it is neither Gothic nor a potboiler. I look at it as a very contemporary novel about modern people who happen to live a hundred years ago.

Michael Lesy's 1973 cult classic *Wisconsin Death Trip* was a strong influence on the atmosphere of *A Reliable Wife*. Was there a similar inspiration for your forthcoming novel?

The new novel is based on a true story. It actually happened, and I knew some of the people involved. It happened a long time ago in a foreign country, but the novel is, in its essential elements, a true story. It was actually harder, I think, to write a novel based on real events than it was to write one that was pure fiction. I felt the obligation to honor the people who had lived through these events, and a real need to understand and communicate the reasons they acted as they did.

In light of the painful disclosures of your memoir, these lines from *Heading Out to Wonderful* seem particularly poignant: "Anyway, it's too late now to go back, to take that rock out of the river, the one that changed the course of the water's flow." Has placing rocks in the rivers of your characters' lives led you to a clearer understanding and acceptance of the pivotal events of your own life?

The final stage of grief is acceptance, or so I understand. Both Sam, in the novel, and I have finally reached a point of acceptance. I live much more in the present and for the future than I ever have in the past. I think that writing this novel was, in many ways, "the rock in the river"—an attempt to rechart the course of the grief that has ruled my life since I was four.

In *Heading Out to Wonderful*, Charlie Beale keeps a diary. Are you a diarist and, if so, how has the habit been helpful to you, and especially to your writing?

I kept a diary when I was a young man. Looking back on it now, rereading those journals, I see clearly how imprisoned I was in the trauma of the events of my childhood, how repetitious the anguish of those events. I don't keep a diary or journal now. I write novels instead. When I was a child, I had a recurring constant nightmare in which there was something terribly wrong with me, and I couldn't speak to describe where the pain was. The journals of my youth were early attempts to find a voice with which to describe the pain. Now I use my writing to elucidate and, I hope, to move beyond that pain.

The new book is set in a small Virginia town in 1948, which is obviously much closer to your own experience than the 1907 Wisconsin setting of *A Reliable Wife*. How did you choose the time and place of *Heading Out to Wonderful*?

There is an actual town of Brownsburg, which the town in the novel resembles only in name. I picked it because I love the real town, and I know it like the back of my hand. Even though the actual events happened in a foreign country, I wanted a setting that was more familiar, and quintessentially Southern. Both of my novels take place in isolated towns. *A Reliable Wife* was my winter novel; *Heading Out to Wonderful* is a summer one. I set it in 1948 simply because that was the year I was born. Nothing more complicated than that.

In a 2009 interview you said that "most writers really have only one or two things to say in their whole lives. But they can't get it out, so they construct elaborate memory palaces to house the simple sentence that they're trying to say. And then, when they finish whatever they're working on, they say, 'No, that wasn't

quite it.' And so they have to write another one." Are you trying to say something different with *Heading Out to Wonderful*, or would you say that your message continues to be "I want to be safe and I want to be heard"?

I think I am trying to say that bad things can happen to good people, just as, in *A Reliable Wife,* good things can happen to bad people. The sentence I am trying to articulate in my life is about the value and constancy of goodness. I'm not sure I've said it clearly yet, but I'm getting closer. In writing, I have found the only safe place I have ever known, the only spot in which it is possible for me to understand people's motivations and to measure my own distance or proximity to what I consider to be the good.

Originally published March 8, 2012, by *Chapter 16.* © 2012 Chapter16 .org, a digital language and literature program of Humanities Tennessee. Reprinted by permission.

QUESTIONS FOR DISCUSSION

1. The novel begins with a first-person narrator who is not immediately identified but is revealed at the end of the story. What effect does his point of view have on the way the story is told? Did you find him to be a reliable narrator? How different do you think the story would have been if it were told from the point of view of a third-person omniscient narrator?

2. The book's opening line is, "The thing is, all memory is fiction." What do you think the author means by that? Do the novel's characters and plot bear out this assertion? Can you remember times in your own life when something that you remembered as true turned out to be false, or when something you remembered as happening one way was later shown to have happened another way entirely?

3. The novel seems to make a distinction between sin and crime, neither of which, from outward appearances anyway, would seem to have established a presence in Brownsburg before Charlie met Sylvan. What do you think is the distinction between the two? What do you think is Charlie's greatest sin, and what is his most heinous crime? Who else in the town do you think is guilty of sin, and what were those sins?

4. In the novel, the town of Brownsburg, circa 1948, is depicted as a nearly idyllic place, "where most people lived a simple life without yearning for things they couldn't have" (page 5). Do you think this kind of depiction is an example of the fiction created by memory, or is this ideal something that American towns once had but have now lost? If you believe the latter, what do you think were the corrupting factors? What has been your own experience in this regard?

5. Early in the story, Will tells Charlie, "When you're young, and you head out to wonderful, everything is fresh and bright as a brand-new penny, but before you get to wonderful you're going to have to pass through all right. And when you get to all right, stop and take a good, long look, because that may be as far as you're ever going to go" (page 16). Does this quote foreshadow the events to come in Charlie's life, or is it merely a caution, a warning, from a wiser, older man? Had Charlie been able to settle for "all right," at what point would he have realized that he had arrived at his destination? How would Charlie's life have been different if he had settled for "all right"?

6. The novel is set just after World War II, in an era and a place where race relations were hardly simple or sanguine, and in the story, the racial divide is an almost constant element, even if it is not a central theme. What does Charlie's willingness to befriend the town's black citizens—as witnessed in his desire to attend their church—tell you about him as a man, and what does it suggest about his past life?

7. Claudie, the black seamstress, was once given a chance to leave Brownsburg to try to find a life outside that town, yet she decided not to leave. Why do you think she made the decision to stay? What do you think would have happened if she had made that leap and left Brownsburg?

8. How does the novel's postwar setting inform the story's mood, plot, and character development? How do you think the story would have played out had Charlie arrived in Brownsburg in the mid-1970s?

9. When Charlie Beale arrives in Brownsburg, he is back in the United States after serving in the Army overseas, and he carries with him two suitcases, one of which is made of tin and has a lock, "because it was filled with money. A lot of money" (page 10). Where and how do you think Charlie got all this money? If you were to create a backstory about what Charlie's life had been like between leaving the service and arriving in Brownsburg, what would that story be?

10. Charlie feels most at home outdoors. What does this connection to nature and to the earth reveal about him? Do you think he yearns to be outdoors out of love or out of fear?

11. When Charlie sees Sylvan, he feels an immediate attraction. Other than her beauty, what do you think attracts Charlie to Sylvan? What attracts Sylvan to Charlie? What do they each seek in the other? Can you imagine a scenario in which their relationship could have a happy ending?

12. The novel seems to suggest that Sylvan's yearning for Hollywood beauty, glamour, and fame is part of a larger American refusal to settle for reality. Do you think this longing was, in fact, a part of the national psyche in the late 1940s, or is it simply the yearning of a girl who grew up without love or even hope? Do you think there is a tendency of lonely people to long for fame today? If so, how is it manifested?

13. "She wasn't a bad girl," the novel contends repeatedly about Sylvan (pages 53, 230, and 256). What do you think? How do Sylvan's courtroom allegations about Charlie color the reader's perception of her? It is clear in the novel that Charlie has fallen completely in love with Sylvan, but do you think she was ever really in love with him? Is it possible that she was—in keeping with her Hollywood fantasies—in love with the idea of being in love?

14. "Childhood is the most dangerous place," suggests the novel (page 112). How might this be true for young Sam? What do you imagine his life was like after what he witnessed as a boy? Do you think he ever came close to reaching "wonderful"?

Robert Goolrick is the author of the novel *A Reliable Wife* and a memoir, *The End of the World as We Know It.* He lives in a small town in Virginia with his dog, Preacher.

Other Algonquin Readers Round Table Novels

A Reliable Wife, a novel by Robert Goolrick

Rural Wisconsin, 1907. In the bitter cold, Ralph Truitt stands alone on a train platform anxiously awaiting the arrival of the woman who answered his newspaper ad for "a reliable wife." The woman who arrives is not the one he expects in this *New York Times* #1 bestseller about love and madness, longing and murder.

"[A] chillingly engrossing plot . . . Good to the riveting end."
—*USA Today*

"Deliciously wicked and tense . . . Intoxicating." —*The Washington Post*

"A rousing historical potboiler." —*The Boston Globe*

AN ALGONQUIN READERS ROUND TABLE EDITION WITH READING GROUP GUIDE AND OTHER SPECIAL FEATURES • FICTION • ISBN 978-1-56512-977-1

West of Here, a novel by Jonathan Evison

Spanning more than hundred years—from the ragged mudflats of a belching and bawdy Western frontier in the 1890s to the rusting remains of a strip-mall cornucopia in 2006—*West of Here* chronicles the life of one small town. It's a saga of destiny and greed, adventure and passion, hope and hilarity, that turns America's history into myth and myth into a nation's shared experience.

"[A] booming, bighearted epic." —*Vanity Fair*

"[A] voracious story . . . Brisk, often comic, always deeply sympathetic." —*The Washington Post*

AN ALGONQUIN READERS ROUND TABLE EDITION WITH READING GROUP GUIDE AND OTHER SPECIAL FEATURES • FICTION • ISBN 978-1-61620-082-4

Until the Next Time, a novel by Kevin Fox

For Sean Corrigan the past is simply what happened yesterday, until his twenty-first birthday, when he's given a journal left to him by his father's brother, Michael—a man he had not known existed. The journal, kept after his uncle fled from New York City to Ireland to escape prosecution for a murder he did not commit, draws Sean into a hunt for the truth about Michael's fate. *Until the Next Time* is a remarkable story about time and memory and the way ancient myths affect everything—from what we believe to whom we love.

"A mysterious, sweeping family saga reminiscent of the work of Meira Chand and Julie Drew, Fox's novel is a suspenseful tale of lost love, rediscovered family, and the importance of history." —*Booklist*

"A taut suspense novel, a history lesson on a people's enduring struggle, and a chronicle of a star-crossed pair's everlasting love."
—Sandra Brown, *New York Times* bestselling author of *Lethal*

AN ALGONQUIN READERS ROUND TABLE EDITION WITH READING GROUP GUIDE AND OTHER SPECIAL FEATURES • FICTION • ISBN 978-1-56512-993-1

A Friend of the Family, a novel by Lauren Grodstein

Pete Dizinoff has a thriving medical practice in suburban New Jersey, a devoted wife, a network of close friends, an impressive house, and a son, Alec, now nineteen, on whom he's pinned all his hopes. But Pete never counted on Laura, his best friend's daughter, setting her sights on his only son. Lauren Grodstein's riveting novel charts a father's fall from grace as he struggles to save his family, his reputation, and himself.

"Suspense worthy of Hitchcock . . . [Grodstein] is a terrific storyteller."
—*The New York Times Book Review*

"A gripping portrayal of a suburban family in free-fall."
—*Minneapolis Star Tribune*

AN ALGONQUIN READERS ROUND TABLE EDITION WITH READING GROUP GUIDE AND OTHER SPECIAL FEATURES • FICTION • ISBN 978-1-61620-017-6

Pictures of You, a novel by Caroline Leavitt

Two women running away from their marriages collide on a foggy highway. The survivor of the fatal accident is left to pick up the pieces not only of her own life but of the lives of the devastated husband and fragile son that the other woman left behind. As these three lives intersect, the book asks, How well do we really know those we love, and how do we open our hearts to forgive the unforgivable?

"An expert storyteller . . . Leavitt teases suspense out of the greatest mystery of all—the workings of the human heart." —*Booklist*

"Magically written, heartbreakingly honest . . . Caroline Leavitt is one of those fabulous, incisive writers you read and then ask yourself, Where has she been all my life?" —Jodi Picoult

AN ALGONQUIN READERS ROUND TABLE EDITION WITH READING GROUP GUIDE AND OTHER SPECIAL FEATURES • FICTION • ISBN 978-1-56512-631-2

In the Time of the Butterflies, a novel by Julia Alvarez

In this extraordinary novel, the voices of Las Mariposas (The Butterflies), Minerva, Patria, María Teresa, and Dedé, speak across the decades to tell their stories about life in the Dominican Republic under General Rafael Leonidas Trujillo's dictatorship. Through the art and magic of Julia Alvarez's imagination, the martyred butterflies live again in this novel of valor, love, and the human cost of political oppression.

A National Endowment for the Arts Big Read selection

"A gorgeous and sensitive novel . . . A compelling story of courage, patriotism, and familial devotion." —*People*

"A magnificent treasure for all cultures and all time."
—*St. Petersburg Times*

AN ALGONQUIN READERS ROUND TABLE EDITION WITH READING GROUP GUIDE AND OTHER SPECIAL FEATURES • FICTION • ISBN 978-1-56512-976-4

Water for Elephants, a novel by Sara Gruen

As a young man, Jacob Jankowski is tossed by fate onto a rickety train, home to the Benzini Brothers Most Spectacular Show on Earth. Amid a world of freaks, grifters, and misfits, Jacob becomes involved with Marlena, the beautiful young equestrian star; her husband, a charismatic but twisted animal trainer; and Rosie, an untrainable elephant who is the great gray hope for this third-rate show. Now in his nineties, Jacob at long last reveals the story of their unlikely yet powerful bonds, ones that nearly shatter them all.

"[An] arresting new novel . . .With a showman's expert timing, [Gruen] saves a terrific revelation for the final pages, transforming a glimpse of Americana into an enchanting escapist fairy tale."
—*The New York Times Book Review*

AN ALGONQUIN READERS ROUND TABLE EDITION WITH READING GROUP GUIDE AND OTHER SPECIAL FEATURES · FICTION · ISBN 978-1-56512-560-5

Mudbound, a novel by Hillary Jordan

Mudbound is the saga of the McAllan family, who struggle to survive on a remote ramshackle farm, and the Jacksons, their black sharecroppers. When two men return from World War II to work the land, the unlikely friendship between these brothers-in-arms—one white, one black—arouses the passions of their neighbors. In this award-winning portrait of two families caught up in the blind hatred of a small Southern town, prejudice takes many forms, both subtle and ruthless.

Winner of the Bellwether Prize for Fiction

"This is storytelling at the height of its powers . . . Hillary Jordan writes with the force of a Delta storm." —Barbara Kingsolver

AN ALGONQUIN READERS ROUND TABLE EDITION WITH READING GROUP GUIDE AND OTHER SPECIAL FEATURES · FICTION · ISBN 978-1-56512-677-0

Coal Black Horse, a novel by Robert Olmstead

When Robey Childs's mother has a premonition about her husband fighting in the Civil War, she sends her only son to find him and bring him home. At fourteen, Robey thinks he's off on a great adventure. But it takes the gift of a powerful and noble coal black horse to show him how to undertake the most important journey in his life.

"A remarkable creation." —*Chicago Tribune*

"Exciting . . . A grueling adventure." —*The New York Times Book Review*

AN ALGONQUIN READERS ROUND TABLE EDITION WITH READING GROUP GUIDE AND OTHER SPECIAL FEATURES • FICTION • ISBN 978-1-56512-601-5

An Arsonist's Guide to Writers' Homes in New England,
a novel by Brock Clarke

The past catches up with Sam Pulsifer, the hapless hero of this incendiary novel, when after spending ten years in prison for accidentally burning down Emily Dickinson's house, the homes of other famous new England writers go up in smoke. To prove his innocence, he sets out to uncover the identity of this literary-minded arsonist.

"Funny, profound . . . A seductive book with a payoff on every page." —*People*

"Wildly, unpredictably funny . . . As cheerfully oddball as its title." —*The New York Times*

AN ALGONQUIN READERS ROUND TABLE EDITION WITH READING GROUP GUIDE AND OTHER SPECIAL FEATURES • FICTION • ISBN 978-1-56512-614-5

Join us at **AlgonquinBooksBlog.com** for the latest news on all of our stellar titles, including weekly giveaways, behind-the-scenes snapshots, book and author updates, original videos, media praise, detailed tour information, and other exclusive material.

You'll also find information about the **Algonquin Book Club**, a selection of the perfect books—from award winners to international bestsellers—to stimulate engaging and lively discussion. Helpful book group materials are available, including

Book excerpts
Downloadable discussion guides
Author interviews
Original author essays
Live author chats and live-streaming interviews
Book club tips and ideas
Wine and recipe pairings

twitter Follow us on twitter.com/AlgonquinBooks
facebook Become a fan on facebook.com/AlgonquinBooks